Natural Prey

ALSO BY EDWARD MATHIS

Dark Streaks and Empty Places (1986)

From a High Place (1985)

Natural Prey

EDWARD MATHIS

CHARLES SCRIBNER'S SONS
New York

JUL 28 1988

Charles Scribner's Sons
Macmillan Publishing Company
866 Third Avenue, New York, NY 10022
Collier Macmillan Canada, Inc.

This is a work of fiction. Names, characters, places, and
incidents either are the product of the author's imagina-
tion or are used fictitiously. Any resemblance to actual
events or persons, living or dead, is entirely coincidental.

Library of Congress Cataloging-in-Publication Data

Mathis, Edward.
  Natural prey.

  I. Title.
PS3563.A8364N3   1987   813'.54   87-9825
  ISBN 0-684-18852-X

10 9 8 7 6 5 4 3 2 1

Printed in the United States of America

This one is for:
Janet, Randy, Casey, and Brian Davis

ACKNOWLEDGMENT

Three times, editor Betsy Rapoport has guided me through the beginner's no-man's-land of hidden pitfalls and inevitable pratfalls.

Thanks, Betsy.

Natural
Prey

1

My parents were born and raised in West Tennessee, an area of wild, unforgiving terrain, rugged and beautiful; a region of unscalable cliffs, sharp peaks, and spiny ridges; a land that mocked the mettle of men and made women old before their time; a land rife with superstition and taboos, with poverty the only abiding tradition.

Superstition and taboos: you didn't mess with women kin closer than a second cousin, and the tricky twilight hour was the time between the dog and the wolf.

For some reason known only to my subconscious I was thinking these irrelevant thoughts as I let the rental Ford slant toward the curb and come to a stop in front of Ralph Kincade's modest three-bedroom frame home. It was the twilight hour on a Friday in late October, in Midway City, Texas.

I turned the switch and the motor died with a jerk and a noisy sigh. I took out a cigarette, pressed the dash lighter, and looked at Ralph Kincade.

He was asleep, or pretending to be, slouched into his corner of the front seat in much the same position he had used since Amarillo.

A slender man of medium height, he had a long, narrow face, still handsome despite the heavy lines crisscrossing his forehead, fanning outward from his lips and eyes. A wide, thin mouth with turned-up edges gave his features a wry, sardonic cast, the look of a man who has firsthand knowledge of pain and tragedy and unrewarding confrontations with both.

I lit the cigarette, snapped the lighter back into the dash. He didn't move. I cleared my throat.

"We're here, Mr. Kincade."

"Ralph," he said. "Call me, Ralph, Dan."

"Okay," I said. "We're here, Ralph."

He chuckled dryly and opened his eyes, lifted his head, and wearily massaged his eyelids with a thumb and forefinger. He blinked at me, blue eyes shot with blood, clusters of white matter at their corners. A doleful look, flirting with humor.

"Thanks, Dan."

"Don't mention it."

"No, I mean it. Thirty hours in this bucket of bolts. You could have flown it in—what, three hours?"

"I don't like to fly either, so it wasn't all for you."

He rubbed his right arm, turned slowly to look at the dark, silent house. "Would you like to come in with me? There's usually some beer. . . ." He let it trail away, a note of doubt creeping into his voice. He had been gone nine months, no way to tell what he might find.

"Thanks, anyway. I drank our last one a few miles back. What I need right now is a shower and about ten hours of sleep."

He nodded, still looking at the house. "What did she say when you called her from Albuquerque?" He knew the answer to that, but he was delaying the inevitable, the action that could make his commitment final.

"She said that she and David would be in Austin this evening. Something about a gymnastic competition. She said tell you she was terribly sorry, but that you would understand how important it was to David. She said they would be home later tonight."

"Did she mention Cynthia, say whether she'd be here or not?" He turned to look at me, squinting, one hand coursing through a curly thatch of steel-gray hair, his face strained.

"No. But she said you knew where the key would be." I hesitated. "She said to make yourself at home. Then she laughed and said that it was your home, after all."

He nodded again, his tight features softening. "She's a nice lady, Dan. And David . . . David's a great kid. I'm really proud of him. He's a terrific athlete, you know."

"I've never met your son, but, you're right, your wife is a nice lady." I hesitated again. "She seemed very happy that you were coming back with me."

He looked pleased. "I hope so," he said gruffly. "We've got a lot to work out." His hand closed on the door handle. He stopped. "I guess I should say I've got a lot to make up for. I made a bad mistake leaving like that. It's time I got back to being a man again."

I shrugged. "You're only human. Humans make mistakes, maybe more than anybody."

He chuckled and shouldered the door open. "Ain't it the truth."

I got out and opened the trunk, helped him unload his valise and the bulky duffel bag. "Need any help with these?"

"No, thanks. I've got them."

We shook hands, said our good-byes, and I watched him walk up the driveway and disappear around a corner of the house, his step slow and somehow uncertain, an ordinary man caught in the sucking undertow of progress. A builder of automobiles for eighteen years, he had lost his job during the early eighties' depression, then, with the advent of alleged prosperity, learned that his job had been automated away. He was fifty-six. No one rushed forward to hire him, and after a period of stubborn rebellion that ate up what little savings he and his family had, he had felt compelled to accept a job at a third of what he had been earning. To save their home, his wife had gone to work for the first time in their married life; his daughter, Cynthia, had been forced to drop out of college and find work. David had taken a job sacking groceries after school and on Saturdays. And still they lived in the haunting shadow of poverty.

Finally, frustrated, humiliated, defeated, Ralph Kincade had taken refuge in flight.

I drove across Midway City to my home, depression nibbling at the edges of my weariness. Ralph Kincade's problem wasn't all that unique. There were thousands, perhaps millions, of Ralph Kincades. People lost in the shuffle of corporate expediency, the race for a bigger buck. People cast aside because their one talent was no longer needed, the disenfranchised with no talent at all—slow dancers in a rock and roll world.

Susie was gone. The house was empty. I knew the moment I stepped through the front door.

No vibrations; the air was still and heavy and cold, no trace of warmth from recent human passage, no lingering aura of kinetic energy.

Lights burned in the kitchen, den, and one of the bathrooms, turned on by the timer at seven o'clock. Dispiritedly, I searched the house anyway, feeling a rising tide of disappointment, a faint, sneaky stirring of resentment. Dammit, her job was beginning to interfere with our lives. Unlike the two blind monkeys in the baobab tree, our encounters were occurring less and less frequently.

Two months before, she had spent ten days covering the Mexico City earthquake; then came hurricane Juan and four days on the Texas-Louisiana coast. Before that it had been the seajacking, which meant a week scurrying around Italy and Egypt. One short day together, and I was off to El Paso on a case. When I returned, she was scrambling around in the Ozarks covering the crash of an airliner.

No way to run a marriage, I thought glumly, especially one barely a year old.

I lit a cigarette and headed for the kitchen and the inevitable note I would find on the refrigerator.

It was there, held in place by a walleyed magnetic frog the color of green bile.

Darling, I'm so sorry—you know how much I wanted to be here tonight when you came home, how much I "needed" to be here! But you know how it is, we're two people short—out with the flu—and, well, after all, it is my job.

I guess you've heard about the floods down in the Valley. That's where I'll be, and don't worry about me. I have Clive working the Minicam and you know what an old mother hen he is.

Damn, sometimes I get so depressed I could just cuss! I never get to see you anymore.

I'll try my best to be home by Sunday evening, but don't worry, honey, if it takes another day.

Sy promised no more out-of-towners for at least a week, so get yourself rested up, big fella—get ready!

I love you, love you, love you,
Susie

Two more days, maybe three. Jesus Christ. The swell of disappointment became a tide. I was suddenly painfully aware of how much I had been looking forward to seeing her, basking in the warmth of dark liquid eyes and fulgent smile, reaffirming my commitment to the impossible fusion of childlike innocence and exotic adult sensuality that characterized my young, globe-trotting wife.

I laid the note on the counter, feeling my body slump, fatigue closing on me like a mailed fist. My back trembled, fire radiating at its base; my buttocks ached from thirty-odd hours behind the wheel of the rental Ford.

Disgruntled, as sulky as a reprimanded child, I made my way to the shower and let the hot, pelting water and cloudy steam work their magic on overstressed flesh and depressed spirits alike.

Unwinding, I thought of the showers we sometimes took together, and felt a budding sense of urgency, a gentle tumescence nosing through dejection like an old hound in a likely patch of weeds. I shut my eyes and let the vivid imagery close on my mind, accepting without resistance that she held me in thrall, that she owned a large part of me.

I toweled off, padding down the hall to the bedroom. I found a pair of pajama bottoms and fell into bed wondering what the shrinks would have to say about a man who became aroused fantasizing about his wife.

I think I was still smiling when I fell asleep.

There were woodpeckers in my dream—red-tufted heads and long, spiky beaks drilling into living wood with hollow, irritating resonance—and mockingbirds that trilled impossibly familiar notes effortlessly, beady eyes alive with sinister derision.

I yelled and thrashed my arms, threw rocks, and finally pleaded, but they would not go away; instead they grew louder, more importunate, tugging me at last through the penumbral veil that separates sleep from wakefulness.

The noises were real: rapping knuckles and the haunting notes of the door chimes playing "Moonglow," the theme from *Picnic*. Susie's choice. I had wanted the theme from "Dragnet," but as usual, I was putty in the hands of a master sculptor.

I groaned, then mouthed a few choice expletives I reserved solely for Police Captain Homer Sellers, my former boss and, at that moment, my former friend. I swung my feet to the cold carpet and held my head in my hands and shivered. I felt cheated; I had all the rotten feelings of a hangover and not one fond memory.

The cacophony continued. Something new had been added: a bass voice impatiently demanding admittance. It was Homer, all right. I had never doubted it for a second. Only he did it exactly that way.

I found my robe in the closet and padded down the hall,

pausing at the thermostat to turn up the heat. He was at it again by the time I reached the front door. I slipped the bolt and jerked the door open in mid-rap, catching him with upraised arm and clenched fist, the beefy thumb on his right hand jammed against the bell, a stubborn grimace on his broad, florid face.

"You can stop now, Homer. I'm up."

He grunted and adjusted his glasses, blue eyes squinting through thick bifocals, the frown dissolving into a grin featuring big square white teeth.

"About time, too. You know it's seven o'clock?" He pushed through the door and brushed past me, backhanding me lightly in the stomach, momentarily obscuring the early morning light, bringing a swirl of biting air in his slipstream. Four inches taller than my even six feet, at least forty pounds heavier than my usual one-ninety, he sometimes seemed overwhelming, larger than life—Raymond Burr with a semi-handsome face.

"I'm sorry, Homer, if I've somehow failed you. I didn't realize I'd left a wake-up call." I closed the door and followed him into the den, then turned abruptly and went back down the hall to the bedroom. I found my cigarettes and put on a shirt, slipped my bare feet into a pair of leather house shoes.

When I got back to the den he was ensconced in my new rocker-recliner, a gift from Susie on my last birthday. The soft-leather chair hugged his big body like a glove.

"You like it?"

"You better believe it. Beats that rickety old thing you had before."

"Nobody ever sat in that rickety old thing but you," I said.

He uttered a short, barking laugh and shucked the cellophane from a tan cigar fitted with a white plastic tip. He rocked gently, rolling the cigar across his tongue, his eyes gleaming behind the thick glasses. He snapped a kitchen match alight with the thumbnail on his right hand and fired up.

I lit a cigarette. "What's going on, Homer?" I sat down across from him—another recliner, an old one that didn't rock. Covered with a soft, ribbed fabric, it was cooler than leather in summer and warmer in winter.

He flipped the match into the fireplace and shook his head, smoke jetting around the cigar as he set the coal just right, his massive head tilted to one side, lank, mud-colored hair askew as usual.

"That's a gas log in the fireplace, Homer. It doesn't burn wood."

"Oops, I keep forgetting. Remind me to get it out when I get up."

"There's only two things that would get you out of bed this early. One's deer hunting, the other one's your job. I haven't noticed any deer around here lately, so I'll ask you one more time. What's going on? Or more to the point, what's going on that affects me?" I should have known better than to push him, but I was cold and hungry, and best friend or not, seven o'clock on a Saturday morning was not my favorite time for social intercourse. Chances were good that there was nothing on his mind more important than a sudden attack of buck fever, a malady that energizes deer hunters during the last weeks before opening day. Homer was more susceptible than most, projecting an infectious exuberance that normally lasted right up to wake-up call on opening morning. He rarely killed a deer; like me, he enjoyed the anticipation, the ritual of preparation, the camaraderie of the hunt more than the reality of violated flesh and bloody skinning knife.

Surprisingly enough, he pursed his lips and nodded, sending ragged puffs of smoke into the slowly warming air. "You're right, son. Ungodly time of day to come calling on a feller. Wouldn't do it if it wasn't necessary."

"Apologies, Homer? Now you're making me nervous."

"Nope, not apologizing. Just stating facts." He squirmed in the chair and crossed thick ankles. "You know a feller named Ralph Kincade?" His voice was matter-of-fact, disinterested, the words accompanied by a deadpan stare I recognized all too well.

Cold ghostly fingers brushed across the back of my head, invaded the narrow places behind my ears: Homer Sellers was in charge of Homicide.

"Is he dead? Or did he kill someone else?"

His eyebrows arched above the rims of his spectacles. "Now, why would you think a thing like that?"

I shook my head, refusing to be baited. "Because you're here. And since you're here, you must already know that I brought him home from California not much more than twelve hours ago. I went out there three days ago, found him, spent a day drinking with him, persuading him to come home. He refused to fly, so I rented a car and drove straight through from L.A. I dropped him in front of his house somewhere between six-thirty and seven o'clock last night, came home, took a shower, and hit the sack. That's it, Homer, my sordid little caper in a nutshell. Now, what's happened?"

He wagged his head and made a clucking sound. "My. All of that just from mentioning the name Ralph Kincade. Wonder what'd happen if I said Naomi Kincade?"

I shrugged and lit another cigarette. "His wife. She hired me to find him."

"Wanted you to bring him home, I expect?"

"If he would come."

"What if he wouldn't? What was the plan then?"

"You'll have to ask her. I don't take anyone anywhere they don't want to go. You know that."

"Yeah, I've heard you say that lots of times. He give you any trouble? About coming home, I mean."

"Not much. I think he was ready, but he insisted on telling me his side of it, telling me all his reasons for riding off into the sunset, a broken and tragic man, misused by his loved ones, abused by society. Those are his words, not mine." I mashed out the cigarette. "What is it, Homer?"

"He's dead." Homer came forward in the chair, elbows on the arms, spatulate fingers laced together in front of him, big head tilted to keep cigar smoke out of his eyes. "Somebody shot him. Somebody who musta liked doing it, 'cause he done it four times." He paused, squinted reflectively. "But maybe that was because it was a small-caliber weapon. Not sure yet, but it looked like a twenty-five, maybe a twenty-two."

I stared at him, the cold fingers roaming at will across the back of my head, a hollow space building at the base of my throat. I found it difficult to swallow.

"About eight last night," Homer said, answering my unspoken question, the faintest hint of a smile shaping his wide mouth. "Best Doc Paris could do until they get into him. Doc said it coulda been as early as seven, as late as nine. Not easy to tell with only body temp, rigor, and lividity to go by. We'll know better by ten o'clock today." He bounced the plastic tip of his cigar off his lower lip. "Funny. Be funny if they find it was seven or thereabouts. That'd mean the killer was probably in there waiting when you dropped him off. Wouldn't that be funny?"

"Funny, but not particularly significant. When did they find him?"

He glanced at the clock above the mantel. "About three and a half hours ago. Three-thirty, give or take a few minutes."

"Who?"

"His wife and son. They'd been down to Austin to some gymnastic meet. Boy's evidently pretty good. His mother said he took third place in the overall something or other."

"She say why they were so late?"

He nodded and took a handkerchief out of his jacket pocket. "Said it was around ten-thirty when they got out of the stadium. They stopped to eat with some other folks out of Dallas. Left for home about midnight. That's about right for Austin, three to three and a half hour hike." He unfolded the handkerchief and blew lustily. He inspected the yield, then bunched the white cloth and stuffed it back into his pocket. He looked up to find me watching, and grinned sheepishly. "Winter coming on, damn sinuses already acting up."

"Were there signs of a break-in?"

"Nope. Whoever went in there went in through the door."

"Robbery, maybe?"

He frowned and shook his head slowly. "Don't think so.

Wouldn't think there'd be much there worth taking. Not that I saw, anyhow. Mrs. Kincade said she'd check, but she couldn't think of anything that'd attract a burglar. Some cheap jewelry, a few pieces of silver."

"Signs of a struggle?"

He frowned again; he wasn't used to answering questions. "Nope. He was killed in the kitchen. Some bologna and bread and cheese on the counter. Looked like he was making a sandwich."

"Cynthia Kincade. You talked to her yet?"

"No. Why do you ask?"

"She's a part of the family. Have you changed the routine since I was a cop?"

"We just haven't caught up to her yet. She didn't come home last night. Her mama said she does that ever' once in a while, stays with a girl friend or something. Or something, probably. I saw her picture there on the chest. She's a purty little thing."

I sighed and took out another cigarette. "They didn't get along, Homer. Kincade told me she was headstrong, had given them all kinds of trouble as far back as the eleventh grade. He said it got worse when she entered college and turned into open rebellion when she had to drop out and go to work to help support the family."

His head bobbed in rhythm with the rocking chair. "Little different story from her mama. Mrs. Kincade said he was way too strict on her, always was. Said the girl blamed him for her breaking up with a boy she planned on marrying when she was nineteen. That musta been not long before Kincade took off." He paused, fingers wrestling with the tip of his large-boned nose. "She said he showed too much difference in how he treated the girl and the boy. Said the boy got all the best of it, especially after he began showing some promise as a gymnast and on the basketball court."

"Where was the boy while she was telling you all of this?"

"Chester had him in the bedroom." He built a quizzical expression and scratched behind his ear. "Why?"

"She just seems . . . talky."

He nodded, lips pursed. "She was a little, I reckon. Cried a lot, but that didn't stop her from talking. You ain't heard much of anything yet."

I got up and wandered over to the patio door. I pulled the drapes and checked out the brightening day. The glass was cold to my touch, the patio damp from the heavy dew that would one morning soon turn into a killing frost. Though curled brown leaves dotted the yard, the oak and elm were still full and green, the grass lush and in need of mowing; a summer's growth of hedge waited patiently for the trimmer. The thought depressed me. I spoke without turning.

"I appreciate your coming by, Homer. To fill me in."

"No big deal, little buddy. I figured you'd want to know, seeing's how you brought him all the way from California, and all."

"Meaning?" I watched a small gray squirrel scoot along an oak limb with fluid ease, poise delicately, and launch himself into the air toward a paper shell pecan tree I had been babying along for ten years. He landed running, caromed off the side of the tree trunk, and disappeared into the foliage. A startled jay fluttered upward, pierced the quiet morning air with shrill obscenities.

"Meaning nothing, little buddy. You brought him over there is all."

I turned to look at him. "It was a job. He wanted to come home and I brought him."

Homer laid the cigar in a nearby ashtray and rubbed his hands together briskly. "You don't feel a little bit of responsibility for what's happened?"

I continued to stare at him; he squirmed a little and gave me a disarming smile.

"No, Homer, I don't feel a damn bit responsible. There's no reason why I should, and you know it. So, why are you trying to lay some kind of guilt trip on me?"

"I'm not," he said placidly. "I just wondered if maybe you wouldn't feel a little . . . well, used."

"Used? You mean you think I was sent to bring Kincade back to be killed?"

"I ain't saying that, but it's not impossible, is it?"

"His wife hired me, Homer."

"I know that. She told me that. Why'd you think I came over here?"

"I don't know why you came over here. I could have told you all I know in a five-minute phone conversation."

"Yeah, I know," he said, a faintly disgruntled look on his face. There was more, and I knew from experience it would come when he was ready and not one second before. Phlegmatic, unflappable as a three-toed sloth, he preferred oblique approaches and disarming guile to straight-line frontal assault. It had always worked well for him, primarily because of his size and the fierce expressions he could muster at will. No one expected finesse from a man who would have looked right at home on "Saturday Night Wrestling." But I had worked with him too long, knew him too well. I returned to my chair, laced my hands together and stared at him. Silence made him uneasy; it was the one inexplicable chink in his well-developed armor.

We sat quietly, smoke boiling around his head, his broad face taking on a darker hue. He pretended to study the hunting prints on the wall behind the couch. I continued to look at him, watching with interest the mounting color and the nervous swipe of a hand through disarrayed hair, a telltale mannerism roughly equivalent to the flick of a rhino's tail.

He cleared his throat and coughed, smashed the cigar into the ashtray. "Well, I guess I was wrong."

"Wrong about what?"

He pushed out of the chair, the pin-striped cloth of his lightweight worsted jacket falling neatly into place around his massive torso. A wary man with a buck, clothing had recently become his one extravagance: tailored suits and imported shoes, shirts that cost as much as one of my corduroy jackets, thirty-five-dollar ties and ten-dollar socks from Washer Bros. A

13

long-time widower, he had never displayed much interest in clothing before, and I suspected the persuasive influence of some comely female. But perhaps I was being overly romantic; maybe it was nothing more than rapidly advancing middle age, midlife crisis.

"About you. About this. Somehow I thought you'd feel kinda bad about it."

"I do feel bad—"

"Somehow I thought you'd want to pitch in and—"

"Whoa, Homer! What's this 'pitch in' crap?"

"Just what it sounds like," he said ponderously, moving to stand in front of the patio door. "I—we sure could use some help."

"Let me get this straight. You're *asking* me to get involved in a murder investigation? Whatever happened to 'murder's police work, old buddy, you tote your little bale and I'll handle the barge'?"

He turned and gave me a reluctant grin. "Did I say that? Well, it never stopped you before."

"At any rate, I don't know why you'd need help on this one. Find the girl."

"You think so? Why?"

"Percentages. You know them as well as I do. Look to the family first."

"I dunno." He stared across the room at the blind eye of my TV, a scowl slowly forming on his heavy features. The thought was unsettling to his sense of the cosmic order of things. Women were nurturers, mothers and wives and daughters, right up there with flag and country and the Dallas Cowboys. For a man who had spent his adult life as a cop, he could sometimes be incredibly naive. "She didn't look like no killer to me."

"Little and cute and cuddly, huh? All you saw was a picture. They're pretty much one-dimensional, Homer."

He gave me a scornful look. "That ain't it at all. That boy David said she took it harder'n anybody when Kincade took off. Said she moped and cried around the house for weeks. If that's so, why'd she want to shoot him when he comes home?"

"Sometimes love turns to hate. Feelings of rejection crystallizing into—"

"I don't need no pop psychology crap. You gonna help me, or not?" He whirled away from the door with the heavy grace you sometimes see in circus pachyderms.

"Maybe," I said, thinking of the two interminable days ahead waiting for Susie. "You haven't told me why you need my help. The fact that I knew Kincade doesn't have anything to do with it, so don't pretend it does. Furthermore, this looks like a pretty routine case to me, so I don't see why—"

"Dammit, Dan, if you'll shut up a minute I'll tell you!" He threw up a hand, fingers splayed. He grabbed his forefinger with his other hand and bent it down. "First of all, them idiots down at City Hall cut our budget by ten percent. When Lynville retired last month, they wouldn't let me replace him. That's one man short. Then there's Melrose—he's out with a ruptured disc operation. That's two men short. That leaves me with two men. We got eight active cases already. I had to pull Chester off for this one, but only on a temporary basis to canvass the neighborhood and sit in on the autopsy. After that I've got to put him back on his caseload." He stopped, all four fingers folded against his palm, thumb jutting in the air. "That leaves me."

"Well, what about you? You work cases all the time."

His breath whooshed; he looked injured, frustrated, and irritated all at the same time. His arms flew wide in a gesture of resignation.

"Jesus H. Christ, Dan! They got me spread thinner'n piss on a hot rock now. When they cut the budget, they dumped Robbery and Bunco on my ass right along with everything else I got to do. I'm working six, seven days a week the way it is."

I clucked sympathetically. "That's a real bummer, Homer."

He stared at me, the injured look predominant. "Look, we're friends, right? Do I ever ask anything of you?"

"All the time."

"Well, nothing important like this. Besides, look at all the stuff I do for you."

"Like what?" I lit a cigarette and grinned into his mock belligerence; his wide mouth struggled to keep from smiling. He knew I would eventually agree to help him, had understood that from the beginning. It was simply the way we had always worked together; benevolent adversaries. It began in a squad car as a way to liven the dull workaday world of the beat cop, continued on into the detectives. It helped us survive, kept our relationship from sinking into the dull complacency of most friendships. It probably had to do with being cops, with male bonding, with our inability to express affection in conventional ways. Whatever the reason, it had become custom so ingrained that we would have been hard put to communicate for very long without it.

"Well?" He buttoned his suitcoat and smoothed the tan silk tie.

"I'm a P.I., Homer. I don't have the authority—"

"Says who?" He chortled, unbuttoning the coat, sliding one beefy hand into an inside pocket. He brought out the hand, something hidden in the wide palm. He reached out and lifted my left arm, slapped the object into my hand.

"There you go." He stepped back and watched me, grinning.

I turned the worn leather case over in my fingers, stared at the badge: number 1224, my old number, my old shield.

"Had it in my desk drawer ever since you gave it to me. It wouldn't fit where you said to put it, even with the axle grease. Kinda brings a lump to your throat, don't it?"

"This doesn't mean a thing. Anybody can carry a badge." I *did* feel something in my throat: a tightness, warmth. It was only an inanimate object, but I had carried it for ten years, and Homer was right—the thing in my throat could have passed for a lump.

His grin widened. "I ain't finished, dammit. Raise that right paw of yours and repeat after me."

"Okay," I said. "I'll give you two days. Susie's due home Sunday night or Monday morning. Either way she'll have some days off coming, and I'm getting her away from here before they send her to Iran to interview Khomeini." I held out the badge. "You don't need to go through this swearing-in bullshit."

"I'll take the two days," he said and pushed back my hand. "Keep the badge; it's yours. And now, hold up that goddamn right hand of yours before I tear it off at the wrist."

"It wouldn't be legal, Homer. You're only a captain."

"It will be soon's I get Chief Hollister's okay." He gave me a long, slow look, eyes glinting. "Now there's two ways we can do this. You can either hold up your hand like I asked you to, or I can whip your ass till your nose bleeds. Your choice."

"Well, since you put it that way, Homer. . . ." I held up my hand.

After Homer left, I showered, shaved, and plodded through a breakfast of toast, cornflakes, and milk. Not my usual breakfast fare, but we were out of bacon and eggs, and I had never mastered the art of making edible flapjacks. Susie apparently had not had time to grocery shop between assignments, another mini–ball of ammunition in the smoldering controversy that would inevitably erupt into open battle. I was selfish enough to want my wife home with me, not gallivanting around the world reporting the miseries of others when I was sitting at home miserable without her.

It was not a matter of her working or not working. I had no objection to a career in her chosen profession of broadcast journalism. During the first few months of her employment with

TNS, the Texas News Service, her job as field reporter had posed no problems—an occasional late evening assignment, very rarely an overnight stay in some outlying city. Minor inconveniences that created only minute ripples in the ever-deepening well of love.

But with an unexpected promotion to special assignment reporter came change, rapid and drastic, her workaday world expanding to encompass the globe and all its many and varied ills, its dangers and catastrophes.

Ecstatic and morose in turn, she had accepted the job after a hard-won commitment from me to a six-month trial period. Five months had passed, and I both anticipated and dreaded the passage of the sixth. She loved the job, and that filled me with fear and insecurity. I found myself constantly seeking reassurance during our too few hours together—either that or acting lofty and unconcerned, futile posturing that served only to aggravate.

I was no longer bothered by the sixteen-year difference in our ages, I told myself, believing it until I chanced to catch sight of my lived-in face in a bathroom mirror close-up, or until she appeared on the tube, enchantingly attractive at her worst, inordinately beautiful at her best. Bittersweet moments. I was sometimes jolted by the sight of her, an overpowering rush of emotion not far behind. Pride was not the least of these emotions; I had come to admit that to myself. Pride of possession, perhaps, pride in the inescapable fact that she belonged to me, and woe betide the sorry bastard who would try to make it otherwise.

I washed the bowl and spoon and wiped up the crumbs of toast. I was threading an arm into my one decent sports jacket, a dark blue mixture of wool and silk, when the phone rang.

I lit an after-breakfast smoke and picked the phone up on the third ring. I inadvertently coughed into the receiver, and my caller accepted that as a salutation.

"Lieutenant Roman?" There was more than a dash of sarcasm in the voice, and I responded in kind.

"Yeah, Chester, this is Lieutenant Roman. By the way, I heard you made detective first. Congratulations."

A heavy silence ensued while he pondered the inequities of the world; then evidently he decided to ignore it.

"Captain Sellers said you'd be working on the Kincade case. Said to bring you up to date. Okay. Still got two men working the neighborhood, but we don't expect anything out of that. Seven to eight is prime TV time, people got everything else tuned out. The girl Cynthia came home a little while ago. All broke up. Cap'n said leave her to you, so she's all yours and welcome to her. I'm gonna sit in on the autopsy—at least that's what we had planned. You wanta do it?" There was a cynical challenge in his tone.

"No, thanks." I refused to be baited into something I'd have nightmares about for a month.

"Okay. I'll get you the preliminary poop and then, according to Cap'n Sellers, I'm gonna be off the case. That the way you understand it?"

"Pretty much. If I need you I'll let you know. Who worked the scene, Ted Baskin?"

"Yeah, Ted and MacReady."

"Did you do anything at all to confirm the wife's story about the time they left Austin?"

"Well, the kid confirmed it and, yeah . . . wait just a second. I got the names here of two people in the convoy I called this morning. They came back in a six-car cavalcade—"

"All right. Include that in your report."

"You got it. Uh, you coming back on the force, huh? Never thought I'd see that."

"Well, you know what a charmer Homer is."

"As a lieutenant, too?" Six years to detective first; I could feel the animosity humming along the line.

"Yeah, ain't that a kick in the ass?" I wasn't at all sure that Homer's little charade with the badge and the swearing-in had had any validity whatsoever, but if I wanted cooperation out of hardheads like Chester they would have to believe it had.

"Hey, I thought you liked being a private eye, all them good-looking broads, the big money—" He broke off, his comradely laugh as false as a hooker's kiss.

"You've been watching too much TV, Chester. It's a cruel world out here. I can't wait to get back to rooting in the city trough."

He managed a laugh, a little too loud and with a little too much sneer. I decided to stroke him a little before it got out of hand; other than being an arrogant twit, he wasn't really a bad cop.

"You were first on the scene, Chester. What kind of vibes did you get? First impressions—you know what I mean."

"Yeah," he said slowly, antagonism fading from his voice. I could hear breathing, a sound like fingernails scratching a stubbled chin. He sucked in a deep breath. "Yeah . . . I was just thinking back. If I had to sum it up, I guess I could do it with only one word." He paused. "Overkill."

"You mean the four gunshot wounds?"

"Yeah. Three in the chest. One looked smack in the heart, the other two not far off. The fourth one was in the crown of his head, a little round bald spot. Not exactly the work of a pro, although the guy was a pretty good shot at that. He grouped the first three real nice. The head shot seemed sorta like an afterthought."

"What caliber would you say?"

"Small. I'd guess a twenty-two. Could be a twenty-five. Not much difference in an entry wound."

"No exit wounds?"

"Nope. All four slugs are still in him. No shell casings laying around, either, so it was probably a revolver. Coulda been an automatic though, and he picked up his casings."

"No signs of struggle?"

"No. There was some bologna on the floor, but I figure Kincade dropped it when he was shot, something like that."

"How big is the kitchen?"

"Narrow, probably four feet between the cabinets and sink on one side and the stove and oven and refrigerator on the other. Fourteen feet long. From the door to where he was standing was probably ten, eleven feet. Looks like he mighta taken a couple of steps toward the shooter, but it's hard to say for sure."

"Okay, Chester, thanks. If you'll drop off the autopsy report with Homer I'd appreciate it. I'll see you later."

"Right," he said and broke the connection.

I hung up the receiver feeling disconsolate, a humid queasiness in my chest. I had been away from it too long. I no longer had the ability to accept the dry, clinical details of murder with objective detachment. Besides, Ralph Kincade hadn't been a stranger. I had spent time with him. We had drunk together, discussed his life in some detail, examined the human condition, the headlong flight of the world to perdition, to extinction. We had even found reason to laugh, to toast the absurdity of it all with the mawkish camaraderie of drinking men everywhere. Dammit, I had *liked* Ralph Kincade, human frailties and all. Maybe running away displayed weakness, but coming home had taken a special kind of courage, too.

He was going home to start again, to make amends to the ones he loved, to "right a great wrong" as he had solemnly told me in the sad, mournful voice of a man who understood futility, who accepted scorn and ridicule as his due.

Nobody had a right to kill him for that.

A green-and-white squad car sat at the curb in front of the Kincade house. An eight-year-old Buick and a low-slung, imitation sports car from Japan hunkered side by side in the driveway, an elegant, graceful behemoth and its genetically distorted offspring.

Tall, threadbare cottonwood and stunted post oak guarded the midsize, bungalow-style frame; a yellowing mixture of Bermuda and St. Augustine grasses provided a less than adequate lawn. Untrimmed privet hedge bounded the small, off-center front porch, and a wooden swing badly in need of refinishing squirmed and wiggled with the chill October breeze. An unkempt patch of roses, long stems profusely laden, bobbed and fluttered their multihued heads like the colorful bonnets of gossipy old ladies. Withered leaves littered the lawn. Gum wrappers and bits of debris caught in the weed-infested grass. Whatever else the Kincades turned out to be, they weren't much shucks as gardeners. But then, neither was I.

I lit a cigarette and got out, looking up and down the street for one of the uniformed cops out of the squad car. Nothing stirred. The street curved gently to the south, tree-lined—noiseless and empty. No children playing. No hearty old men stumping along, catching the warming sunshine. No gawkers. Unusual.

Somebody once said that news of tragedy spreads with the speed of wildfire. There should be gawkers, I thought. If nothing else, a small clutch of neighbors to speculate on the sudden demise of Ralph Kincade, to shiver a bit and cluck their tongues, to finally conclude that it must have had something to do with a woman—or with drugs. Or both.

But nothing stirred, and I flipped the cigarette into the gutter and walked up the ragged blacktop driveway feeling oddly misused, out of time and place, acutely aware of the badge in my pocket and an overwhelming sense of déjà vu. It all seemed vaguely familiar, like a spot I had stopped at before on my way to somewhere else.

Damn Homer Sellers, anyhow.

4

A boy opened the door, a slender, compact youth with a handsome face that bore more than a passing resemblance to Ralph Kincade's. Close-cropped blond hair, clear blue eyes, freckles, and a full-lipped, turned-up mouth combined to give him a perennial expression of good cheer that I guessed would be hard put to express sorrow on this or any other sad occasion. Shorter than me by a good three inches, his body tapered from comparatively wide, heavily muscled shoulders to a small waist and narrow hips. He wore dark jeans and a white T-shirt with the legend NUMBER ONE BROADJUMPER.

He had the kind of body I would have killed for at his age; still might.

"You're Mr. Roman," he said, his tone somewhere between a question and a statement. "I'm David Kincade."

I nodded, and he stepped back, swung open the door.

"You're the man who brought Dad back from L.A.," he said flatly, no accusation that I could detect. He didn't offer to shake hands.

"Redondo Beach," I said, "but that's close enough." I closed the door behind me.

"I'll get Mom," he said and moved out of the small entry alcove. He swung one well-muscled arm toward a square expanse of room off to our right. "Have a seat. It won't take a minute."

I stepped into the room, but decided to wait standing; it would save having to get up when the lady of the house entered. In this era of women's rights, of total equality between the sexes, I was never sure what the new, revised amenities should be, so I usually came down on the side of caution, avoiding, whenever I could, situations that had once demanded masculine gallantry. I often wondered how Sir Walter Raleigh would have fared in today's bright new world. Or Genghis Khan.

In direct contrast to the house's exterior, the living room was neat and orderly. A nubby, rust-colored couch hugged one wall, bookended by matching wooden tables and lamps. An occasional chair, well-worn and comfortable-looking, sat at right angles to one of the smallest wood-burning fireplaces I had ever seen. A large family portrait hung above the fireplace, and five trophies, four brass and one silver, adorned the narrow mantel. A modest room, but homey, marred only slightly by glaringly new, garish carpeting, a black and wine mixture that did nothing for the color scheme. An antique rocking chair jealously guarded one corner, and framed photographs of David in gym gear literally papered one wall.

"Good morning, Mr. Roman." Naomi Kincade swept into the room, pale and composed, hand extended, the three-quarter, voluminous sleeve of the jade-green robe she was wearing drifting back to reveal a well-tanned, firm-looking forearm.

"Good morning." I gripped the hand briefly and found it surprisingly warm; somehow death and grief and cold always seemed to go together.

"Won't you sit down?" I thought I detected puzzlement in her voice, a trace of wariness. It occurred to me that she had not been told that I would be investigating her husband's death.

"I'm sorry about your husband. I liked him."

She nodded and moved her lips in a silent gesture of thanks. Her gaze sought mine, clear gray eyes intent.

"I appreciate your kindness, Mr. Roman. I especially appreciate your coming by like this." She made the faint smile again. "Although, I must admit to a bit of curiosity."

I killed a moment by crossing my legs and rubbing the toe of one scuffed boot with my palm. Her directness was infectious.

"This isn't a social call, Mrs. Kincade. I've been. . . ." I hesitated, briefly considering *drafted, conned, coerced,* before returning to the false, but less contentious, *retained.* "I've been retained to investigate your husband's death."

Her eyes widened. "Well . . . I—by whom?"

"The police department," I said as if it happened every other day. "Specifically, Captain Homer Sellers."

"Captain Sellers? Is he a large man with untidy hair?" She ran a hand across the contours of her own smooth upsweep as if the thought engendered unpleasant memories. The hair was a deep dark brown, too deep and too dark for a woman her age.

"That's an apt description. He also has sinus problems."

She nodded absently, gazing around the room slowly, as if seeking comfort in familiar things. "I didn't know they did that—the police, I mean, bringing in outside help."

"They can use all the help they can get." I was sidestepping her question and I wasn't certain why. I'd been sworn in, hadn't I? "They're understaffed right now and short of funds."

She huffed a small, meaningless laugh. "I can certainly understand that. I'm short of funds quite often." A rueful smile softened the somber features, added an appealing touch to a face that had survived her forty-eight years very well, tiny crow's feet at her eyes and smile lines the only visible encroachment of advancing age. A wide smile and white, well-kept teeth enhanced the youthful image and attracted attention away from plain, strong features. I had a feeling that soft-spoken, almost deferential Naomi Kincade could be a rock when the occasion demanded.

"I understand you and David drove down to Austin Friday afternoon—"

"Morning. We left early, as a matter of fact. A little after eight as I remember. At any rate we arrived before noon."

"Why so early?"

"Coach Satterly's request. Most of the boys went down with him in his van, but David didn't want me to drive all that way by myself. Coach Satterly wanted us to leave early in case of car trouble. He said to call the stadium if that happened and they'd get someone out to pick us up. Actually, he didn't much like the idea of David going with me. He was afraid something would happen, I suppose. David is his best all-around gymnast; he's particularly good on the parallel bars, and the coach was depending on him to make the difference."

"He came in third?"

"In the individual standings, yes." She stopped and sighed. "He had a bad night. His timing was off. He fell to a nine-six on the parallel bars and a nine-seven on the vault. He took a ten on everything else. Only seven-tenths of a point overall, but it was enough to drop him to third place. The team carried second place and would have been first if David—" She broke off, a shadow of the rueful smile back on her face. "I think it might have been the excitement of his father's coming home."

"He was happy about it, then?"

The quiet gray eyes lifted to mine. "I told you, Mr. Roman,

when I hired you that David was the principal reason I wanted you to find my husband. He was terribly upset when Ralph left. . . . We all were. But in some ways it was worse for David than for Cynthia and me. Cynthia had—Cynthia and her father had been having trouble for a long time. I don't mean to imply that she didn't love him, because I'm sure she did. But Ralph and David were, I think, unusually close."

"That happens sometimes," I said, remembering the summer my father and I built a hunting cabin on four hundred acres of land he had deeded to me when I was born. It had been one of the best times of my life, maybe *the* best time, certainly the closest I had ever felt to the small, quiet man who had labored beside me, taught me the craft passed on to him by his father. Near the end of that summer I discovered that my father was a secret drinker, an incipient alcoholic, and things had never again been the same.

"A few weeks ago David came to me and said he was going to California to find his father. I talked him out of it, persuaded him to go ahead and start college. I promised him I'd see what I could do about—but you know all this. I told you when I hired you."

"Most of it," I said. "You said a few weeks ago. Why did you wait so long?"

The smile turned wintry. "A matter of finances, Mr. Roman." One capable-looking hand drifted to the hollow of her throat. "And speaking of finances, I'm sure the thousand dollars I advanced you wasn't enough to cover your fee and all the expenses, so if you will remind me before you leave—"

"It's enough. All told, I only spent a couple of days looking for your husband." God don't mind the little white lies, and anyhow, it was partly true. The third day we had spent drinking, and everybody knows drinking's supposed to be recreation.

She looked skeptical, but I could see the relief in her eyes. "Are you sure?"

I nodded. "Okay, you reached Austin about noon. Then what?"

She folded her hands in her lap. "Well, then I dropped David off at the stadium with Coach Satterly and the other boys. I headed for the Ramada Inn where we had our reservations—"

"Reservations? You meant to spend the night?"

"Oh, no. We—the families from Dallas and Fort Worth who have boys in the competition always share a room so we can have a place to freshen up before the meet. We, the ladies, usually go shopping in the afternoon, or play cards in the room. The men . . . well, we suspect they spend most of their time down on Sixth Street where all the bars are."

I nodded and smiled, remembering a few football weekends of my own in Texas's capital city. Sixth Street—historically, Old Pecan Street—is the heart of Austin nightlife, a bustling, rambunctious, carnivallike atmosphere that Dallas has long envied and will not in the conceivable future be able to match. Laid back, smoothed out. Music poured out of every bar along the street, running the gamut from jazz to Willie Nelson's country to punk rock.

"What time did the game start?"

She smiled. "The competition. It started at seven o'clock."

"And lasted until ten-thirty?"

"Ten. Sometimes they run a little over."

"You left Austin around midnight?"

"Yes, very close to midnight. We went back to the motel and had a sandwich in the dining room before we left. Then we loaded up and came home. One of David's friends, Mack Rutledge, rode back in the car with us. There were six cars in all, I believe."

I looked around the room; no ashtrays. "I understand your daughter came home a while ago. I'd like to talk to her for a moment."

A frown flitted across the wide, smooth forehead. "I'm not sure it's a good time, Mr. Roman. She was terribly upset by her father's death. I—I'm afraid I gave her—" She broke off and grimaced apologetically. "One of my Valiums. She is probably asleep."

"I wouldn't think one Valium would be that strong, Mrs. Kincade. Basically, I only need to ask her one question."

She stared at me for a moment, then wet her lips. "What?"

"Where she was between seven and nine last night."

She went blank, then let an incredulous look take possession of her face. "Why, that was the time—" She broke off, lips tightening. "I can tell you that," she said, her voice a few degrees cooler on the scale. "She spent the night with a friend of hers named Terri."

"Man or woman, and what was that last name?"

"It's a woman, of course." She bit her upper lip. "But I'm not sure—I don't remember hearing her last name, although I must have."

"That's why I need to talk to her," I said gently.

"Surely, you can't believe that Cyn would—"

"No, ma'am. I don't believe anything. Not yet. The first rule of detecting: you eliminate the people who could not have committed the crime. That leaves you with the people who did." It was a logical statement, I thought, if a bit oversimplified, but she wasn't buying any part of it.

"Do the police believe Cyn had anything to—" She stopped again, seemingly unable to bring the thought to fruition. She looked a bit off-center, her eyes slightly out of focus. It was a radical departure from her former cool reserve and it bothered me. Interviewing family members of murder victims had been a part of being a homicide detective I had hated. It hadn't changed over the years; neither had I. But it was a necessary part of it, and I wasn't doing myself or Mrs. Kincade any favors by beating around the bush.

"I have to talk to her, Mrs. Kincade. I'm sorry."

"Well . . . if you think you must." She pushed up from the couch and stood looking at me. "I must warn—"

"I'll get her, Mom." David materialized in the doorway, a scowl marring the tanned forehead.

"Well . . . fine. Thank you, dear." She sat back down. David disappeared without a word.

"I'd like to talk to her alone, if I might, Mrs. Kincade."

"Why?"

"It just works better that way. She's an adult, isn't she?"

"Yes, of course, she's twenty-one."

"It would be better alone," I said. "If you don't mind."

"No, of course, I don't mind," she said severely, and rose to her feet again. She nodded without looking at me and left through the door where David had stood.

I looked at the small pile of ashes in the fireplace and thought about sneaking a few puffs on a cigarette. But caution prevailed. You just couldn't tell about people anymore. For all I knew I could be afoot in Indian country, alone with a houseful of health nuts, clean-air freaks, or, what would be even worse, ex-smokers.

/ 5 /

The first thing I noticed about Cynthia Kincade was that she was smoking, a pack of Trues and a throwaway lighter clutched in her hand, the cigarette held at right angles to her body à la Bette Davis. She was lean and willowy, no bust to speak of, long black hair in dire need of grooming. She didn't look at all sleepy, and if she had been grievously wounded by her father's death she hid it well behind features that might have been pretty had they not been seized in a petulant scowl. Jeans and a tight yellow sweater emphasized her slenderness; a graceful walk accentuated her femininity.

I stood up.

She drew up short, a startled expression wiping out the scowl. But only for a moment: she made a fierce negative gesture and curled her lip as if deeply affronted by my gentlemanly attitude.

"Sit down. You don't need—"

A phone rang. She jumped, then looked embarrassed at being startled and strode angrily toward the doorway to the kitchen.

She leaned around the doorjamb and snapped the receiver off the wall.

I moved to the fireplace and took out a cigarette.

"It's for you," she said crisply, stretching the cord around the jamb and rattling the receiver on the wooden table beside the door.

"Thanks." I smiled at her, but she had already turned away, doing her Bette Davis thing again, complete with nervous, jerky puffs and clouds of smoke. She took my spot at the fireplace.

"Roman."

"Hard at it, huh?" Homer Seller's rumbling bass. "That the girl or the wife answered the phone?"

"Number one," I said.

"Sounded a mite upset. You scratching around in the short hairs, or what?"

"Or what. Do you have something on your mind?"

"Don't be so snippy, little buddy. 'Course I've got something on my mind. Ted Baskin's up here in my office. Found a little something in Kincade's suitcase we thought might interest you a mite."

"What?"

"Insurance policy on old Ralph's life. That make you perk up your ears a little?"

"How much?"

"Twenty-five thousand."

"Gee whiz," I said. "That much."

"Well, don't turn up your nose, son. I know people'd kill for half that—hell, for a tenth."

"Wrong kind of people, Homer. At any rate, if it was in his bag then it was his policy, right?"

"Well, not exactly. Amalgamated Surety, Inc. issued the policy, but it looks like it was paid for by the Chosan Construction Company in L.A."

"That was his employer."

"Uh-huh. There's a rider says the policy will terminate

within ten days after termination of employment or on the last day of the month during which termination occurs, whichever comes first."

"Pretty standard stuff. Any limitations, restrictions?"

"Only one. Won't pay off on suicide."

"Yeah, well—"

"Pays off on murder, though, and it's still in force, looks like."

"Thanks for calling, Homer."

"You don't seem very impressed by all this."

"I'm not."

"Well, maybe this'll make you sit up and take notice. Who do you think the beneficiary is?"

"No idea."

"Uh-huh, well, it's the girl Cynthia. That unplug your drain a little?"

"Not much." But it was a lie. After the wife, I'd have bet on the boy ten to one. "That it, Homer?" Cynthia was glaring into the fireplace, drumming impatient fingers on the mantel.

"Nope. Got another tidbit or two. Autopsy's finished. No surprises there, although Doc Paris set the time of death between seven and eight. He told Chester he thought it was closer to seven than eight, but he didn't commit himself on the report. Dug out the slugs—twenty-five caliber. Got a couple of beauties for ballistics comparison if we ever find the gun."

"Good. I'll get back to you."

"Don't forget the policy."

"What policy?"

"Ain't you at least gonna mention it to them?"

"I'll do that, just for you." I hung the receiver in its cradle and lit the cigarette. Cynthia was still at one end of the mantel, staring up at the family portrait and flicking her cigarette. I moved back across the room and stopped at the other end.

"I'm Dan Roman," I said. "I—"

"I know who you are. Why are you here asking all these

questions?" Her head lifted, and I saw that she had her father's blue eyes.

"I haven't asked you anything yet."

"I thought you were working for us—for Mother?"

"I was, and maybe I still am. I'm certainly not out to harm you in any way. If I don't ask questions, the police will, and I'm a pussycat compared to them." I made my tone light and humorous, but it elicited no response. She drew the last gasps of smoke from the cigarette, threw the butt into the fireplace and began lighting another.

"Mother said you wanted to know where I was last night, that that was all you wanted from me."

"That's mostly it, yes."

Her head swung, the blue eyes meeting mine, long black hair sliding across her shoulder. For the first time, her face had smoothed to its normal attractive contours. "I was with a man," she said, her voice just above a whisper. "I won't tell you who."

"Why not?"

She shook her head.

"Let me guess," I said dryly. "He's married. He's got a wife and three kids and he's the president of some—"

"No. It isn't like that. He's had trouble with the police before. He can't stand—no, he'd hate me if I brought the police to him."

"I'm not the police, remember. If you can prove where you were between seven and nine last night it doesn't make any difference who you were with. Okay!"

"I can't, not without bringing him into it. Why? Why does it matter? You—the police surely can't believe I'd harm my daddy." The shell was cracking a little around the seams; there was a quiver in her voice, a suspicion of moisture in her eyes that she blinked rapidly away.

"It's not a question of believing or not believing. It's procedure. You, David, and your mother make up his immediate family. Your mother and David were in Austin. You're the only one not accounted for, and they'll want to know. I'm sorry, you don't really have a choice."

She straightened, swung away from the mantel. "I have a choice. I choose not to tell." Face set, head high, she made it all the way to the door before stopping. She stood poised for a moment, then slowly turned. "I'll—I'll ask him."

"Good. But tell him the truth. I'm not a policeman, but I'm working for the police. We don't want any misunderstandings."

"All right."

"One other thing. Had you communicated with your dad at all since he went to California?"

"No."

"Did anyone in the family hear from him? Maybe through a friend?"

She shook her head. "No, nothing."

"Did you know where he worked in California?"

"No. We knew he was somewhere in the L.A. area. He sent money home sometimes. Always a money order from a different bank in Los Angeles." She hesitated. "He never wrote a note or anything in with the money order, never listed a return address."

"He worked as a laborer. I don't suppose there was all that much extra money to send."

She nodded. "He didn't send much at a time, and he always apologized by writing the word *sorry* on the paper he wrapped around the money order." She stopped and sighed. "It's hard to picture Dad working as a laborer. He had a very technical job at General Motors and, too, he always had a horror of high places." A faint trace of humor crossed her face. "It was a standing joke: Mom patched the roof while Dad stood out in the yard yelling instructions." She brought a thumb to her mouth and nibbled at a hangnail. "David wanted to go to Los Angeles to look for him, but Mother talked him out of it. It's such a big place, and we had no real idea where to look."

I nodded. Mrs. Kincade had told me that much when she hired me. Checking my contacts at both the IRS and Social

Security offices had given me the same employment information, the same rooming house address. Finding him after working hours had proved a little more difficult; there were a lot of bars in and around Los Angeles, and that's where Ralph Kincade had spent his free time.

"Before he went to California. Did he have any enemies that you knew about?"

"No. Everyone liked Daddy. That wasn't his problem. He just felt he wasn't needed anymore. He was angry most of the time, but it was at ... well, everything, I guess, the people who shuffle other people's lives around like kids playing with toy soldiers. He was scared all the time. You could tell that."

"Scared of what?"

She shrugged and leaned a shoulder against the doorjamb, the light from a large picture window in the opposite wall highlighting her features, lending character to the small, shapely face. "Life, I guess. Himself. I don't know."

I dropped the cigarette butt into the ashes. She pushed away from the doorjamb, fiddling with the cigarette pack and lighter, watching me with an unwavering stare.

"You don't really believe I had anything to do with Daddy's death?"

"No, I don't think you did, for what it's worth. But somebody killed him. An amateur, most likely, but an amateur who wanted him dead beyond a doubt. He was shot four times, Ms. Kincade. I don't know if anybody told you that. Four times is overkill, and that comes usually from nervousness or hatred."

"Maybe it was a burglar?" Her tone betrayed her; she didn't believe that any more than I did.

"It's possible. Was anything of yours disturbed, missing?"

She shook her head with a small, hollow laugh. "I don't really have anything worth stealing." David appeared in the doorway behind her. He looked relaxed, the handsome face on the verge of a smile, an expression that looked right for him, normal.

"Well, a burglar wouldn't know that, would he? It's not always the big houses that get hit. A junkie's not particular when he needs a fix. He'll steal anything he can pawn."

"The Rolands down the street got hit," David said. "They took their portable color TV, the toaster, some silverware, a whole lot of little stuff like that."

"It happens," I said.

"Mom laid down," he said, idly stroking his sister's unruly hair. "She said if you needed her—"

"No, let her rest. Maybe you'd like to walk out to the car with me?"

"Sure, you bet." His face struggled to regain a solemn mien.

"I'll call you, Mr. Roman." Cynthia Kincade extended a hand.

"I'm in the book. I have a recording machine," I said. "If I'm not there, just leave a message." Her hand was cool, her grip surprisingly firm.

"All right." She gave me a small smile and ducked under her brother's arm.

Outside, the sun had taken the bite out of the autumn air. The street had finally come alive. A knot of women stood talking a few doors away, ubiquitous jeans and sweaters, rolled-up hair bound in colorful scarves. At the corner a short, fat postman angled across the street, leaning away from the bulging bag that threatened his equilibrium, one chubby fist clutching a bundle of mail. Midway down the block, three screaming tykes pummeled a playmate riding for his life on a tricycle. A flop-eared brown-and-tan hound chased after them, tongue extended through a happy beagle grin.

I stopped halfway down the driveway to light a cigarette. David drew up a few feet away.

"Would I be right if I said I figured you heard everything that was said in there just now?"

"Pretty much," he said, and smiled. "It's a small house, Mr. Roman. I was in the kitchen. It's just off the living room."

"Did you hear anything that you might want to talk about?"

He looked puzzled. "I don't think I understand."

"Anything that didn't sound just right. People sometimes forget, get things mixed up, don't always tell it exactly right afterwards."

"I didn't hear any lies, if that's what you mean," he said coldly.

"You heard your sister say where she was last night?"

"Not all of it. But I knew where she was, anyway."

"You know who her friend is?"

"No," he said, the blue eyes meeting mine without flinching.

"You said you knew where she was."

"I didn't mean *where* exactly. I meant I knew she'd been seeing some guy. I was sure she was with him."

"You've never met him, seen him?"

"No," he repeated, but the eyes wavered, flicked away. He rubbed his right arm briskly, then the left. "Colder out here than I thought."

"Your mother tells me you and your dad got along well. Why do you think he left?"

He took a moment to consider, eyes fixed on the noisy group of youngsters out on the street. "I'm not sure. His lousy job for one thing. Never any extra money. He wasn't used to that. None of us were, I guess. Trouble with Cyn . . . they fought a lot. He wanted to know where she was every minute, like that. She wouldn't tell him. They were too much alike, I think." He sighed. "But it was the job, I guess, more than anything else. Mom having to work, Cyn dropping out of college, even me working after school. I think that shamed him somehow."

"He couldn't find another job here?"

"No. He was always looking, but that shipping clerk thing was the best he could find. It was the kind of job you start out with, not end up trying to support a family on."

"He found a job in California in construction. He seemed to like it pretty well."

He smiled. "I guess most anything would have been better than what he had. He was ashamed to tell people what kind of work he was doing."

36

"You both liked outdoor sports, I understand. Did you do any hunting?"

"And fishing. A lot of our free time was spent doing one or the other." He rubbed his heavily muscled arms again, smiling apologetically. "I should have slipped on a jacket."

"Yeah, you'd better get back inside. One more question: Have you had any contact with your dad since he left nine months ago?"

"No," he said quietly, and this time he had no trouble meeting my gaze. "Is that all, Mr. Roman?"

I nodded and smiled, and he put out his hand. I took it, prepared for a bone-crushing grip. It was almost limp, not as strong as his sister's.

I went down the driveway and climbed into the Ramcharger, sat watching as David Kincade cleared the porch steps in one lithe bound and disappeared inside the house.

He had lied about not knowing his sister's lover. Maybe they had never been formally introduced, but I'd bet an eighty-dollar hubcap that he'd seen them together somewhere, or more likely, had made it his business to find out who the man was. He'd impressed me as being a very capable young man, even if he wasn't much shucks as a liar.

6

I ate lunch at Margo's, as far as I knew the only place left in the world that served old-fashioned open-faced roast beef sandwiches with mashed potatoes and real beef gravy.

I lingered over a second bottle of Miller's, watching the harried lunchtime crowd wolf down chicken-fried steak and double-decker hamburgers, hot dogs and greasy-looking enchiladas I wouldn't have eaten on a bet. Young people for the most part, midline executives with tanned skin and good teeth, up-and-comers with glossy shoes and button-down collars that had been popular when I was a kid. Dilettantes at life, they were insecure except among their own kind and would swarm a restaurant one week, abandon it the next. Moving on, always seeking, they really weren't all that much different from their predecessors; it was just that there were so damn many of them.

I made my way to the cashier's desk, paid up, and strolled outside to my truck. The day had ripened: a gentle breeze, and a perfect seventy-two degrees on the marquee of a nearby bank. I shucked the jacket and climbed inside the truck. I lit a ciga-rette and went over what I had learned from a morning with the Kincades.

It didn't take long, and it wasn't much. Nothing that I hadn't already known, except for Cynthia's mystery boyfriend. One way or another I would have to find out about him, speak to him face to face, make up my own mind about him. I had no real suspicion that Cynthia had had anything to do with her father's death, but it was a dangling thread and until it was snipped I would have to worry it like a sorry old hound.

With that in mind I retraced the route I had taken from the Kincades'. I had a hunch that Cynthia would be feeling a grow-ing need to explain things to her boyfriend, and what with the smallness of the house and a younger brother lurking around, it wasn't likely she would use the phone. One on one would be the logical way, maybe even a few tears despite the brittle de-meanor, a chance at the kind of comfort a mother and a brother couldn't provide.

That was assuming, of course, that she, or he, or both of them, hadn't committed the murder.

I found a ragged little park at the north end of the curving street. I pulled the Dodge over the curb and left it parked in a well-worn set of ruts leading deeper into the trees. I took a pair of small binoculars from under the seat and wandered around, stopping occasionally to peer into the trees. I found a picnic table that afforded a view of the Kincade driveway, lit a cigarette, and settled in to wait.

I figured I had about thirty minutes before some nervous housewife got on the phone to the police, another fifteen before the beat cops got around to checking me out. I wasn't worried about that, but it would attract attention and might come at the wrong moment.

Cynthia Kincade was nobody's fool and, while I wasn't at all sure she knew what type of vehicle I drove, if she saw me talking to a cop only a block away from her house it might make her a tad suspicious and a hell of a lot more wary.

But it couldn't be helped. Crime stats being what they were, people were scared, entire neighborhoods banding together to keep a weather eye out for potential criminals, strangers first and strange-acting neighbors second. Time was, a lone male could sit for hours in a neighborhood park and not draw more than a half-dozen curious glances. No more.

Within minutes I was experiencing the crawling, tingling sensation that comes from being watched by hostile eyes. It was an old familiar feeling I had noticed first in Vietnam. Skeptical at first, I had cultivated it, refined it, until it had become a part of my defensive mechanism almost as important as my eyes and ears. Sixth sense, ESP, or pure paranoia, it had proved to be right more often than not, and I had come to trust it.

Five minutes later I almost laughed aloud as two men stepped out of a house across the street and came toward me.

Big men, tall, with wide shoulders and thick chests running to paunch. They wore jogging togs, but I couldn't visualize them jogging; they carried baseball bats and neither could I visualize them playing ball. The one behind had a catcher's mitt on his left hand, and the one in front tossed a ball up and down. That made me want to laugh again, but not for long.

They wore grim expressions on fat, shiny faces and, except for the fact that one of them was black and the other one was white, they could have been brothers.

I lit another cigarette and pointed my binoculars into the

trees. And that fooled them just about as much as the ball and mitt fooled me.

They drew up a few yards away, shoulder to shoulder, Adidas planted wide apart, neighborhood champions doing what was right, defending the womenfolk, the elderly, the kids. And they *were* doing what was right, I told myself, and tried to curb the impulses taking root in my mind.

"Afternoon." The white one tossed the ball to his friend, placed the butt of the bat on his right toe and folded his hands around the handle. "Purty day, ain't it?"

"Beautiful," I agreed, wondering how they would approach their subject.

"Thought we might bat the ball around a little." He had bad teeth and a button nose, and at some time during his adolescence he had fought a losing battle with acne.

"Good day for it."

He nodded and looked at his black friend as if he had exhausted his repertoire of small talk.

"I see you have binoculars." The black man's voice was soft and cultivated in direct contrast to his pugilistic features, an off-center nose and eyebrows thickened by scar tissue. His smile was affable and wide, revealing a glimpse of gold.

"Bird-watching." I crushed the cigarette against the heel of my boot, got up and tossed the filter into a nearby trash barrel. I went back and sat down.

The white one looked dubious. He made a quick survey of the nearby trees. "I ain't never noticed any birds much over here except them little blackbirds and a lot of sparrows."

I shook my head and chuckled. "You just don't know how to look. Not more'n ten minutes ago I saw a silver-throated red garfinkle."

"Red garfinkle, huh? I don't reckon I ever—" He broke off at a sound from his companion, turned to look at the smiling face, then turned back to me, his skin taking on a dull pink glow. He straightened to his not inconsiderable height.

"I guess you're puttin' me on, mister. That ain't hard to do. I ain't too bright sometimes. But now that we've broke the ice, so to speak, we're gonna have to ask you what you're doing in our park."

The black one just stared, top-level cool; he had wise eyes, long arms, and his unwavering smile said "try me."

I lit another cigarette, stalling, using the time to sort through and cast aside several smartass answers before deciding on the truth.

"I'm on stakeout," I said.

The white man's hands tightened on the ball bat, shifting to a swinging grip. The flush died away. He bumped the toe of one shoe like a golfer practicing a putt.

"Me and Mike here are elected officials of the neighborhood crime watch program," he said seriously. "I reckon we're gonna have to ask you to move along now."

"Look, I really am on stakeout—"

"Mike here has got a mind like a steel trap. He's got your license number already memorized, and according to our rules we're gonna have to report your truck to the police as a suspicious vehicle."

"TKF 924," Mike said proudly. "Texas license. Dodge Ramcharger, color black. Wire wheels and high performance tires. Whitewalls."

"You've been in the immediate area more'n thirty minutes without a logical explanation," the white man said, obviously pleased with Mike's recitation.

"Look, fellas, I'm sorry if I—Look, I really am on stakeout—"

"Of course, you don't *have* to move along," Mike said gently. "But take it from someone who used to walk occasionally in Central Park in New York, parks can be dangerous places filled with unpredictable people. Unpleasant things just seem to happen in parks."

"Like broken arms," the white one said. "And concussions."

"All right," I said, irritated, more at myself than at them. "You've scared me enough, okay?" I shoved a hand inside my coat. "I have I.D."

They might have looked like a couple of Babe Ruth rejects,

but they moved like Too Tall Jones, surrounding me before I could blink, bats lifted high, faces tense and frightened and determined.

"You bring anything out of that pocket that cuts or goes *bang bang*, and we're gonna hurt you, mother!" Mike's face was shiny with sweat, eyes wide and unblinking, pink tongue caught in one corner of his mouth.

I nodded carefully, brought my hand out with the case between two fingers. I flipped it open, showed him the badge.

He studied it for a good ten seconds; it seemed longer. Then he made a whooshing sound and let the bat fall to the tabletop. "Son of a bitch, Lenny, he's a cop!"

"Whoops," Lenny said, backing away, grinning so hard I could see his molars. "Why didn't you say so right at first?"

"Lack of good sense."

"Hey, no hard feelings, all right?" Lenny advanced again, holding out a pudgy hand. Down to our left I caught a glimpse of movement, of color: the red Toyota backing out of the Kincade driveway.

I gripped Lenny's hand, moved on to Mike's. The Toyota gunned up the street toward us. I turned my back as it sped past, then whirled and dashed to my pickup.

"Hey, where you going?" Lenny, bat still balanced on his shoulder, stared at me open-mouthed.

I said something inane about another red garfinkle, but luckily it was lost in the noise of the truck's motor. I bumped over the curb and into the street, powered around the last segment of curve in time to see the Toyota's stoplights blink at the corner.

She turned right.

I followed.

7

The Sunrise Arms started out in life as a motel. Built during the early sixties to meet the needs of an ever-expanding, migratory population, it had been slapped together by illegal labor out of cheap Mexican brick, plywood, and the crumbling mortar of profit motive. Sixteen single buildings built in the shape of a U facing old Highway 183, a squat, flat-roofed building in the center that served as lobby, manager's apartment, and recreation center.

By the midseventies the fragile buildings teetered on the brink of total vacancy and sad decrepitude, waiting with bated breath for the next high wind, or the advent of some unwary tenderfoot, whichever came first.

High winds were notoriously unreliable, but tenderfeet came every day in dribbles and spurts, all shapes and sizes and sexual identification.

Jud Harmon, late of the U.S. Navy, thirty years of doing what was right, thirty years of salutes and no back talk and green water that made him sick. Free at last. On his own and looking for something to fill all those empty hours that energetic men find themselves burdened with when they retire.

He bought the Sunset Motel, began a program of refurbishment, then watched with horror as the Airport Freeway parted company with Highway 183, skirting his motel a mile to the north, taking with it the lifeblood of his business.

Undaunted, Jud Harmon switched gears, changed direction, added to each of his sixteen cabins a ten-by-twelve-foot combination kitchen and dining alcove, installed proper plumbing, a stove, a refrigerator and, seven months from the day he began renovation, had each of the units rented as one-bedroom efficiency apartments.

All this and more Jud Harmon told me the first time I met him. A lot more than I needed to know to find his runaway spouse. I didn't find his wife, but he never seemed to hold that against me on the rare occasions when we chanced to meet.

He was a rumpled little man, a smile as fiercely phony as a trained chimpanzee's, the lighthearted strut of a contented rooster.

It was to the domain of Jud Harmon that Cynthia led me, to the fourth cabin on the right leg of the horseshoe-shaped compound. I caught a glimpse of her slender figure disappearing through a caramel-colored door.

I drove down to the next light, made a U-turn, and came back up the other side. I parked on the shoulder of the service road, lit a cigarette, and settled in once more to wait.

I could see the front of the cabin, the red Toyota and an ancient battered Mercury listing on failed springs like a tired old horse, its paint so faded and dull it refused to reflect the sunlight. Next door, a matter of a few grassless yards away, a gleaming, showroom-new Chrysler station wagon suffered in silent misery, as out of place in these surroundings as a dowager queen at a bag lady soiree.

Tired, lonesome, I sucked on the cigarette and wondered what the hell I was doing here, playing at being a cop again, prying in the sordid business of other people's lives. I had my own life to think about. Not that it was sordid, but it was growing more worrisome by the day. I wanted my wife at home where I could get at her, at least occasionally, as selfish and chauvinistic as that might be. I needed the comfort of warm, loving arms, safe refuge from a hostile world. I needed passion in my life, reassurance, a little ego boost every now and then. I needed *her*, dammit, and the only solace I could find was knowing she felt the same about me. Small consolation for a brooding libido.

The afternoon staggered by. Along about three o'clock I ran out of cigarettes and crossed the median to a 7-Eleven. Fast service and high prices, a nervous nod from a thin-faced man with a South American accent who rattled my change all over the counter. He mumbled profuse apologies and swept up the coins like a nimble-fingered kid playing jacks, a bead of sweat on his upper lip, moist black eyes refusing to meet mine.

I was halfway back to my truck before I figured out the reason for his agitation. We had been alone in the store, and I had wandered around for a while looking for something to eat. Eventually I had returned to the counter empty-handed and asked for cigarettes—modus operandi of countless bandits over the years. He had believed I was there to rob, and had been scared spitless, and somehow the thought saddened me. I thought about going back to apologize, but that seemed pointless. We didn't speak the same language, didn't live in the same world.

I made my way back across the highway and climbed inside the truck. I broke the seal on the new box of Carltons and sent a casual glance toward the Sunrise Arms. The Toyota was gone.

I sat still for a moment, acutely aware of the rumbling roadway a few yards from the truck, the belch of exhausts, the susurrus of spinning tires, the ear-shattering roar of a semi accelerating away from the light, the raw hum of power unleashed.

I talked myself out of cussing, out of being upset with myself. It wasn't Cynthia Kincade I needed to see, it was her lover and, with any kind of luck at all, he was still ensconced in his miniature apartment, hopefully unaware that he was being stalked by old Bulldog Roman himself.

I got out and crossed the street again, angling across in front of Jud Harmon's office apartment. I was almost safely past when the door popped open and Jud came bouncing out, all teeth and a face as wrinkled as his baggy pants.

"Howdy, Dan! What the hell's going on, buddy?" Gone were the clipped, nasal accents he had brought from New Jersey, the staccato delivery. Sometime during the years since I had last seen him, he had become a Texan, complete with scruffy, run-over boots and John Deere gimme hat.

I spoke and we shook hands. I lit a cigarette and listened to his new drawl for a few minutes, then asked him the name of the man in apartment 4.

His eyes lit up. "That one, huh? Big, good-looking guy, but I don't cotton to him much, you know what I mean? Kinda cool and arrogant. Like somebody told him once his shit don't stink and he ain't never got over it. You're working, huh?"

"You know his name?"

"You bet. Know all my people by name. Name's Gregory Knutson. Blond-haired and purty strong looking. Bet it's that little filly comes to see him all the time. She somebody's wife?"

I shook my head. "Did you see her leave a few minutes ago?"

"You bet. Purty little thang, ain't she? Kinda shy when it comes to tits and—"

"Was she alone?"

"Yep. He's still in there far as I know. Usually gone during the day. He's got a job down at the Cresson Sheet Metal Works, but he didn't go in today for some reason." He gave me a sly look. "Maybe a little matinee."

"Do you know if she was here last night, all night, or any part of it?"

He shook his head regretfully, frowning. "Went into Dallas yesterday. Didn't get home till about ten this morning. First time that's happened in I don't—"

"Have you ever noticed her spending the night before?"

"Once in a while. Not often. She's over there a lot at night, though."

"How long has Knutson lived here?"

He lifted the cap and ran a hand through thin brown hair. "Four months, maybe a little less." He replaced the cap and gave me his wide, artificial grin. "I got him tabbed for an ex-con. You know what I mean. He sorta looks at you out of the corner of his eyes, talks a lot without moving his lips. Guys in the navy who spent a lot of time in the brig had the same habits. Something about being locked up changes a feller."

"It does," I agreed, and hit him lightly on the shoulder. "Thanks, Jud. Nice seeing you again. You're looking good."

"Thanks," he said, and self-consciously hitched up his sagging pants. "I got me—well, I found me another woman."

"That's great, Jud. A man wasn't meant to live alone." There was a soft, ironic beat to my words that he didn't hear, wouldn't have understood if he had.

"She's sorta a lot younger than me. I'm an old reprobate, you know that. But. . . ." He drifted off, then swept one arm in an all-encompassing circle. "But, hell, look what I got to offer."

"There you go. It all evens out. She's a lucky girl." I backed away, nodding and smiling; he was a hard man to get away from. "I'll see you later, Jud."

He followed a couple of steps, then stopped. "You're working on something big, huh?"

"Nothing big. Routine stuff, dull."

He bobbed his head and winked. "I gotcha. Just don't go messing up my apartment, okay?"

"No gun battles or fistfights," I promised solemnly and walked toward apartment 4. Another cop show addict, I thought, reruns of "Mannix," "The Rockford Files," and "Harry O," the newer, more sophisticated mayhem of "Magnum, P.I." and "Miami Vice." Exciting stuff. Obviously, I was doing something wrong. Maybe I needed an office above a liquor store in downtown Dallas, blinking neon lights outside my window, an office bottle of Vat 69, a roscoe or a gat, and a secretary with curves all the way around her body. I'd have to have a seedy, semicomic sidekick, make friends with all the losers on the streets, and have a financial relationship with prostitutes, junkies, bag ladies and bartenders. It all seemed like a lot of trouble just to lead an exciting life.

8

Gregory Knutson was big, all right. Good-looking in a surly, arrogant way. That much of Jud Harmon's description was accurate, but if he had done time recently he had been out long enough for the summer sun to erase his prison pallor. Brown as bread crust, he leaned against the edge of the open door and waited for me to speak, pale blue eyes wary under thin, spiky eyebrows. A palm-sized swatch of blond hair curved across his wide forehead in casual disarray; small, fleshy lips parted slightly from the outward pressure of a moderate overbite. Scowling, he looked mean enough to bite and tough enough to hold on.

"Mr. Knutson? My name is Dan Roman—"

"Sonuvabitch!" He slammed the butt of his palm against the doorjamb, shaking the wall, rattling a nearby window. I managed not to jump.

"Hey, you've got a good eye," I said, smiling amiably. "Most folks don't notice that right away."

"Goddammit! I told her it was stupid to come running over here, bringing the damn law nosing around. Now lookit what—" He broke off, his expression suddenly crafty, sneering. "But you ain't the law, are you? You're that peeper that brought back her daddy from L.A."

"You've got me pegged," I said. "But I don't understand your problem. Didn't Cynthia tell you all I wanted from you was confirmation that she spent last night with you?"

"That ain't none of your damned business. That's our private business."

"Okay, you're right. But how about the hours seven to nine last night? That is my business. Was she with you?"

He raked a hand across his jaw, fingered the corners of his mouth. "Yeah, she was with me."

"Here?"

"That ain't none of your damned business."

"Where then?"

"I told you, none of your damned business. She was with me, that's all you need to know, all I'm gonna tell you, anyhow."

"Why is that all I need to know? What significance does that two hours have to—?"

"I ain't stupid. That was the time her daddy was killed. It was on the TV, and anyhow, she just told me." His upper lip rolled back in a triumphant grin; I decided he wasn't all that handsome after all.

I sighed and looked toward the highway. Jud Harmon slouched against the corner of his office building, carefully looking everywhere but at us. I took out a cigarette, pondering my options. I could back off, put in a call and have a squad car there in five minutes. Knutson seemed to fear the law, and that might shake him enough to loosen his tongue. On the other hand, it might make him more stubborn. Sometimes it worked that way. I lit the cigarette and studied his belligerent face.

Why was he afraid of the law? He didn't appear to be hiding, so it apparently wasn't something he had done recently. Recently . . . maybe that was the key. If I was any kind of judge, Jud had been right, Knutson had the look and mannerisms of an ex-con. And that almost always meant parole for some length of time.

I blew a little smoke in his direction and smiled. "It seems to me you're being unduly hostile, my friend. I would think you'd want to help out your girlfriend. Makes me wonder a little. Are you just naturally ornery, or are you afraid your parole officer—"

"Shit!" He wilted, recoiling as if I had just launched a physical attack, the new tan leaching to a pasty beige. "She tell you—?"

"She didn't tell me anything, but you just did. Did you violate your parole last night, Gregory?"

He looked past my shoulder, pulling his lips together, then rubbing them with his tongue. "Okay, she was with me. All night, all right?"

"No, not all right. I need to know where you were. In the beginning I was willing to take your word for it. Now that I know you're an ex-con I'll have to verify what you tell me. That's a hard fact of life, Gregory. Maybe it's not fair, but there it is."

"Hell, all we did is fly down to the coast."

"That seems innocent enough to me. Where on the coast?"

"Thing is . . . well, I'm not really supposed to leave the county without getting permission. Hell, that's a crock and you know it."

"I agree. Where on the coast? Exactly."

"Galveston."

"Where did you go in Galveston?"

"Motel out on Highway 45. Ramada Inn." He stepped away from the edge of the door. "You wanta come in? The place is—"

I shook my head. "How did you register at the motel? Your name?"

He gave me a sardonic look. "You kidding? Mr. and Mrs. Gregory Smith."

"Original. Why, Gregory? You fly all the way to Galveston to go sit in a motel room? It's a little cool for the beach."

He smeared his annoyed expression with a swipe of a big hairy hand. "Naw, we had a . . . well, a little party, you know. Buddy of mine from the . . . the old days met us and we had some laughs, a little wine, you know."

"Just the three of you?"

He took a deep breath. "No, there was four. We took an old friend of mine along with us as a sorta date for Patches."

"Who?"

"Patches? Guy I did some time—"

"No, who was the girl you took along?"

He shifted his weight and wet his mouth again. "Just an old friend. Name's Maggie, Maggie Lane."

I stared at him for a moment, feeling a minute tremor of shock. "Maggie Lane? The girl who used to sing in Charlie Cole's Zero Club?"

He nodded, an oddly cynical look on his face. "Yeah. You know her?"

I didn't answer. I put the notebook away, hooked the pen in my upper jacket pocket. I knew her, or more correctly, had known her. Maggie Lane née Margaret Belchor. A bright-eyed young woman fresh from a failed marriage to a potato farmer in Indiana; strawberry-colored hair, curves, and a low, sultry voice in the Peggy Lee tradition. It didn't take me long to discover that the light in her eyes came from star-wishes, that her one abiding dream was to be a singer of songs in places where it mattered. But she had cast her loop too high; the rope played out, and she was left to dangle. One of the ones who wanted so much it hurt, she had settled for less because it hurt more not to. The last time I saw her she was standing in the booking line in the Midway City jail, head high, wearing a mink stole around lovely freckled shoulders, and an aloof, disdainful smile that said, "I may be nothing but a hooker, but I'm still a class act."

"Do you have her address?" I took out the pen and notebook again.

He shrugged. "I got her phone number. I ain't never been to her place. I can't afford her." He rattled off the number, then curled his lip. "You'll take a hooker's word, huh?"

I had a sudden desire to hit him. Instead, I turned and flipped the cigarette into his bedraggled patch of lawn.

"Hey, man, you're not going to turn me over, are you? I been cooperating."

"Not unless you're lying." I stepped off the small concrete stoop and walked toward Jud Harmon. He still loitered near a bed of wilting roses, snipping, whistling tunelessly through the gaps in his teeth. He looked up and grinned as I approached.

"Well, I see you talked to the big'un."

"That I did," I said, nodding, walking on past.

"Found out what you wanted to know, I guess." He trotted along beside me.

"That I did," I said.

"I don't suppose you'd want—"

"No, thanks, Jud. It's a little early for me. Maybe next time."

"Huh?" he said, and pulled up short at the edge of the highway. "What I meant was—"

"Never touch a drop before dark," I said, lifting a hand and smiling at his perplexed face. "Man's got to have some order in his life, some rules. That's one of mine. Catch me next time." I angled out into the traffic.

If he spoke again it was lost in the ponderous roar of an accelerating diesel. I paused at the door of the Ramcharger. He was still standing there, arms akimbo. Catching me looking, he threw one arm into the air, fist clenched, index finger extended.

I smiled and waved, climbed into the truck and drove off, the thought of seeing Maggie Lane again a warm sweet taste on the back of my tongue.

$$9$$

The day had matured like a beautiful woman, the air as crisp and pleasant as a lover's first kiss. A smell of woodsmoke, the tart flavor of charcoal and mesquite as countless husbands slapped brisket, chicken, and ribs on low-burning barbecue fires. A day for relaxation and domesticity, smiling wives and rosy-cheeked kids, romping dogs and the normal hubbub of Saturday living.

But I was lonesome. Tired and lonely and feeling a kind of

seething self-disgust. All the way home across Midway City I had thought about Maggie Lane, remembering the way she had been when I first met her, remembering what she had been the last time I saw her. Coolly and with logical detachment. An old, sad story over and done. Not even particularly unique. She had wanted too much without knowing what exactly and had paid too high a price for what she got. I had watched it happen and couldn't stop it, although I tried. She had inflicted great pain, but it wasn't intentional, and I had shut down that part of my mind where she once lived. She was yesterday's dream, a failed chance, a sorry ending long forgotten.

But our minds betray us constantly, store old wounds like odds and ends in a bureau drawer. There's no accounting for the circuitous routes they take in springing their little surprises, and, suddenly, mired in the cranky Saturday traffic, thinking about Maggie Lane, I wanted her. A fierce unbidden desire swept through me like a hot, dry wind. Memories flooded me, vivid images flowing: silken, sweet-smelling hair, a taut, quicksilver body, dark green eyes that made promises that were always fulfilled.

It lasted only a moment before guilt came flooding in. I lit a cigarette and sucked hot smoke into my dry mouth and thought about Susie, let myself revel in self-disgust for a while. I couldn't stop my body's betrayal, but I didn't have to aid and abet.

But the moment had unnerved me, so I drove to my house, showered, shaved, and dressed again in cleaner, sweeter-smelling clothing.

Then I went looking for Maggie Lane.

She didn't answer the first time I called. Nor the second or third. Not at home, I wondered, or busy and not answering the phone? Busy at what in the middle of a Saturday afternoon? I wouldn't let myself dwell on that.

I called Homer's office instead. His secretary, Mitsi, answered.

"Oh, hi, Danny. I hear you're back with us again."

"Don't believe everything you hear, Mitsi. Is Smokey the Bear in?"

She chuckled. "No, he isn't, Danny. Can I help you?"

"Will he be back in, do you know?"

"Oh, yes. They're working us to death. I haven't worked on Saturday since . . ." She let it trail away. "Golly, I don't remember when."

"Chester told me he would leave the Kincade autopsy report with Homer—"

"He did, Danny. It's on Homer's desk along with the file. Do you want me to look up something?"

"No, I don't think so. I'll pick it up later. In the meantime, could you punch some names in the computer for me?"

"You bet. Let me get—okay, Danny, shoot."

"Gregory Knutson." I spelled it for her. "All four of the Kincades if it hasn't been done already. Their names are in the file. Maggie Lane aka Margaret Belchor." I thought for a moment. "One other thing. Chester said he had the names and phone numbers of two of the women who were in Austin with Naomi Kincade. See if you can find them on his report."

"Are you at home, Danny?"

"No, let me call you back. How long, do you think?"

"Oh, it shouldn't take long. Fifteen minutes?"

"That's fine, Mitsi, thanks a lot."

"Don't mention it. Gee, this is nice, seems like old times, Danny."

"Old hard times," I said, and she laughed and broke the connection.

I found another 7-Eleven and bought a Pepsi and a Twinkie. A tough-looking old bird with scarred, knobby hands took my money and looked me in the eye. No fear here. I traded weather information for a meager smile and left wondering what he might have within easy reach under the counter: a 3.57 with a feather pull or a sawed-off twelve-gauge pump?

I gave Mitsi a full twenty minutes before I called her. This time she was crisp and authoritative, all business. "Nothing at all on Ralph or Naomi Kincade. Cynthia Kincade was ticketed once for DWI, but she fought it in court and the case was thrown out. David Kincade is coded for some sort of juvenile record, but it was sealed when he turned eighteen. We can get in, Danny, but we'd have to have authorization."

"Okay, we'll leave that to Homer. How about Knutson?"

"He's serving a fifteen-year sentence in Huntsville for armed robbery. He and—"

"Not any more. He's been paroled for four or five months. See if you can find out who his parole officer is, will you?" I cleared my throat. "Maggie Lane?"

"Let's see . . . Maggie Lane. She's been arrested twice for prostitution. The first time about three years ago and then again a year ago. Fined both times and released." She whistled softly. "She must be doing pretty good at it, judging by her address." She ended with a grudging little laugh.

"And that is?" I took out my pen and little pad.

"Well, it's been a year and she may not live there anymore, but it's 1818A Perelmann Lane. I think that's one of those fancy duplexes just off Windmere."

"Sounds about right," I said. "Phone number?"

"None listed, Danny." She uttered the little laugh again. "I'm reading between the lines, but she must be one of those high-priced call girls."

"What do you know about call girls, Mitsi, high-priced or not?"

"You think I've been sitting here for twenty years with my eyes closed and my ears plugged, Danny? I may be a little old lady, but I know what goes on out there." She cut loose with her full-throated, whinnying laugh, a terrible thing to hear—especially over a phone.

I let it wind down a little, then thanked her and broke the connection. Fiftyish, a cherubic face and a round little body, she handled her job with enthusiasm and verve, handled big hulking Homer almost as well. She knew everything that went on in his life—including a lot of things she probably shouldn't—and, of late, I had begun to wonder if there could be something between them besides a glass-topped plywood partition.

I cycled another quarter through the phone, called Maggie Lane's number again. It was busy; a definite improvement. At least she was home and tending to business. I winced a little at the thought.

While I waited, I punched out one of the numbers Mitsi had given me, a woman named Gloria Strand, an address out in Valley Oaks, one of Midway City's better developments. Silk Purse Alley the old-timers called it, mostly carpetbaggers and opportunists and such, damn Yankees one and all.

But the voice that answered the phone wasn't Yankee, damn or otherwise. It was soft and musical, with as much charm as you could pack into one word.

"Hello."

"Mrs. Strand? Gloria Strand?"

"This is Gloria Strand. May I ask who's calling, please?" A voice that could break your heart, as Texan as windy tales and black-eyed peas, elongated vowels and attenuated consonants, liquid honey and just as sweet.

"Mrs. Strand, my name is Dan Roman. I'm working with the police on the death of Ralph Kincade—"

"Oh, yes, wasn't that a terrible thing?"

"Yes, ma'am, it is. Now—"

"A detective named Chester called me earlier this morning. Are you aware of that?"

"Yes, ma'am, I am. I just wanted to clarify a few points he didn't get into—if you have no objections."

"No, of course not. I'll be glad to help any way I can."

"Thank you. Why don't I tell you what I know and you stop me if anything doesn't sound just right. Then we can go on from there."

"That'll be fine, Mr. Roman."

"I understand you, all of you, arrived in Austin around noon. You had lunch and then the men went their own way and you ladies—"

"That's not exactly right. We all had lunch together and then the men drove us into downtown Austin, *then* they took off on their own."

"Okay, fine. You ladies went shopping. About what time was that?"

"Oh, I'd say one-thirty or a quarter to two."

"And you shopped until when?"

"Five," she said promptly. "We decided beforehand. That would give us time for a leisurely dinner before going to the stadium. Austin has some fine restaurants."

"Yes, ma'am, I've been there. So, you finished eating at about what time?"

"Quite close to six-thirty. We asked the maître d' to have a cab waiting out in front at six-thirty. We only had to wait about three or four minutes."

"One cab? Wasn't it a little crowded? Six people seems—"

Her low, musical laugh was well-controlled and ladylike. "Six? My heavens, no. There were only five of us in the beginning, and then poor Naomi got that migraine headache and went back to the motel. Four of us. It was a bit crowded even so. Molly Seegram had to sit up front with the driver." She laughed again at that, and I chuckled along with her.

"Migraine headache, huh? That was certainly bad luck. When did it hit her?"

"Oh, we were shopping. . . . I'd say around four o'clock. Poor thing. We offered to go back to the room with her, but she wouldn't hear of it. She was determined not to spoil our day. She said quiet and a nap were the only things that would help. So we put her in a cab and . . . I really hated to let her go like that, but she wouldn't have it any other way."

"Did it work? The nap and the peace and quiet, I mean?"

"Oh, yes. When we saw her later at the stadium she was feeling fine. She looked tired and kind of . . . drawn, you know, but she was enjoying watching David and the other boys—"

"When was that, around seven?"

"Well, no . . . it was closer to nine, I suppose. She overslept at the motel and got to the meet a little late. It was very crowded, so she just took the nearest seat and waited until she

57

saw Molly and I going to the restroom. Then she joined the gang and had a fine time—"

"Around nine. But you saw her before that? You could see her from where you were sitting?"

"No, not really. We looked for her, but it's a big place and there were a lot of people. . . . Why, what does this have to do with Mr. Kincade's murder?"

"Background," I said. "You know how it is with bureaucratic red tape. Dot all the i's and cross all the t's."

She laughed again. "Tell me about it. I just went through three weeks of frustration trying to get a permit to put in a satellite dish. You wouldn't believe the restrictions—and the forms to fill out."

I clucked in sympathy, and we talked a few more minutes before I thanked her and broke the connection. I lit a cigarette and opened the door on the booth, then sat there and added it up in my head. Four o'clock until nine o'clock. Five hours. A shuttle flight from Austin to Midway City would take forty minutes at most. Then a cab and delivery to a nearby shopping center, perhaps. Or a rental car and the same destination. Even an Airtrans bus would have taken her within walking distance of her home. Entry into her home without being seen would have been chancy, but by no means impossible. At that time of day people were eating, getting ready for the prime TV hours just ahead. Besides, if I remembered correctly, that area of town, one of the oldest in Midway City, had been laid out with alleys bisecting the rows of houses. But maintaining the alleys just for garbage pickup had proved to be too costly to the city and they had been allowed to run wild, ragged strips of weeds and saplings that would have provided perfect cover for Kincade's killer. It was something I would have to check.

All conjecture, I told myself, flipping the butt into the street. Shaky conjecture at that. From a phone booth in Albuquerque I had given Naomi an estimated time of arrival of six o'clock, and missed it by about forty-five minutes. It could have been three hours, or four . . . or all night, long-distance automobile trips being what they are. Or it could have been an hour earlier, or even two.

On the other hand, my ETA was all she had. She had no choice but to depend on it if, in fact, she had a pressing reason for doing her husband in, and at the same time establish what she thought would be an iron-clad alibi. What pressing reason? The only thing that came to mind was the twenty-five-thousand-dollar policy that would have lapsed in a few more days.

Twenty-five thousand dollars. That wasn't much money, was it? Or was it? Maybe it was all relative. It didn't seem like much if you had some. Maybe if you didn't have any, it would loom like the mother lode. It would go a long way toward putting a son through college, a new car, having the house painted.

I felt a tremor in my stomach, a tendril of nausea working upward. Dammit, I didn't believe Naomi Kincade was a killer, I didn't want her to be the one. I wanted some nameless, faceless villain whom I could slap in irons without a second thought, march off to his just deserts with never a qualm.

I sighed and fumbled in my pocket for another quarter. Just living life was getting more worrisome all the time.

10

After the third busy signal I said to hell with it, climbed into my truck and drove out to the address on Perelmann Lane. Reluctantly. I wasn't sure I wanted to see Maggie Lane again, murder investigation or no murder investigation. She was a part of my personal history. Not the happiest part or the worst, but maybe one of the saddest.

I parked out on the street and walked up the short, extrawide driveway feeling exposed and vulnerable, looking down at myself and seeing shabby, scuffed boots and rumpled clothing, a thickening around the waist I hadn't noticed before. But it was only Maggie after all, I reminded myself. She had seen me at my worst and at my best; there was not much I could do to fool her, even if I'd wanted to try.

Maggie Lane's duplex was a meticulously crafted arrangement of Old English brick, glass, and gleaming white wood topped with hand-worked cedar shingles. Low and rambling, at first glance it appeared to be a single private home, a dwelling that declared without equivocation the status and sophistication of its occupants. It wasn't until you noticed the two entrances, deeply recessed double doors set twenty feet apart, that you began to consider other possibilities. I chose the left wing because of a small, elegant sign above the entrance, gold-embossed letters that stated simply: M. Lane.

I stepped through the doorway into cool, shadowy gloom. I wasted a few seconds looking for a bell, then, finding none, lifted the heavy brass ring set into the door. I lifted it and dropped it three times, stepped back, feeling a gentle thrust of adrenaline, a faint acceleration of my heartbeat. My mouth was dry; my face felt warm. I found myself grinning at my own foolishness; it was only Maggie, after—

The door popped open on silent hinges. Caught with the idiotic grin, skewered like a specimen bug by clear green eyes, all I could think to do was stand there, smirking like a prodigal son, heat building in my cheeks, watching the lovely tanned face swing from cheery welcome to shock to something I wasn't sure about.

"Danny! I thought you were—" She chopped it off, shaking her head, glossy strands of delicately tinted auburn hair spilling forward, curling just above her breasts. She wore a simple sheath dress, sleeveless, form-fitting, but otherwise almost demure. A single white flower peeked out of a deep wave at the side of her head, and finely molded lips seemed to quiver as they vacillated between humor and disapproval. "Danny. What are you doing here?"

"Just happened to be passing by," I said, letting the smile die the death it deserved. "And I saw that little sign above the door there and I thought to myself, I wonder if that could be the Maggie Lane I used to know, sweet Maggie Lane who used to sing like an angel, who ran off to California to be a superstar—"

"Cut it out, Danny," she said, her voice oddly muted. She moved backward, either an involuntary reaction to my adolescent nonsense or an invitation to enter. I didn't know which and didn't much care. I stepped through the door, a long-dormant pocket of resentment expanding, bursting, dusting my mind with unreasoning anger. The violence of it shook me; I felt walls tumbling, old scar tissue rending.

"I don't believe you," she said, voice still small and flat. "You never do anything without a reason." Her head lifted, the green eyes smoky, almost opaque. "I'm sure you know what I am, what I do. Did you come here for that? If you did, then I'm sorry. I have a five o'clock appointment." She brushed a shimmering column of hair back across her shoulder, her features suddenly relaxed, a quirk of humor at the corners of her mouth. "I'm a businesswoman, Danny. There are rules."

"We all have rules," I said lightly, the anger draining as rapidly as it had begun. "But old friends should be exceptions to the rule."

She settled to a seat on the arm of a brown velvet chair and studied my face, her hands picking at each other on the rounded swell of a thigh. "I can't believe you did, but if you came here for sex, I'm sorry. I don't want you as a customer."

And there it was again—rejection. Rejection from a hooker. How do you top that? I wanted to laugh, but found I couldn't.

"Old lovers and old dogs. Nobody cares."

She looked up quickly. "I didn't mean that the way you think. You'd just complicate my life again. I don't need that."

"Dammit," I said, and found that I didn't know what else to say. How do you explain the unexplainable? Finally, I said, "I'm married, I don't—"

She laughed. "I know that. So, what's new? Half my customers are married."

There was no way to answer that one, either, not without sounding pompous and self-righteous.

She glanced at a tiny silver-banded watch on her wrist. "We have time for a drink, Danny. Still scotch rocks?" She stood up, gave me a crooked little smile.

"Black Jack ditch," I said with only a moment's hesitation. It was still early, but it had been a long, hard day.

She turned away, then turned back, the small smile broadening. "You can sit down, Danny. I know you're tall." There was a hint of the old coquettishness, a teasing lilt to her voice; the green eyes sparkled as she turned once more, the lithe body still as supple as willow wands, as sensuous as an Italian love song.

I sank into the chair she had vacated, surveyed the surrounding area for ashtrays. There were none. I sighed and checked out the large, airy room instead, admiring the subtle blending of brown and gold and beige, the off-white carpeting that must have required cleaning once a month. Sandstone-colored draperies covered one entire wall and two medium-size windows flanked a fieldstone fireplace that looked as if it had never fired a log. Three multicolored masks that looked Asian adorned the wall above the fireplace mantel and a vividly green hanging plant provided a splash of contrasting color. Small, gilt-edged original paintings hung everywhere, and a large Oriental rug protected the carpeting between facing velvet sofas. There was a lushness about the room, a feminine ambience that was almost an aphrodisiac. A room for seduction, I thought, watching Maggie Lane's well-formed figure come toward me from the small wet bar in the corner, feeling once again the sense of loss and desolation I had felt that night in the Midway City police station.

"Here you go," she said, smiling, handing me my drink, our fingertips touching for one electric moment before she hastily moved away. Then she turned, came back and put down her drink on the end table beside me. She reached down and deliberately picked up my empty hand, held it in both of hers, a small lopsided smile forming on her lips.

"You still have marvelous hands," she said. "Did I ever tell you what exciting hands you have?"

"I don't think so," I said. "A man wouldn't forget a thing like that."

She smiled and let the hand slide free. She picked up her drink and moved away again.

I sipped my drink. "Thanks, I needed that, it really hit the spot," I said, aware that I was talking in clichés, unable to stop. "You haven't lost your touch."

She was sitting on the edge of the sofa facing me, playing at drinking: her lips were moist, but I didn't see her swallow.

"Thank you."

I nodded and sipped again, looking everywhere in the room except at her. The silence grew. She looked at her watch, winced, looked at me.

"Danny . . ."

"Oh, yeah, your customer. Mustn't keep a good customer waiting, must we?"

She brought back the crooked smile, put her drink on an end table, rose slowly to her feet.

"Where were you last night?"

She looked startled, then puzzled, then angry, color flooding upward from her neck into her cheeks. "I don't think—"

"I'm sorry," I said, and stood up. "That was a rookie thing to do. But it's important, Maggie. It's not nosiness; I need to know. Please trust me."

She stared up at me, eyes wide. "Can't you tell me—"

"I will after you answer my question."

She blinked, wet her lips. "I was—I went down to the coast—down to Galveston."

"Who with?"

"A girl. A girl friend of mine . . . and her boyfriend. Cynthia Kincade—this has something to do with her father's murder, doesn't it?"

I nodded.

"I heard about it on the radio this morning. I tried to call Cynthia, but. . . ." Her voice trailed off. "The man's name was Greg. I don't remember his last name."

"When did you go to Galveston?"

"About six last night. We stayed all night."

I wanted to ask her about the other man, but I didn't. He had nothing to do with the murder and it was none of my damned business what she had done in that motel room on the bay, none of my damned business what she was going to do with the good customer as soon as she brushed me out of her hair.

"That was it, Danny? That was why you came?"

I nodded, feeling a hollow spot in the pit of my stomach, a rough, abraded place somewhere in the back of my mind.

"You could have called, you know." She took my arm and herded me gently toward the door, looking around and into my face, the sparkle back in her eyes. She squeezed my arm. "But I'm glad you didn't. I'm glad you came. At least now I know for sure that you know about me, and I don't have to wonder anymore. You're all married and everything, and I have my business and everything's fine."

"Fine as frog's hair," I said, wondering what I would do without clichés.

"Be good," she said, shaking one of my marvelous hands. She smiled the crooked smile, then raised quickly on tiptoe and kissed my cheek. She stepped back and closed the door.

I stood for a moment in the gathering twilight, breathing deeply, staring blankly. I lit a cigarette and started down the driveway just as a car door slammed out on the street. A foreign car, sports car—Porsche, Maserati, Anna Maria Alberghetti—one of those.

A man pranced up the drive toward me, custom-fitted clothes, glossy shoes, an old school tie. Big, big as me, but fatter, smoother, probably a banker, a lawyer, or a broker—one of that ilk.

He started smiling ten feet away, nodding pleasantly, holding the smile right up to the time I reached out and grabbed a handful of his colorful tie, yanked him right up into my face.

"That lady in there, asshole—that's Maggie. You know Maggie, you son of a bitch? Well, that lady is my woman, man! I've been gone, but now I'm back! You got that, you tub of shit?" I turned him loose and shoved him away. "You still want to go in there?"

"Oh, hell—oh, no, not at all. Uh, as a matter of fact—can you believe it? I have the wrong address." He gave me a sickly, loose-lipped grin and trotted down the driveway, keys rattling like hail on a metal roof as he fought the locked car door.

I walked back to Maggie's door, took a hundred-dollar bill out of my billfold, and quietly slipped it through the mail slot. Maybe it was a low-down, mean-spirited thing to do, but, dammit, it felt *good*.

11

From Maggie Lane's I drove to the police department. I parked in back and climbed the rear stairs to the second floor. Except for two men talking near the coffee machine, the entire second floor was empty. Homer's office light was out; Mitsi was gone.

I turned on Mitsi's desk light and pawed through her supply drawer until I found a pad of field investigation reports. I whipped the cover off her battered Selectric and filled out a report on everyone I had talked to.

As far as I was concerned, Cynthia Kincade was off the questionable list. Her alibi was now as solid as seasoned oak. And that left her mother. But I didn't want to think about that, not for a while. I was tired and hungry and lonesome, and I'd had enough prying and poking into people's lives for one day.

I left the F.I.R.s on Mitsi's desk under her stapler, covered her typewriter, and clumped back down to my truck.

Darkness had fallen, bringing a chill to the air. A tinge of fire singed the horizon in every direction except north. North was still open land, patches of oak forests and acres of cotton, ranchlands with grazing cattle, fields of winter oats.

But the Metroplex was a giant spreading stain, constantly on the move, sucking the life out of the land, absorbing, reshaping in its own sterile image. One day, not in my lifetime I hoped, it would take a half tank of gas and a belly filled with true grit just to reach the country.

My house was dark and silent, brooding quietly in the early night. I went around turning on lights, the kitchen radio, and the TV in the den. With my stomach growling like a bad-tempered dog, I broiled a porterhouse steak and microwaved a potato. I tossed everything green and crunchy I could find into a bowl for a salad, added sliced tomatoes, chopped green onions and croutons, and by the time the six o'clock news came on the tube, I was ensconced in my favorite chair eating from a rickety TV tray. Plain fare fit for a king, or at the very least, a count.

As usual, the news was frightening: murders and rapes and assorted mayhem, kids missing, a volcanic catastrophe in Colombia, twenty-five thousand dead. Not conducive to good digestion. I flicked the remote control and settled for a rerun of "Lassie."

An hour later I was punching around on the control, looking for something with enough bite to keep me awake. I had about decided on an old movie that looked promising when the delicate notes of "Moonglow" penetrated an inane commercial message about the relative merits of hot versus cold water in washing dirty clothing.

I sighed, turned down the sound, and got up, padded barefoot to answer the door, saddened by the thought that I would never know the answer, would undoubtedly be consigned to that small, wretched group forever doomed to wear tattletale gray.

As I worked the lock and undid the chain, some small quixotic part of my mind whispered the name Maggie Lane, and something thudded in my chest, shivered in my stomach: a mixture of excitement and dread that defied rational analysis.

But it wasn't Maggie Lane standing there; it was David Kincade, handsome face fixed in an apologetic expression, hands shoved deep into the pockets of a navy blue windbreaker. He ducked his bare, tousled head and gave me an ingratiating smile.

"Mr. Roman. I'm sorry to bother you this way, here at your home, I mean. But I thought I should come and talk to you about Mom. . . ." He let it trail away as a gust of cold wind spilled hair across his forehead; the acid air nibbled at my toes like tiny, hungry teeth. I stepped back.

"No problem, David. Come on in. It's chilly out there."

"It sure is," he said, stepping through the door, hunching his shoulders in an exaggerated display of misery. "Kinda sudden after that nice day we had."

"Texas weather," I said, leading the way back to the den. "I wouldn't trade it for a broken baseball bat. Keeps you on your toes. Sit down, David."

He laughed and perched on the edge of the couch, unzipped the windbreaker. Another tight T-shirt, black, with no inscription that I could see. He had exchanged the faded jeans for dark blue corduroy pants. He looked exceptionally good in the dark blue clothing, and I had a sneaking hunch that he knew it, another hunch that dates to the proms had never been a problem for David Kincade.

I lit a cigarette and settled into my chair. "Now, what's this about your mother?"

"She's upset, Mr. Roman. Really upset. One of her friends, Mrs. Gloria Strand, called her this afternoon. She said you had been asking a lot of questions about Friday afternoon down in Austin—"

"And that upset her? That's odd. They were just routine questions."

Something moved across his face, leaving the even features more compressed, a stern, disapproving look that was almost comical on his youthful visage.

"They're not dumb, Mr. Roman. Neither one of them. Mrs. Strand told Mom you were very casual and passably clever, but that it didn't take a genius to see that you were interested mainly in where Mom spent the afternoon and early evening."

Score one for the lady with the honeyed voice, I thought. "What did your mother say to that?"

"I told you. She was upset. It just hadn't occurred to her that you might think she had anything to do with Dad's . . . Dad's death." His voice quivered near the end, and I suddenly recalled how it felt to be eighteen and lose a parent.

"It doesn't mean that, David. Not necessarily. I intend to see your mother in the morning. There must be someone she saw or who saw her during that time—"

"There is," he said quickly, loudly, sitting stiffly upright, muscular hands gripping his kneecaps. "Me. That's why I'm here. I saw her in the stands—"

"About what time was that, David?"

"Seven. Just before we started. I had been looking for her and I finally saw her over near the entrance. The stadium was crowded and I guess—"

I slapped the arm of my chair. "Well, by golly, that's fine, David! That sure clears that up. I don't mind telling you I never thought for a minute that your Mom wasn't where she said she was, but you know how cops are. They see a dangling thread, they gotta pull on it."

He took a deep breath and smiled, the blue eyes sliding away from mine to the silent figures dashing across the TV screen. "I'm glad," he said. "Mom was really upset." He looked at me, bringing back the apologetic grimace. "But you know how women are. It doesn't take much sometimes."

"You've got that right," I said, suppressing a smile.

He turned to look at the TV again. "I'm sorry. I'm making you miss your movie. Isn't that *Strangers on a Train*?"

"I think so. It's an old one from the fifties. Something to fall asleep by."

He shook his head, his face serious. "I've seen it before. It's a good movie. I like the old ones better than what they're making today. Too much junk about dope and high school sex or something far out like *Star Wars*. The old movies were more realistic, more about people."

Value appraisals and moral judgments; this was one serious-minded kid.

"Changing times," I said. "What can you do?"

He stood up and zipped up the jacket. "Have you seen it before?"

"What?"

"*Strangers on a Train*?"

"No, I guess I missed it first time around."

"Well, if you don't see the first part of it, it won't make much sense. I'm really sorry I interrupted."

"Hey, that's okay. I'd probably be asleep by now, anyway. I'm like an old hound with fleas. It's easier to sleep than scratch."

He smiled and moved around in a small semicircle, running the zipper up and down on the jacket. He still seemed reluctant to leave.

He cleared his throat. "This fixes up everything for Mom, then?"

"I don't see why not. I need to talk to her, but—"

"Why?"

"Normal routine," I said. "It's called a follow-through interview. People never seem to remember everything the first time."

"Will I have a follow-through?"

I laughed and stood up. "We've just had it, David. See how it goes? The first time around you didn't tell me about seeing your mother in the stands."

"I didn't think it was important."

"No reason why you should. And I didn't know enough to ask."

He nodded solemnly. "You suspected Cyn, didn't you?"

"In the beginning everyone's a suspect of sorts, David. Most murders are committed by close family members, friends, or other relatives. In this case you were the only one exempt. That is, unless you had a twin brother out there doing your stunts for you. The greater part of a murder investigation is ruling out the ones who can't be guilty for one reason or another. That's what I've been doing all day. I've established your sister's alibi, and you've just corroborated your mother's story. So that means we have to start looking further afield. That's one reason I need to see your mother again. I need the names of some of your father's friends and other relatives."

"There aren't any other relatives. I can tell you that much." He paused and shook his head, his face troubled. "And I don't think Dad had many close friends. Oh, there were some guys out at the factory he used to have a beer with now and then, but nobody special that he used to hang around with, like that."

"Everybody has friends, David. Sometimes they just don't know it."

"I guess so. You think it could have been somebody looking to rip us off?"

"I don't think it's likely. Your dad still had his wallet in his pocket with more than two hundred dollars in it. That doesn't necessarily mean a lot. The killer could have been too frightened after he shot him to worry about anything but getting away. On the other hand, maybe killing your father was the only reason he was there at all."

David's eyes closed momentarily, as if he could shut out the thought. "I—I just can't believe anyone would want to kill Dad."

"People kill for all sorts of reasons, David, and a lot of times it has almost nothing to do with the victim."

"I don't understand what you mean."

"Random murders. Killing for the sake of killing, for the way it makes them feel. At one time not so long ago, you could look to the victim's family, friends, or other relatives, and in eighty percent of the cases find your killer. No more. Stranger murders are climbing steadily, and not all of them are connected with robbery or rape."

He shifted his feet uneasily, face bunched in an uncertain frown. "Sounds like a lot of weirdos, sick people."

"Some of them are, but just saying they're sick and writing them off is too easy." I stopped, suddenly realizing how young he was and how heavy the conversation had become. I reached out and thumped him on the shoulder. "Don't worry about it, we'll find out who killed your dad." It was sheer bravado and he probably knew it, but there were times when a little show of confidence didn't hurt.

He nodded, looking dubious. "Well, I won't take up any more of your time, Mr. Roman. I sure appreciate you listening to me like this."

"I've done more talking than listening," I said dryly, moving behind him toward the entry hall. "You're all dressed up tonight. Heavy date?"

He flashed his ready grin. "Sort of. Just some guys from school. We're going to drive around, hang out, you know."

"I can barely remember."

We shook hands at the door. I closed it behind him and went back to my chair in the den.

His handshake hadn't improved, but then, neither had his ability to lie.

I had barely settled into my chair when the doorbell went off again; the poignant notes of "Moonglow" were rapidly losing their charm. I flipped off the sound on the TV again and made my way to the door, a little slower this time.

I more than halfway expected it to be David—some little lie he had forgotten to tell me, a dead battery, perhaps.

But the man standing there was about as different from a David Kincade as you could get. Tall, narrow-shouldered, lean to the point of emaciation, he had a good-natured, ugly face with a big nose, receding chin, and a prominent Adam's apple, and fit perfectly the mind's-eye image I had drawn of Ichabod Crane the first time I read *The Legend of Sleepy Hollow.*

"Howdy, Dan'l." My next-door neighbor for seven years, he was a retired engineer from Bell Helicopter Company, a widower who lived alone with two haughty Siamese cats and an intelligent German shepherd named Rowdy. His name was Hector Johnson and he was the closest thing I had to a fan.

"Hello, Heck. How you doing? Come on in."

"Hate to bother you so late like this, Dan'l," he said, giving me a wide, toothy smile that told me he didn't really mind at all.

"Hey, pard, no bother. Come on in and hunker a spell. I'll see if I can rustle us up some brews." As always with Hector, I found myself slipping into a mangled cowboy patois. As an Easterner—he was from Indiana or Iowa, one of those flat, muddy midwestern states—he expected no less, had, in fact, become almost Texanized himself during the ten years he had spent in our wild and woolly West.

He stalked ahead of me into the den, cowboy heels clacking on the terrazzo tile. "Can't stay. Just come aborrying, as usual."

"What are neighbors for?" We drew up in the middle of the den.

"Well, I'm ashamed of myself. I promised you last year I'd get me one before this year, but you know how it is with us pensioners—"

I clapped him on a bony shoulder. "Which one, Heck? The Remington semiautomatic or the little Noble double?"

He brought back the grin. "I like that little double. My boy's taking me to one of those shooting preserves for my birthday, and we're gonna be hunting quail and maybe even some pheasant. I like the way that little sucker swings. Just seems to fit this skinny shoulder of mine."

"Good choice. Hold on a second, I'll get it for you." I padded out of the room and down the hall to my gun closet. I took the double off the rack and found a gun case that fit, then rummaged around and located a full box of shells. I went back down the hall grinning a little, wondering if he had been as good an engineer as he was a con artist. For each of the seven years he had lived next door, he had borrowed one or the other of my shotguns, keeping it usually for the entire hunting sea-son, vowing each time to get himself one before the next year rolled around.

I didn't mind. He was a good neighbor. Quiet, industrious, with a well-kept lawn and a willing pair of extra hands when the need arose. He minded his own business and always brought the guns back in spic-and-span condition. What more could you ask of a neighbor?

He was still standing in the center of the den, staring down at the silent TV.

"Dang it, Dan'l, I hate this. I'll bet I'm causing you to miss your movie."

I shook my head. "I've already missed most of it, I think." I handed him the gun and the shells.

"Well, I've seen it already. You ain't missing much. Supposed to be a mystery, but there ain't no mystery to it. You know right away these two guys are gonna kill each other's wives—"

"It's on cable," I said. "They run them over and over. Maybe I'll get another chance at it."

"Yeah, that's right. Well . . ." He suddenly seemed to notice the box of shells. "Hey, man, I'm not going to take your shells, too. I can afford my own shells."

"I know that, Heck. I bought way too many last year. They're liable to go bad on me. I'd hate to see them go to waste."

He gave me a quick, suspicious glance, then hefted the box of shells in one thin, gnarled hand and turned toward the door. "Well, I sure do thank you, Dan'l. Tell you what, I'll bring you a brace of quail, or maybe a pheasant. How's that strike you?"

"My favorite birds. You might make that three quail, though, I have another mouth to feed now, you know."

"By grab, that's right. Mighty purty mouth it is, too." He laughed, a surprisingly melodious sound from such a scrawny neck. He stepped through the door into the crisp night air. "Don't worry, I'll take care of your gun."

"I know it. Have fun, Heck. I'll see you later."

He ambled off across his driveway, a thin, shambling figure in worn denims and a colorful cotton shirt. A self-professed agnostic, he saw himself as a free thinker, held steadfastly that the laws of physics were not immutable, that reincarnation was not only possible but probable, that man with all his millions of words to the contrary had not produced one tiny fragment of substantive evidence that his presence on this earth meant more to the living universe than the existence of the lowly earthworm.

True or not, it was still a sobering thought.

I dozed off and on through the rest of the movie. David had been right; it didn't make a lot of sense. At nine o'clock I gave up. I went into the bathroom, shaved, brushed my teeth, and took a long, hot shower, then gradually adjusted the water until it was running cold.

I was trying to stay awake until ten o'clock. Susie would be on approximately midway through the newscast. A three- to five-minute report, depending on the severity of her current disaster. Floods weren't exactly unknown in the Valley, but they were coming off a two-year drought, and that made it more newsworthy.

At ten o'clock I opened a bottle of beer and settled in once again to find out what was going on in the world. The news was no better than it had been at six, but this time I bit down on my jaw teeth and stuck it out:

A six-month-old baby and a new baby-sitter are missing in Fort Worth tonight. Police believe a baby-selling ring may be involved. Police are searching for the woman. . . .

Two unarmed men were shot and killed in a grocery store holdup in Fort Worth this afternoon—police are following up promising leads, but have no suspects. . . .

One man is killed and two are injured in a gunfight in a liquor store parking lot—one man is in custody in Dallas. The two injured men were rushed to Parkland Hospital in critical condition. . . .

A woman was raped in Midway City. The assault occurred a little more than an hour ago in the young woman's apartment, and certain elements of the crime lead police to believe it was the work of the same man who has terrorized the south side of Midway City over the last two years. The man, dubbed Batman because of his dark clothing and Batmanlike face mask, is suspected in at least nine similar crimes. . . .

Fort Worth police are looking for a gunman who walked into a west-side beauty salon brandishing a small-caliber weapon and shot three women patrons and two beauticians, then turned and walked out again without saying a word. Juanita Lopez was pronounced dead at the scene. The remaining four victims were taken to John Peter Smith Hospital, where their conditions remain undetermined at this hour. . . .

Midway City Police are still investigating the murder of Ralph T. Kincade, a lifelong resident of Midway City. Police spokesman Captain Homer Sellers told reporters there were some promising leads and that the case had been assigned to one of his most experienced investigators in hopes of a speedy solution. . . .

There was more, but I had stopped listening. Promising leads, my ass. Fairy tale time. Stonewalling gobbledygook. Homer had no idea what had happened in the case, which, I had to admit, wasn't a hell of a lot. One unlikely suspect replaced by one even more unlikely suspect—and, if her son could be believed, no suspect at all. David had lied about seeing his mother at seven o'clock. I was almost certain of that. But that didn't mean she hadn't been there. By all accounts the stadium was large and crowded. One face would be almost impossible to find, especially from the floor. I had no real feeling that Naomi Kincade had killed her husband, had sensed none of the cold, calculated cunning she would have to possess to initiate and execute such an intricate plan. But that wouldn't stop me from seeing her again, to try to establish beyond a shadow of a doubt her whereabouts at that crucial time.

The newscast ground to a halt for a commercial. I got up and went to the toilet. On my way back I detoured through the living room and opened the drapes on a window.

The street was quiet and dark, the stars bright. A clear, cold Texas night, as peaceful as sleep. It was hard to imagine that murderers stalked this once sleepy city, that bandits and rapists and muggers roamed almost at will. Like all the other small towns and cities in the Metroplex, Midway City had burgeoned during the sixties and seventies, unheralded growth that had caught the city fathers by surprise.

Mostly merchants or businessmen of one stripe or other, city councilmen had stayed awake nights trying to figure out how best to encourage growth. They welcomed developers and speculators with wide open arms and tax breaks galore. As a result, this once placid bedroom community had zoomed from ten to something over ninety thousand souls in twenty years. Growth equaled progress, everybody knew that.

But growth also equaled poverty, a hard core of unemployables and welfare recipients, maddening traffic, more bars and liquor stores and topless night clubs, porn shops and sex movie houses. Progress meant entrepreneurs, the kind that carried briefcases and the kind that carried guns; hustlers, hookers, and pimps were well represented, as were winos and the people who lived on the streets because they had no other place to go.

Personally, I had no quarrel with progress; it was as inevitable as old age. But my homeowner's taxes had quadrupled during the last fifteen years, and I damn sure had plenty to say about that.

I drew the drapes and circled through the kitchen to the den, then pulled up short in the doorway, transfixed by the husky-harsh sound of Susie's voice, by her lovely, beaming face on the TV.

"This is Susan Roman on the road in Wellesville, Texas, for TNS. Goodnight, Don and Alice." Her picture shrank to quarter-size, then slowly faded as the local anchor team cho-rused, "Goodnight, Susan."

Dammit. I had fooled around and missed her, the bright spot I had counted on to erase the murky day. It was more than enough to make a good man cuss.

But I didn't. I turned off the TV, dumped the rest of my beer down the sink, and trundled down the hallway to the bedroom, weary and disconsolate.

Sleep came, but it was late, and I had to wait shivering in the darkness.

12

I was up before eight Sunday morning, feeling rehabilitated if not happy after almost eight full hours of sleep. Another cool, clear day ahead, no rain and no smog in the forecast, a pre-dicted seventy-four-degree high. A perfect day for being out-doors, for everything from pecan hunting to picnicking to watching the Cowboys in Texas Stadium. A good day for lolly-gagging with the one you loved.

After breakfast I called Naomi Kincade. I gave her the same line I had given David about follow-up interviews, and she agreed to an appointment at nine o'clock, saying that anything later than that would interfere with church. Her voice was low and noncommittal and gave no indication that David had told her about his visit. I was inclined to believe that he hadn't, and that was just as well.

I smoked a leisurely after-breakfast cigarette and read the Sunday paper for a half hour or so. Fifteen pounds of advertise-ments and one pound of news, more than enough words to make up a couple of good mystery novels. All my favorite com-ics were long gone: Li'l Abner, Alley Oop, and the Katzenjammer Kids. More progress. Now we had so-called biting satire and relevant issues, pithy caricatures of quotidian existence.

At eight-thirty I folded the paper and gave up in disgust. I went into the bedroom, dressed, and drove across Midway City for what seemed like the hundredth time in two days.

Not a bad drive on a quiet Sunday morning: a dearth of traffic, only a few pedestrians on the streets. Nevertheless, out of habit I avoided the thoroughfares and wended my way through the neighborhoods, a rich mix of affluence and indigence, ostentatious displays of wealth and pockets of poverty existing within easy shouting distance of each other. Traditional enemies; the answer to the question of which was the prey and which was the predator depended solely on who was doing the talking.

Both automobiles were gone from the Kincade driveway, but I still parked out on the street. The house looked deserted, draperies closed, the Sunday paper on the bedraggled lawn. I finished my cigarette and climbed out of the truck, wondering if maybe I wasn't being stood up.

But she was there, dressed modestly in a belted beige dress with three-quarter-length sleeves and a bit of lace on the collar. A single strand of pearls encircled her short, strong neck, the long-fingered hands unadorned except for her wedding ring, an expensive-looking digital watch around her wrist.

Naomi Kincade smiled without showing her teeth and worked the latch on the storm door. "Good morning, Mr. Roman."

"Good morning," I said, and handed her the Sunday paper from the lawn. "You're lucky. My delivery boy usually throws mine on the roof."

She acknowledged my weak attempt at humor with another small smile. "It's chilly again this morning." She closed the door and led the way into the large front room.

"The sun's hacking away at it," I said. "Supposed to be in the seventies again today." Without being asked, I sat down in the chair I had used the day before. She moved to the couch, perched stiffly on its edge, smoothing the tan dress over her knees. She regarded me quietly, her features more striking than I remembered, a faint blush of color in cheeks that had been pallid, in well-shaped lips that had seemed lusterless before.

"What was it you needed to ask me, Mr. Roman?"

"Well, a follow-through usually covers the same—"

She lifted one hand in an impatient gesture. "Please, let's not play games. I've talked to Gloria Strand, and I think I know why you're here. Why don't you just come out and ask me what you want to know?"

"You got it." I leaned forward. "Where were you between four o'clock and nine o'clock on Friday? To be more exact, where were you around seven o'clock" I leaned back. She leaned forward.

"I was in Austin in an automobile driven by a Mr. Sam Bellows. We were on our way from Micki Maguire's—that's a restaurant out on Highway 35—to the stadium. We were running late and Sam was speeding. He got a ticket, which delayed us even more, and we didn't arrive at the stadium until about seven-fifteen. I was there until ten-thirty."

"Sam Bellows?"

She sighed and looked into the dead fireplace. "I was hoping I wouldn't have to bring Sam into this. But, of course, when Gloria told me the kind of questions you were asking, I knew it would come to this sooner or later."

"Come to what? I don't care who Sam Bellows is. All I want is confirmation that you were in Austin at the approximate time of your husband's death."

Her lips moved in a smile totally devoid of humor. The gray eyes turned to meet mine. "Then I am a suspect?"

"Who is Sam Bellows, Mrs. Kincade?"

"I thought you didn't care."

"I don't care what he is to you. If you were with him and he'll confirm it—that's all I care about."

She took a deep breath, focused her eyes on the painting

above the fireplace. "Sam is an old friend of Ralph's—and of mine. He worked with Ralph at the auto factory. He was laid off at about the same time. But he was more fortunate than Ralph. He had a brother in the building supply business in Dallas. He took Sam in as a partner, then when he died two years ago, he left his part of the business to Sam. Sam offered Ralph a job, but Ralph was too . . . too proud, I guess. He turned Sam down. I didn't turn him down when he offered me a job." She stopped and looked at her hands clasped loosely in her lap. "After Ralph left, Sam began asking me out. I—we had lunch a few times before I let him take me to dinner. We've been going out to eat once or twice a month since—well, for the last six months or so."

"That doesn't sound so terrible. Was it just a coincidence that he was in Austin Friday?"

She looked up, smiling wryly. "No, of course not. He's been going to David's competitions for the last couple of years. He started going with Ralph. When Ralph left he . . . he continued to go. He's a great sports fan." She paused. "Sam's wife died more than five years ago."

"He didn't go with you to Austin?"

"No. He flew down later in the day. He rented a car and picked me up about four-thirty at the motel. We drove around Austin—the Capitol Building area—then went to eat at Micki Maguire's. We lingered too long over dinner, and that's why Sam received the speeding ticket."

"You got rid of the migraine, huh?" It was dirty pool, but I couldn't stop myself from asking.

Her lips tightened. "There was no headache."

"All right," I said meekly; it was as close to an apology as I was going to get. She had lied to me about Austin and that was going to create a lot more work. Sam Bellows would have to be checked out and maybe even the speeding ticket.

"We're not lovers, Mr. Roman," she said severely, as if in answer to an accusation.

"I'm sorry."

Her lips pulled even tighter, then relaxed in a low, humorless laugh. "Are you being sarcastic?"

"I don't think so. What you and Mr. Bellows do is no business of mine. I would like to know where I could reach him."

"You mean now, today?"

"Today would be fine."

She nibbled at her lower lip. "I think—I may have his phone number—"

"That will do if you don't have his address."

She started to rise, then settled back, looking confused, a little out of sync. "Oh, what's the matter with me? Sam's in the phone book. He lives here in Midway City. You can get his address from the book."

"That'll do it." I pushed to my feet. "Thanks for seeing me, Mrs. Kincade."

She nodded distractedly and followed me to the door. "Mr. Roman?"

I turned, one hand on the doorknob.

"Cynthia knows about Sam, but David doesn't. I'd appreciate—"

"He won't hear a word from me."

"Thank you."

"You're welcome." I pushed through the storm door onto the porch.

"I'm sorry I lied to you. I should have told you about Sam and the dinner yesterday."

I nodded and smiled and walked down the driveway to my truck.

Not a large lie, I thought, mostly one of omission. Even understandable from her viewpoint, although going to dinner with a widower seemed not much of a transgression in a time when sexual promiscuity was as common as rice at a wedding.

But Naomi Kincade had been born and raised in an earlier time, a different climate of morality, and like many who lived on the edge of poverty, had little beyond pride and an unblemished name. Maybe that accounted for it.

13

Sam Bellows lived no more than two miles from my house, in a relatively new subdivision of middle-income houses that had been stacked along arrow-straight streets like hotels on Park Place and Boardwalk. The elevations were different, but there was still a cookie cutter sameness about the homes that spoke of speed more than quality, that spoke of profit motive more than a sincere desire to create serviceable housing.

Sam himself was short and rotund, as ugly as dried mud until he flashed his engaging smile—small, deeply imbedded brown eyes twinkling, radiating sincerity and good cheer. A thick shock of wavy silver hair framed his large head like the ruff of a startled lion, added an aura of dignity and stature to his unremarkable body.

Dressed in a sloppy sweatshirt, faded denims, and tattered Puma jogging shoes, Bellows greeted me cordially, pumped my hand with a hard, knobby fist, then led the way into his living room, a rectangular space across most of the front of his house filled with new modern furniture, plastic and glass, and solid-colored sofas and chairs with seat cushions at least a foot thick. It looked hard and cold and color coordinated, not the kind of room I'd want to spend a lot of time in.

"You got here pretty fast," he remarked, waving me toward one of the puffy chairs, selecting for himself a black recliner facing a giant television screen. The sound was off, but gaily colored figures dashed across the screen in seemingly wild disarray. I recognized the Cowboys, the hulking shapes of the New York Giants.

"I live fairly close by," I said. "I'm sorry to break in on your game like this. I called before lunch, but I guess you weren't home from church."

He gave me a crooked grin. "Jogging. Figure my body needs more help than my soul." He picked up a beer can from the coffee table. "Beer?"

"No thanks, I'm fine."

He put the can back down. "I don't need one, either. Cowboys getting their ass whupped to a frazzle. Kinda takes the fun out of it. Them Giants come to town looking for Cowboy ass and it looks like they found out where they hid it."

"It looks bad," I acknowledged.

He sat down abruptly. "Well, Mr. Roman, I don't mind telling you that Naomi called me earlier today. She said you'd be wanting me to tell you that me and her was together around seven o'clock Friday night."

"Only if you were."

He cocked his leonine head. "'Course we was. That's what she told you, wasn't it?"

"Yes, she did."

"And you didn't believe her?" There was truculence in his voice, a bit of impatience, a frown building on the plain, rough features.

"That isn't the point. I need corroboration."

"Well, I ain't sure what that means, but I'll tell you straight out she was with me from around five to about seven, maybe a little later."

"Mind telling me what you were doing?"

"I don't mind telling you, but I want you to know I don't think it's any of your business."

"All right, strike that, it isn't important. But I would like to see your copy of the speeding ticket."

He nodded, then brought back the scowl again. "You don't believe anybody, do you?"

I shrugged. "I believed Nixon and look what happened."

The frown dissolved into a reluctant smile. He returned my shrug and reached into his left rear pocket. His billfold was brown and worn, curved to fit the contour of his rump. He dug around inside, peering nearsightedly, then came up with a thin rectangular slip of paper. "You can't have this. I've got to send it in with my fifty dollars."

"I'll need to make a copy for the record, but I'll see that you get it back." The date was right, the time and location, and Sam Bellows's name was scrawled on the bottom of the ticket. It looked good until I noticed that the small square block beside the word *passengers* was empty.

"Mrs. Kincade was with you when you got this, right?"

"'Course she was. We were on our way to the stadium and running late. That's why—"

"This ticket doesn't indicate that."

He shrugged again. He looked a little surprised, but not concerned. "I can't help that. I was hurrying the cop as much as I could. Maybe he just forgot. Let me see."

I gave him the ticket, pointing out the unmarked square. "Should be a one in there."

He grunted and handed it back. "Big deal. So he forgot. Nobody's perfect."

"That's true, but cops in general are pretty careful about things like that. It can get their ticket thrown out of court."

"Yeah?" His face lit up. "Maybe I oughta—aw, hell, for fifty dollars it ain't worth the trouble."

I folded the slip of paper and put it in my wallet. "I'll see that you get this back tomorrow." I put the wallet away. "Did you and Mrs. Kincade sit together at the stadium?"

He shifted in the recliner, a disgruntled look crossing his face. "Naw. Her boy don't know we been seeing each other. She didn't want to take a chance on him seeing us come in together." He squirmed again. "Hell, ain't nothing to be ashamed of. We hadn't done anything wrong. After all, Ralph run off and left her and the boy and we didn't know if he was ever coming back or not. She had every right to have a little fun in her life." He fixed me with a baleful gaze. "That's one damn fine woman, mister, and don't you forget it."

"I agree," I said.

"And you cops running around making out like she mighta had something to do with Ralph's murder, well, that pisses me off some, I guess you know that." The color was slowly receding from his ungainly features, leaving a muddy pallor that made him look almost satanic. His fuse was short and appeared to be burning. I wondered why.

"I can understand that. Man feels the need to protect the woman he loves." I said it easily, giving him a chance to back away or charge. He charged.

"You damn right! And let me tell you something else. If you cops think she's an easy mark just because she ain't got no money, if you think you can wrap up your case by pinning it on her, well then, by god, you've got another think coming! I got money, a lot of money, and I'll spend every damned dime—" He broke off, breathing heavily, tongue raking across dry lips, face working as he made a visible effort to bring himself under control.

I sat and looked at him until I was sure he was finished. Then I stood up, took out my cigarettes and lit one.

"Thanks for your cooperation, Mr. Bellows."

He stared at the television screen, his pallid face immobile. He gave no indication that he heard me, made no move to look up, stand up, or shake hands.

"Don't bother," I said. "I'll find my way out."

He looked up then and nodded, looking sheepish. "Sorry about blowing off there—"

"Don't sweat it. We all have tender spots."

He didn't answer, his eyes back on the silent screen, seemingly absorbed, as Danny White disappeared in a sea of dark jerseys.

I crossed to the door and let myself out.

The day had blossomed to perfection: a mild breeze and warm sunshine. But it was winding down, with dark only a couple of hours away.

I decided I might as well make my last report on the Kincade case, finish up the two days I had promised Homer with a whimper instead of a bang. Homer could take the speeding ticket one step further if he thought it necessary. I didn't. I had no doubt that Naomi and Sam Bellows had been together in Austin Friday evening; my only doubts were relative to what they had been doing.

But that was only the cynical side of my nature rearing its ugly head, and I pushed the thought out of my mind and drove to police headquarters.

The second floor was deserted again. I filled out the last two F.I.R.s and struggled through a detailed account of my activities for the file, a lot of words that came down to a one-line conclusion: in my opinion, none of the Kincades had a part in the death of Ralph Kincade.

Satisfied I had done all I could do, yet vaguely dissatisfied that I hadn't accomplished more, I was putting the cover back on Mitsi's Selectric when the sound of clumping footsteps echoed in the corridor. They seemed familiar. Seconds later a loud sneeze and the prolonged blowing of a nose told me more, and I went into Homer's office, turned on the lights, and settled into his visitor's chair.

He came lumbering in, big feet smacking the tile like a beaver's tail slapping water. His broad face looked tired, blue eyes deep-sunken and red-rimmed, a full day's stubble on the heavy jowls. He was wearing his contact lenses again, which accounted for the red and weeping eyes, but the weariness seemed to come from within, as if his inner reserves had been exhausted and he was running on sheer will alone.

"What's happening, old man?"

He grunted and fell into his chair, slapped his case notebook on the blotter, clasped his hands, and fixed me with a bleary glare.

"You don't wanta know," he said, then proceeded to tell me. "Another goddamned murder. Two goddamned murders. Old man LeClair himself. That's bad enough, even though he was old as God and about ready to die, but his granddaughter Julie was only seventeen."

"Jesus H. Christ," I said hollowly.

"Don't blame him," Homer said, his voice rasping. "Blame the sick bastard who put three bullets in each one of them."

14

Pausing occasionally to blot his eyes with a clean handkerchief, he told me about it, as much as he knew from the preliminary investigation, his voice rough and strident at times, sometimes profane, in an attempt to relieve feelings he had never learned to hide very well.

"The old man was upstairs in his study, right off his bedroom. We figure he was sitting at his desk when the killer came in the room. He evidently stood up, maybe because he saw the gun, maybe to greet someone he knew. Anyhow, he was lying across the desk, sorta catty-cornered, his head almost hanging off. He'd been shot twice in the chest and once in the back of the head." He washed his face with one big hand, then brought it up across his head and down the back of his neck. "Daughter-in-law said he was seventy-nine. Had arthritis and a heart murmur, hardening of the arteries. Still worked two or three days a week, though. Stubborn old coot, just wouldn't give up."

"I met him once," I said. "Way back when I was in a squad car. I stopped him for speeding. He was driving a ten-year-old Chevy. You wouldn't have thought he had a dime. I found out later who he was when he came to court to fight the ticket."

Homer nodded absently and leaned back in his chair. "The girl was at the foot of the stairs. We think she came home and maybe heard the shots upstairs and ran up there. She either saw what had happened and turned and ran, or saw the killer coming out of the room and turned and ran. We know she was upstairs because we found the little hat she wore to church on the top step. He musta caught her there and they struggled. That's when the hat came off. She got away and ran down the stairs, but he caught her at or near the bottom. He shot her twice in the back at fairly close range, then after she fell, shot her again in the back of the head. That was up close, too. It burned her hair and the bullet came out her mouth. We found it in the parquet flooring."

"Big caliber?"

He shook his head. "It was damaged some, but Ted Baskin says it's a twenty-five caliber. From an automatic. He found a shell casing with ejection marks. The killer evidently picked up the other five."

"Same size used in the Kincade murder."

We stared at each other for a moment while he blotted the edges of his eyes. Finally he nodded. "Yeah, it is. But I don't see much of a connection. This was a robbery, looks like. Some cash money's missing from a safe in the old man's den, and some negotiable securities are gone. Don't know how much yet. Some valuable securities according to the daughter-in-law."

"Where was she?"

"Church. Her and the girl and the son Paul. Paul plays the organ and the mother sings in the choir. Church starts at ten o'clock and usually winds up around eleven-thirty, quarter of twelve. The mother and son found them about twelve-thirty."

"Have any idea about time of death?"

"Medical Examiner said he'd guess around eleven—"

"Then what was the girl doing home?"

"I hadn't got to that yet. She got up this morning feeling a little bad, like the flu coming on or something. But she decided to go on to church. About ten-forty she got to feeling worse, and one of her friends ran her home. The friend dropped her at the door and went on back to church. She said Julie wasn't feeling bad enough to need aid, but that she thought she'd lie down for a while to see if that would help."

"And she walked right into it."

"That's what it looks like. The friend, her name's Carol something, says she thinks she saw a car parked out on the street down a ways from the house, but she don't have any idea what kind or what color, except that it was light-colored and old."

"Nothing from the neighbors?"

"Nothing so far. You know how it is out there in Sunnyvale. Too much distance between the houses, too many hedges, trees. That small a gun, I doubt anyone would have heard the shots out on the street, much less a hundred yards away. That's about the distance to the nearest neighbor. Only chance we got is to pick up something on the car. They got a neighborhood crime watch program going. Maybe somebody took down the plate numbers or something. We still got some men working the area."

I nodded and fingered the sheaf of reports I had been holding. I reached across and laid them on his notebook. "There's my last reports. I didn't do you a hell of a lot of good, but I think I've established an alibi for all the family members. You may want to go one step further on Naomi Kincade—you'll see what I mean in the report—but personally, I think they're clean. Maybe it was a thief after all, some junky looking for silverware to pawn. Or maybe a random stranger murder, and Kincade's luck just ran out."

He grunted, pushed at the reports with one spatulate finger. "You're quitting, huh?"

"I'm not quitting. I promised you two days. This is the end of the second day. Be fair; that was the agreement."

"I don't remember any agreement like that. You said you'd take the case, and after all the trouble I went to getting your badge, getting you reinstated—"

"Bullshit, Homer! You went through some hokey swearing-in scene that meant about as much as a fart in a high wind.

I've been running around acting like a cop, even pretending to be a cop, when you know and I know it isn't so. People go to the slammer for that, buddy, and I—"

"You know I wouldn't let nothing like that happen."

"I *think* you wouldn't let it happen. I don't know it for a fact. You're only a captain, after all."

He gave me an injured look. "I don't go around knocking your job. Much as I think it's a silly profession for a grown man, I don't call you *just* a private eye—"

"You've called me a lot worse."

"—with all that sarcasm in my voice. Besides, since you was the one brought Kincade back, I thought you'd—"

"Cut it out, Homer. You're not going to lay that guilt trip on me a second time. I've paid my debt to Ralph Kincade, if I ever owed him anything. I'm sorry I couldn't solve the case for . . . but that's just the breaks sometimes, buddy. You win some, you lose some." I stood up and lit a cigarette.

He crashed forward in the swivel chair. "Tell me about it. The harder I work, the behinder I get." He looked up with a tired grin. "Give Susie my love, huh?"

"I hope I can," I said. "She's due home sometime tonight if the lower half of Texas doesn't slide off into the Gulf or something."

"I watch her program every chance I get," he said. "She gets prettier all the time." He gave me a critical glance. "You don't deserve her, you know that?"

"We've discussed that; but we decided I do."

He snorted, then let it segue into a laugh. He shook his rumpled head and picked up my reports. I took that as a hint that the impromptu meeting was over. I turned and sauntered to the door.

"Thanks, Dan," he said. "I appreciate what you did. You saved me a lot of man-hours and at least now I know where not to look."

"Don't mention it, but don't forget it, either."

He looked up and grinned again. "Okay."

"I'll see you," I said, and opened the door and left.

I saw the silhouette of her low-slung Dodge Lancer the moment I turned the corner. It was parked haphazardly in the right lane of the driveway, as if she had been in a hurry.

Rectangular blocks of golden light fell from the front windows of the house, and the amber porch lamp beamed a welcoming glow. For the first time in days it looked cozy, homey, inviting.

I slammed to a halt beside her car, only inches away, feeling a jet of adrenaline coursing in my blood, a warm tightness in my chest. I wondered if the grin on my face looked as foolish as it felt.

I let myself in quietly, easily—too easily; she hadn't bothered locking the door. A stern lecture on the dangers of unlocked doors would be in order, I told myself, then lost the thought as I crossed the small entry hall in two strides, peeped around the den door, and saw her curled on the couch.

Asleep, as I had suspected when she hadn't run to greet me, her face almost hidden behind one tawny outflung arm and a cascade of raven hair. Her right leg lay perilously near the edge of the couch, her left folded somewhere beneath the green ankle-length robe I had bought for her twenty-second birthday. Her favorite she said, out of a dozen or so hanging in her cramped closet, exotic creations from around the globe, from Sak's, Giorgio's, and Gucci, imported silks, handcrafted originals.

I wasn't altogether sure I believed her, but the fact that she was wearing it was a good omen, the unmistakable aroma of Roman Nights perfume another.

Once, half-drunk, overcome with whimsy, I had bought her the perfume more for its name than for its smell, which was somewhere between old, musty roses and stump water. Compounding the felony, I had somehow convinced her that I found the aroma to be an irresistible aphrodisiac. So I was stuck with it. I had noticed, however, that she never wore the perfume outside the house—never wore it inside the house except on those rare occasions when she felt I was being unduly neglectful and the spirit of Messalina fluttered in her stomach and prickled in her blood.

Sometime soon I would have to tell her the truth about that perfume. But not tonight.

"Peeping Tom." Her voice was dry and husky-harsh from sleep, and dark eyes peered warmly through silken strands of black hair that complemented exactly the olive skin. She smiled and raised her arms. "Come here."

There was a note of welcoming joy in her terse command, and I dropped to the edge of the couch, wriggled my hips into the soft curve of her stomach. I brushed the hair out of her face, leaned into her sleepy warmth to find her lips. Cool and soft, pliant, they warmed to their task as seconds clicked by on the clock, opening in search of more than a kiss could ever bring.

I broke away, finally, and smacked my lips. "The taste is familiar. Now, what was that name again?"

She laughed and squirmed into a half-upright position against the arm of the leather couch, face glowing, eyes bright and dancing. She reached out and collected one of my hands in hers, brought it to her cheek.

"I've been waiting," she said, with a note of mock reproach, "for two hours. I almost fell asleep."

"Almost?"

"Well, I suppose I did doze off, but I heard you come in the door."

"So, you were playing possum."

"I was half asleep. Anyway, I wanted to see how long you'd stand there and look at me." She nipped the end of my thumb, then laved it with the tip of a pink tongue.

"If you hadn't spoken I'd still be there, awestruck and transfixed with wonder."

She sat upright and kissed me. "What a nice thing to say."

"No big deal," I said modestly. "They don't call me ol' silver tongue for nothing."

"You could give an accounting of yourself. You're not working on another case?"

"Not anymore. I was doing some work for Homer—"

"Homer? Homer Sellers?"

I nodded. "You remember the man I went to California looking for? Ralph Kincade? Well, I found him and he decided to come back with me—"

She covered my lips with her fingers, smiling. "If it's bad, I don't want to hear about it right now. As a matter of fact, I don't want to hear any more about anything right now. We've been away from each other for almost two weeks and I, for one, am . . ." She let it trail away, color rising in her cheeks.

"You am what?"

"I am waiting for you to welcome me home properly."

"Well, golly, I hugged and kissed you. Twice. I don't have a fatted calf, so I don't know what else I can do—"

"Think about it, old man," she said, gripping the back of my neck with both hands, tugging my face toward hers. "I'll bet you can come up with something—" She burst out laughing. "No pun intended."

"Well, I never," I said, the rest lost to soft lips and heated breath, a quickening in my body that had little to do with conscious, rational thought.

We broke apart; her features were soft, almost formless, eyes heavy-lidded.

"Do I have time for a shower?" I asked, whispering.

"Just barely," she whispered back. "If you hurry."

15

We came together from opposite sides of the bed, all traces of awkwardness gone, our bodies assuming long-accustomed positions, our hands finding familiar things to do. The mechanics seldom changed, but somehow each time she made it different; that was her magic.

At no time was she more beautiful than when she was sexually aroused, an inner incandescence giving her skin a feverish glow, lips dry and warm and tumescent, dark eyes electric, sparking with their own internal fire. I could have told her it made me feel young and fierce and foolish just to look at her, made me feel humble just to touch her. I could have, but I didn't.

Once, caught up in the rhythmic cadence of our bodies, she made a sound—a soft, joyful cry more stirring than breathless exclamations or urgent obscenities could ever be.

I held her tightly, lost in the moment, a part of me waiting and watching for her other face. A face that only I could see, flushed skin and tightly clenched eyes, lips pulled downward at the corners in a sad clown's mouth. An involuntary expression of total involvement, fulfillment, it was her secret face, but it was my secret.

Moments later, teetering at the outer limits of human endurance, I saw her secret face beginning to form and felt the need to say something, anything, as long as it was meaningful and conveyed the rich ambience of the moment. But a blank mind is not conducive to arcane elocution, and the moment passed in golden silence, blended with other moments that went on and on and on. . . .

* * *

We got around to eating at nine o'clock. Arby's beef sandwiches she had picked up on her way home from the airport. Heated in the microwave, along with shoestring potatoes and a cold beer, they tasted marvelous, much needed energy for exhausted lovers.

We fed each other shoestring potatoes and warm glances, acting in general like newlyweds after that all-important first night. I watched her lovely mobile face and thought strange thoughts about burned-out old men and new beginnings, about insouciant youth and lofty, breathless dreams. I felt guilty somehow for feeling so good, afraid that I was cheating her, that the best of me had come and gone, lost somewhere in the years she knew nothing about.

Once, when she lifted my hand to her lips and nuzzled it against her cheek, I wanted to tell her my misgivings, reassure her of my love, reassure her that marrying her had not been a selfish act of masculine vanity, an aging libido seeking resurrection. But emotional outbursts had never been one of my failings, and I just sat there smiling until my cheeks began to hurt.

"You can tell me now about Homer," she said. "About Mr. Kincade."

"Later. It's a long story and a sorry one. We've got plenty of time. I'll tell you all about it tomorrow. Okay?"

"Okay," she said quickly, too quickly, suddenly absorbed in cleaning up the remnants of our simple meal. I reached out and caught her arm.

"We do have plenty of time, don't we?"

She let her breath out in a gentle sigh, slipped slowly back into her chair, her right hand catching mine in midair as I released her arm. She mauled my hand, avoiding my eyes, examining intently the knuckle I had once broken against a hairy jaw.

I watched her in silence, leaving the ball in the air on her side of the net.

She tossed her head and looked up, face pale, a defiant tilt to

95

her chin that usually preceded calamitous news. She made a wry face, bounced my hand a couple of times on the table top, wet her lips and cleared her throat, all signs of agitation, frustration.

"Honey, I have to . . . to go to work tomorrow—now, wait! Let me explain. Ellen Wernitz's father died. She had to leave tonight for Minnesota. So that leaves us with no one to cover that late hurricane in the Gulf—Curt, I think it is. It's supposed to make landfall sometime tomorrow afternoon near Galveston—"

"And you're on the welcoming committee." I felt a surge of disappointment, a tiny rill of anger, the plans I had been formulating disappearing like smoke signals in an unexpected wind.

"I knew you'd be mad," she said miserably, slicing at my palm with a razor-edged thumbnail.

"I'm not mad, Susan," I said, taking back my hand to dig cigarettes out of the bathrobe pocket. "But don't those damned idiots over there know that hurricanes are dangerous? They spawn tornadoes, floods—"

"That's why I have to go," she said quickly. "Dangerous or not, it's news, and that's what they pay me for, Danny. I can't let being a woman stand in my way or I'll never get anywhere."

I used up a few seconds lighting a cigarette, cooling down, marveling at how swiftly we had gone from loving glances to the edge of hostility. I felt a spike of pain above my left eye, a sinking sensation in my chest.

"Where is anywhere, Susan?" I had my voice back under control, a slow friendly drawl as false as government growth statistics.

Her lips tightened. She cupped her chin in one hand and stared into the darkness outside the bay window. "I told you about the rumor. That we're going to a twenty-four-hour day, that we're going to break it up into eight three-hour segments. Well, it's going to happen January first. That means they'll need four new anchor people. I have a good shot at one of those jobs, Danny." She paused, looked at me. "Actually, I've got better than a good shot. Sy has already told me that I'm one of the four being considered. So, you see, honey, I can't let up now, even if it is unfair to . . . to you."

"Sy," I said lightly. "He that big curly-headed guy we met at the Rangers' game?"

She nodded eagerly. "Yes. You'd like him, Danny. He's a deer hunter and a sports enthusiast, and he likes to camp out, rough it, all the things you like to do. You'd have a lot in common."

"I doubt it. He's bigger than me, a lot younger, and too damned pretty to be a man. Besides, he wears too much jewelry."

A smile flashed across her face, brightening her eyes. "Danny! You're jealous!"

"Jealous? Naw, I wouldn't wear all that stuff if somebody gave it—"

"That's not what I mean, and you know it. You're jealous of Sy and me." A look of delighted surprise gave way to wide-eyed incredulity. "Danny, you can't be!"

"Yep, I am," I said. "Where you're concerned, I'm jealous of anybody who's younger than me or better-looking than me— and that's just about everybody I've ever seen on television, especially that station you work for."

Her laugh was a mixture of disbelief and reproof. "I don't believe you. Aren't you forgetting something? I was in love with you a long time before you were even aware of me—as a woman, I mean."

"Not true. You were twenty when I met you, and there was nothing wrong with my eyesight or my woman-sensing radar antenna. Nobody had to point out how sexy you were. I figured that out all by myself. I was enthralled from the beginning."

"You had a fine way of showing it." Her tone had turned light and breezy. We were back on familiar ground, safe territory, and I could sense relief nudging through her anxiety. She had expected more resistance from me, bitterness, and my easy capitulation had thrown her into a state of mild euphoria.

But it wasn't capitulation; it was only my usual clown-and-pony routine, hiding my true feelings behind nonsense and persiflage. Maybe the shrinks would say it wasn't healthy, repressing things, but it was the only way I knew to keep something I couldn't bear to lose.

"You were a sassy rich kid," I said. "Heavy on the sassy. And I was just a lowly P.I."

"You were a lonely P.I.," she said, her face as soft as her voice. "That's the first thing I sensed about you."

"Sob, sob."

"Yes, you were. No matter how hard you tried to cover it up with those tough guy routines you and Uncle Homer were always doing. I knew it right away. I could see it in your eyes, hear it in your voice, in the way you were always kidding around."

"How come you call Homer uncle? I know you're not related." I knew the answer to that, but the conversation needed a new direction.

"Habit, I guess. He was Daddy's best friend on the force before Daddy got killed. Homer just sort of took over the family after that. He looks like an uncle ought to look, and was probably nicer to us than most uncles would have been. We didn't see him much after Grandmother died and we moved to Waco, but the habit just hung on."

"He thinks the world of you and your mother—" I broke off, jumping a little as the telephone shrilled from the wall behind my head.

I glanced at the clock over the sink. Ten-twenty. I looked back at Susie. "Ten to one this is the devil we've just been speaking about." I lifted the receiver in the middle of the second ring. He didn't wait for me to answer.

"Hey, little buddy. Didn't get you out of bed, did I?"

"Yeah, you did. I thought I told you Susie was coming home." I ducked a shoestring potato from across the table. I grinned; Susie made a menacing face and held up a fork.

"Oops, by golly, you did." He guffawed; not a pleasant thing to hear at the best of times, up close it almost blew off my ear.

"Well, just hunker down there on your heels and rest a little. Got something I know for a fact you'll want to hear."

"I doubt it."

"Well, I'm gonna tell you, anyhow. You know Ted Baskin? Sure you do. Well, he sat in for me at the LeClair autopsies today—nice job for a Sunday afternoon, huh? But old Ted, he's a good old boy when it comes to things like that—"

"You want to get to the point, Homer?"

"Yeah, the point is, Ted helped tag the slugs as they took them out, and you know how he is, he got to thinking about them being twenty-fives and about the Kincade murder weapon being a twenty-five, and he went back to the lab and ran a comparison and—you with me so far, boy?"

"And they matched," I said, feeling suddenly cold all over.

"How'd you guess?"

"Are you sure?"

"'Course I'm sure. Just got back from there myself. You know what kinda eye I got."

"Yeah, I know. That's what worries me." I was speaking mechanically, trying to piece this new information into the fabric of the Kincade murder. Like an optical illusion that changes shape if you stare at it long enough, the Kincade mosaic had suddenly shifted, a new beginning, a different direction.

"You know Ted," Homer was saying quietly. "He don't make mistakes about things like this."

"I know." I took a deep breath, let it out. "Well, my friend, looks to me like you have yourself a whole new ball game."

"Yeah, don't we," he said, and fell silent.

I listened to him breathing for a while, then, suddenly angry for no reason I could fathom, I reached up and dropped the receiver into its cradle.

16

Susie's plane was scheduled to leave at eight o'clock Monday morning. She chattered gaily through our early breakfast and declined my offer to take her to DFW Airport.

"I don't know what time I'll be in tomorrow night, and if I drive my car I won't have to bother you or wait around on a cab. You know what a hassle that can be." She gave me a sidelong glance as she stacked the dishes in the dishwasher. "What do you think about going down to the cabin for a few days? We could leave early Wednesday morning. I told Sy I was taking five or six days off. He agreed that I needed some time off after these last two months—"

"Nice of him. He's got little glittery eyes but it sounds like he's got a big heart."

She smothered a laugh and came up behind my chair. She slipped her arms across my shoulders and nibbled on an ear. "Come on, honey. Don't be like that. You're not going to sit around and sulk for the next two days, are you?"

"Children sulk. I might pout a little."

She kissed my cheek, nipped my ear again. "You didn't say what you thought about the cabin. It's beautiful down there this time of year. We could take long walks, pick up pecans and hickory nuts, light a big fire in the fireplace and . . . and anything else that might come to mind." She chuckled and blew in my ear.

"Sounds good, but I may be busy."

"Busy? You're not on a case."

"I told you, I've been working for Homer."

"You said you were finished, that you only promised him two

days." She moved back to the dishwasher and punched the buttons, disappointment clouding her face.

"That was when I thought we'd be going somewhere today. What do you think that call was all about last night? There's been another murder—two, in fact—and there seems to be a connection."

"You could tell him no. It's not your job anymore, Danny."

"That's right, it's not, and I could turn him down. But Homer does a lot for me, Susan, and this is one of the first times he's asked me for help. He wouldn't do that if his back wasn't against the wall. Besides, we've been friends for a long time. That matters to me."

"I know it does. You could give him two more days." She smiled brightly and slipped into the lightweight nylon jacket she liked to use for plane travel. Her lucky jacket; she was convinced it helped keep the plane in the air.

"Maybe that's all it will take," I said. "The first twenty-four hours are the most important."

I carried her overnight bag out to her car. We embraced, and she scooted under the wheel of the little Dodge with flushed cheeks and shining eyes. I wanted to think the excitement stemmed from our parting kiss, but I watched her drive off down the street and knew otherwise. She was off on another adventure, on her own and doing what she did so well. Still too young to recognize the danger, to understand that life wasn't just five minutes on the ten o'clock news, that living was simply a series of false starts and stops, an occasional surge to make you careless, to make you feel lucky and anointed by the gods before the knobby hand of personal disaster smashed you flat. Sometimes, just watching her exuberance made me feel my years like rusty padlocks and chains, made me feel old and tired and used up; at other times she made me come alive, made me feel young again, revitalized, an ancient spirit in a new incarnation.

Morose, chilled, I went back inside the house. I rummaged around in the storage cabinet above the oven and came out with the unopened bottle of Wild Turkey. I put it in the center of the kitchen table, sat down at my usual place and stared through the bay window at the leaf-pocked yard.

I had a decision to make. I had come to a fork in the trail, a place that mattered. I could back up my lofty words to Susie and call Homer, offer my services once again. Or I could sit here and get drunk, slide into that amber-colored world where fantasy ruled and there were no cops or murderers, no beautiful young wives who dashed off to other, more interesting lives among the shakers and the doers.

The phone jangled. I jumped and swore. Sometime soon I'd have to do something about that damned phone, find one that chimed or tinkled or buzzed pleasantly.

It rang a second time. I lit a cigarette and snatched the receiver off the hook.

"Hello, dammit!"

A voice clucked sympathetically. "Not feeling any better this morning, huh? Thought maybe you might. But I guess Susie just left and that'd make any man feel ornery—"

"How the hell did you know that, Homer?"

"Well, she called me yesterday evening when she got in, looking for you. We chatted a bit, and she told me she had to leave again this morning early. She was worried about how you'd take it, her leaving again so soon, but I told her you were a growed-up man and understood about responsibility to a job—"

"Thanks a bunch. Why didn't you tell me last night you'd talked to her?"

"Hadn't when I saw you. She called right after you left."

"What's on your mind, Homer?"

"Nothing much. Just thought I'd run over and we could talk about the case, these new killings—"

"My two days are over. I've got some pressing business."

"Like what?" he asked bluntly. "Getting drunk? Surely you ain't gonna let Susie having to leave to do her job piss you off enough to get—"

"Homer, butt out. Just butt the hell out. It's my damn business if I want to get drunk or not get drunk."

"Yeah, you're right," he said coldly. "It is." He broke the connection.

I stared at the humming receiver, resisting an impulse to slam it against the wall. Sometimes being Homer Sellers' friend was a hard and rocky road to ride. But, on the other hand, being my friend probably had a few drawbacks now and again.

I sighed, punched out his number on the phone. I chatted with Mitsi a few moments before she put me through.

"Sellers."

"Get your big ass over here. If I have to come and get you, you're in trouble, old man."

He chuckled as if nothing had happened. "Be right there. Gimme about ten minutes to get my ducks lined up, as them Yankee fellers like to say. Okay?"

"Ten minutes," I said, and hung up.

I put the bottle of whiskey back in the cabinet. No point in giving Homer the satisfaction of knowing he had been right. He thought he knew me too well the way it was.

I sat back down and watched the blooming day through the bay window. Another nice one shaping up. Three in a row. Must be some kind of record for late October, a time of year noted for sudden changes, temperamental irascibility.

I flicked on the radio, lit a cigarette, and waited. Ten minutes, he had said. I'd give him thirty.

17

It took him more than ten minutes, but less than thirty.

We sat down at the kitchen table with the surprisingly thick file folder on the LeClair murders. Homer busied himself lighting a cigar while I skimmed through the field investigation reports to date, the crime scene photos, and the autopsy reports.

Grim reading, stark and factual and cold. Violent endings reduced to bare essentials, three necessary questions already answered: where, how, and when. The mechanics had done their work, the vital questions of who and why would fall to the detectives, those supposedly superior beings whose knowledge and experience lifted them a notch above their fellow officers. Actually, persistence, curiosity, and skepticism were the rudimentary tools a detective needed, along with a modicum of talent and insight. Foot-slogging police work and tipsters solved more crimes in a week than all the intellectual divination throughout the history of man.

"Paris set the time of death between ten-thirty and eleven," I said. "That's a little tight, isn't it? Especially for him."

Homer grunted, sending a pale cone of smoke in my direction. "We know they had breakfast at eight o'clock. Doc Paris said that gave him something definite to work with. First time I've ever seen him commit to anything less than a one-hour swing either way."

"Who's Dr. Phillip Thorne?" I held up one of the small stack of F.I.R.s.

"Pastor at their church. Three more in there from the same place. A guy named Lansing, the choir director, and two ladies in the choir. They all say Madge LeClair never left the church during the service. Same thing with the boy. He played the organ this week. He's some kind of hotshot piano player, some kind of prodigy, from what they told Chester. Nineteen years old and won about every kind of competition around by the time he was sixteen. He's already had concerts in most of the big cities, including Dallas."

"Paul LeClair? I never heard of him."

He shrugged. "Neither have I, but that don't mean much. Only piano player I know of is Liberace, and I wasn't too fond of him."

"Other children? Close relatives?"

"An older son named Robert. Evidently out of LeClair and his first wife. Nobody seems to know exactly where he is."

"I thought you said Paul was Timothy LeClair's grandson?"

"That's right. Old Tim's second son, Marvin, was Madge's husband and the father of Paul and Julie. He's been dead five or six years. The old man was grooming him to take over the family business, which is mostly oil-drilling supplies and real estate. The first son, Robert, apparently liked spending money more than making it, and him and old Tim parted company a long time ago. Paul said he thought his uncle had been gone for about twelve years, but Madge said it was more like fifteen. Last time anybody heard of him, he was in Alaska."

"How about servants? If I remember correctly, that's one of the biggest houses in Sunnyvale."

"Yep. They got a chauffeur, a housekeeper, a cook, two maids, a full-time gardener, and a part-time helper. Sunday's the help's day off except for the chauffeur. He's off on Thursdays." He leaned back, arms straight, big hands splayed on the table. He beamed at me around the cigar. "How's that for a steel-trap memory?"

"You're learning, Homer. What I don't understand is why the girl had a friend drive her home if the chauffeur was working? Didn't he drive the family to church?"

He nodded. "Yeah, he did. I asked Madge LeClair that same question. She said the chauffeur—name's Peter Johnson, by the way—belongs to the same church. She said Julie probably didn't want to disturb him in the middle of the service. He's old and crotchety and she said Julie was halfway afraid of him. He's been with them for twenty-five years and he always made the kids walk the chalk, especially after their daddy died. You know the type, faithful old family retainer taking it out on the kids for having to kiss the boss's ass all them years. He is a crotchety old bastard. I talked to him myself. He told me there wasn't anything wrong with Julie except a little cold and he'd have told her to get back up there in that choir where she belonged until church was over." Homer pursed his lips and frowned. "Didn't seem to bother him a lot that she was dead. He took on some about the old man, though." He pushed to his feet with a grunt. "Gotta make a pit stop." He adjusted the lapels of an expensive-looking brown worsted I hadn't seen before and disappeared from sight in the den.

I picked up the LeClair crime scene photos again. Clear and graphic, they depicted an old man in wrinkled flannel trousers and a workingman's shirt with the sleeves rolled up above the elbows. He lay sprawled across a battered wooden desk, face down, arms outflung, one gnarled hand still clutching a ballpoint pen, the other trailing off the edge of the littered desk. An irregular pool of blood had gathered beside the body, dark and glossy with beginning coagulation. A wispy fringe of white hair encircled the back of the old man's head, and high up on the bald crown, a small black hole leaked a thin dark rivulet of blood.

"Pretty, huh?" Homer sank into his chair across the table. "Good pictures, though."

"Who took these? Baskin?"

"Naw. That short fat guy who works for him. Can't ever remember his name. Dresses like a rodeo cowboy."

Reluctantly, I turned to the pictures of Julie LeClair. She, too, lay facedown, her body twisted awkwardly at the foot of a broad circular staircase. One hand was caught beneath her body, the other stretched alongside her head, fingers clenched as if in a last act of self-defense. She had been shot twice in the center of her back, the dark dots no more than an inch apart, enclosed in a dull brown stain the size of a saucer.

The hem of her full-skirted dress lay across the small of her back, the long slender legs widespread. She wore no panties, and her small feet were bare.

"Was she molested?"

Homer shifted in his chair across the table. "No, not if you mean raped. If he did anything at all, it didn't leave any signs or marks. I think we have to assume she was wearing panties or panty hose, and if she was, then the killer took them with him. She didn't look like the kind of girl who wouldn't wear them." He paused, stubbed out his cigar. "I didn't ask her momma. Maybe I ought to."

"Yes," I said. "What happened to her shoes?"

"We found one on the stairs, about halfway up, one about six feet from the body."

"Physical evidence? Prints?"

"Nothing except for the one casing. He probably wore gloves, otherwise we think he'd have left prints on the safe and maybe on the stair railing. Nothing there but family prints and a lot of smears."

"Was the safe blown?"

"No. The old man musta had it open. Either that or the killer knew the combination."

"If the safe was standing open, then it may not have started out as a robbery. Maybe he just seized the opportunity to pick up some easy cash and at the same time make it appear to be a burglary that got out of hand."

Homer flexed his fingers, laced them together, and began popping his knuckles. "Sounds logical except that LeClair had four hundred and seventy-five dollars in his wallet in his back pocket. The pocket was still buttoned. A pro would have checked."

I shuffled the photos and papers into some semblance of order and put them back into the folder. "You know yet how much money was in the safe?"

"Probably won't. LeClair liked to keep some cash on hand but nobody knows how much. His daughter-in-law guessed between four and five thousand. His personal accountant is checking on the negotiable securities. He thinks it won't amount to much—ten, maybe fifteen thousand."

"Not much? I guess it depends on where you're standing."

"Yeah." Homer snapped one last knuckle and splayed his fingers on the table again. "Well, what do you think? You know about as much as I do now."

I smiled faintly and lit a cigarette, blew smoke across the table. "I know more than you do, Homer. Always have, but that's beside the point. You want a beer?"

He scowled and glanced at his watch. "Little early for that bull—yeah, I'll take a can."

"No cans, only bottles." I pulled the tops off two dark amber bottles and gave him one. "What do I think? Okay, I'll tell you what I think. We need to look for some sort of connection between the Kincades and the LeClairs. I don't believe this was a robbery any more than the Kincade murder was. Too damn much coincidence. Same gun, same overkill. Same M.O. The girl coming home was unexpected and didn't fit into the original plan to kill LeClair. The killer took the money for appearance's sake, or maybe because he's greedy, and when the girl came in I think for a moment he considered raping her, maybe before he shot her, maybe while she was dying."

"Could be coincidence," Homer said a little belligerently, taking, as usual, an opposing view. "If the guy's a thief and didn't get anything at the Kincade place, maybe he thought he'd try a place with more possibilities, and you gotta admit that fits the LeClair mansion."

"The report says no sign of forced entry. How did he get in, Homer?"

"We don't know that, not yet."

"It suggests a key, though, doesn't it? How many doors?"

His face bunched thoughtfully. "Five, as I remember."

"Five, not counting French or sliding doors opening onto balconies. If I remember, that house has several balconies."

"Yeah, it does."

"That's a lot of keys."

"That's the housekeeper's job, managing the keys. We haven't talked to her yet." He looked at his watch. "Not unless Chester managed to get over there this morning, but I doubt that. He's up to his ass in that Bowart killing Saturday night. Looks like it might be drug-related—"

"How about the rest of the help, the maids and the cook?"

"Nope, not yet. Only one we talked to is the chauffeur. I told you that."

I sighed and stubbed out my cigarette. "I'll need some help with this, Homer. Too much for one man to handle. We need to run makes on everybody, including the man and the girl. We need to check for a connection between the Kincades and LeClair. From what I read in the reports, even the interrogations of Madge LeClair and her son were pretty skimpy."

"Well, hell, Dan, they were all tore up. There's a limit to how much you can push people under those circumstances. We had to get the LeClair family doctor over, the way it was. He gave both of them sedatives. They couldn't have been involved and I couldn't see treating them like they were criminals. These are important people—"

"Rich people, you mean. I never knew you to make distinctions in the old days, Homer."

"Dammit, I didn't, and I still don't. But you know as well as I do the pressure is gonna be a bitch on this one, already is, as a matter of fact."

"Then don't you think you should have one of your men heading up the investigation? I'm no longer a cop. We can pretend from now until doomsday, but—"

Homer slapped the table, grinning broadly, big white teeth and squinted eyes giving him a ludicrous look of boyishness. "Don't sweat it. Ted Baskin is the detective of record. He's a sergeant, and that's enough rank to take the heat, if there is any. And he doesn't mind working for you. He's hell on wheels in the lab or at a crime scene, but he's also smart enough to know his limitations when it comes to dealing with people."

I shook my head, feeling helpless. "That's fine, Homer, but it still doesn't alter the facts. This is likely to be a high-profile case, and I don't have authority—"

"Yeah, you do," he said, the grin growing broader, if possible. "I talked to Cliff Hollister last night. He's appointing you special investigator out of his office to assist in this case."

I stared at him blankly, stunned. Cliff Hollister, Midway City's chief of police. A long-ago friend who had left his pride and good looks on the banks of the Trinity River under the methodical pounding of my fists during an ancient ritual: two enraged men fighting over a woman. The woman had been my first wife, Barbara; the ritual one that has existed since the first time one man tried to take the woman of another. Since that time, I had always thought of Hollister as an enemy, when I thought of him at all.

"I don't believe it."

"God's truth," Homer said, and raised his right hand. "Look, Dan, I think you got old Cliff all wrong. I don't exactly know what went on between you two back—"

"Let it lay, Homer."

He shrugged and lifted both hands, palms up. "Okay. Your business, I reckon. Any other little problems you got with this? Just run 'em out here, boy, and I'll squash 'em for you." He chuckled, a fatherly chuckle that generally set my teeth on edge. This time I ignored it.

"No, no more problems."

18

I found Ted Baskin in his small spartan office adjoining the crime lab. An old metal desk, two swivel chairs, and a large Walleco safe took up most of the room, making it next to impossible for him to entertain more than one visitor at a time. Hunting dog pictures adorned one dingy green wall, glossy prints of his two Labrador retrievers and an orange and white Brittany spaniel. Half a dozen framed certificates from forensic and criminology courses he had completed formed an irregular line on the wall behind his chair.

He was hunched forward over the desk, one hand over his eyes, the other holding a telephone receiver crammed against his ear. He had tightly curled, sandy-red hair, and every exposed inch of his skin was covered with freckles the size of dimes. We had been partners back in the early days, two rookies with the zeal of oracles for the law. As detectives, we had been teamed up again in the Homicide Division, not quite so bright-eyed and eager as before, but still convinced that being a cop meant something despite a judicial system that seemed hell-bent on hamstringing law and order. Quiet-spoken, reserved, almost shy around strangers, he had leaped at the chance to take over the technical squad when thirty-year veteran Amos Tierney retired. For several years Baskin had been the only member of the squad—crime scene technician, photographer, and lab technician. But population growth inevitably brought more crime, and the last time I had talked to him, his squad had grown to four and he had been promoted to sergeant.

He looked up as I sat down across the desk from him. He lifted his eyebrows and flashed the infectious grin that had made me forget his homeliness the first time I saw it. He lifted one finger and spoke into the phone with a rush.

"Gotta go, babe, the boss is here. See you later, bye." He cradled the receiver and shook his head, the smile still working. "Women. They're so damn sweet when you first get married, you wish you could eat them. A couple of years later, you wish you had." He leaned across the desk, and we shook hands.

I laughed and took out my cigarettes. "You, too, huh? I wonder why that is?"

He took an ashtray out of his desk and set it in front of me. "I haven't seen you for a while. I hear you got married again. Jesus, Dan, I thought you were smarter than that."

"Had to. All my clothes were getting dirty, the house was a pigpen, and I broke my last Taiwan back scratcher." I lit a cigarette, watching him laugh, remembering that one of the reasons I liked Ted Baskin was that he thought almost everything I said was funny. At times that had proved to be embarrassing.

"Well," he said, still chortling, stubby fingers fiddling with the two file folders in front of him. "Well, I guess you and me are gonna be working together. You volunteer, too, or did Homer sweet talk you into it?"

"*Bulldozed* would be a better word." The idea of Homer sweet talking anyone into anything was almost enough to make me laugh again.

"Yeah, I know. I volunteered, but only after he had me backed into a corner I couldn't get out of." He opened the top folder and shuffled the papers. "Homer said you were up-to-date." He stopped and grinned. "So, where do we go from here, boss?"

"I thought you might have some ideas. You're the one who came up with the ballistics match. What caused you to make the comparison, anyway?"

He shrugged, clearly pleased at the question. "Time. Nosiness. I'd just finished checking the Kincade bullets and here comes another murder with the same caliber weapon, same kind of overkill. The back-of-the-head shots seemed similar and not all that usual, outside of some bandit shooting a store clerk to eliminate a witness. And, too, twenty-five-caliber weapons aren't your run-of-the-mill guns in a killing like this. Anyhow, I had some free time and I got nosy."

I nodded my approval. "And now we have three murders connected by the same gun. That could be coincidence. Homer's taking that position, that both crimes are the result of a burglary gone wrong."

Ted shook his head. "I don't know about that, Dan. I've worked a lot of burglary murder scenes, and usually one of two things happen. The thief gets so shook up at having shot somebody that he takes off without a thing, or he keeps his cool and goes ahead with it. That coulda happened at the Kincades' since he didn't get anything, but at the LeClairs' there was all kinds of small stuff around he coulda stuffed in a pillowcase. I understand all he got was some cash from the safe and some securities, and we don't know how much of that. Maybe none. Nobody had the combination to that safe except the old man—"

"I didn't know that."

"It's true. Not even his daughter-in-law or grandson. At least they're not admitting it if they did." He shook his head again.

"Dammit, it just didn't feel like a robbery." He massaged his chin, green eyes reflective. "And don't you think it was a funny time for a burglary?"

"That had occurred to me. I don't think a thief would go into a house like that blindly, without casing it first. If he had watched enough to know the servants were off on Sunday, then he should have known that the old man would be there, that he was semi-invalid and never attended church. If he had inside help, someone who tipped him, then he would also have to know the money and securities would be in the old man's bedroom study. No, I think you're right, Ted. Homer's grasping at straws. He doesn't want to face the fact that he may have a crazy running around Midway City with a gun. Besides, Homer's getting torque from the brass and he hates that."

"Is that what you think? A crazy?"

It was my turn to shrug. "I don't know what I think. I worked two days on the Kincade case and it dead-ended. All I did was clear the family members."

Ted nodded. "I read your reports." He lifted an eyebrow, then added a thoughtful frown. "You think we have to go the same route with the LeClairs?"

"I don't see that we have a choice at this point. With no evidence and no leads it's a brand new game despite the gun connection, no matter how remote."

"My job," he said quickly, bringing back the crooked smile. "I'm hell on wheels with paperwork and evidence, all the dull stuff. You're the boss, so you oughta get the exciting stuff, like talking to the people . . . anyhow, rich people make me nervous."

"You're too kind, Ted. I'd forgotten that about you, how generous you are."

He laughed. "That's why we were such a good team. I've got an eye like a hawk and a nose like a ferret, and you've got a mouth like—"

"Careful."

"—like Perry Mason."

"Never met the gentleman," I said and pushed to my feet,

returning his smile, a little appalled by the exuberance on his face. Something else I had forgotten about him: he had always said there was nothing like a good murder to start all the old juices flowing and, judging by his expression, his pop-off valve was about ready to blow.

I leaned across the desk and patted his shoulder. "Easy, boy, we're still at the gate."

He boomed another laugh and sprang to his feet. He was short and stocky, with a hard, round body that rarely needed tending to maintain its muscular tone and normal weight of one hundred and eighty pounds. He ate enough for two teen-agers, loved all kinds of junk food, and never seemed to gain an ounce, a constantly irritating fact throughout our years as partners.

"Man, me and you together again," he said, grinning so hard I could see flashes of gold-capped molars. "Some gun-happy prick don't know it yet, but he's on his way to a mainline event at Huntsville Prison. Maybe we oughta call a press conference; he might just go ahead and give hisself up."

"Uh-huh. Well, before we declare the case solved, why don't we see if we can find out who LeClair's attorneys were? Might be interesting to see what's in the old man's will."

"Can do." He made a notation in the top folder. "By the way, my oldest boy went to school with the Kincade boy. Rick was a year behind, but he knew David pretty well. He said David was real cool, real popular with the guys and gals both. In fact, he said David was the senior class's number-one broadjumper last year."

I studied his grinning face for a moment. "I take it you're not talking about athletics."

He shook his head. "Lady-killer, I guess. I notice Rick is showing a great deal of interest in gymnastics this year."

"David's a good-looking kid," I said. "Built a lot like me when I was his age." I crossed the short distance to the door.

Baskin moved the top folder aside, opened the other one. "Anything we need to do on the Kincade case? I read through it, but I don't see a lot unless you want to follow up on the speeding ticket."

"Not at the moment. I'm ninety-nine percent sure Mrs. Kincade's telling the truth. I think we should concentrate on the LeClair murders. At least that case is new and we've got somewhere to go with it. If one perp did both crimes, he'll be just as caught if it's for the LeClairs."

Ted nodded and came around the desk. He leaned one hip against his lone filing cabinet and folded his arms. "I read your comments about Cynthia Kincade's trip to the coast." He paused, a quizzical half smile on his face. "Sounded like you don't know what that trip was all about."

"I didn't much care as long as she was there. Why?"

He shrugged. "She's a hooker."

Shock reaction held me motionless. I stared at his brown-speckled face and felt tiny switches clicking as understanding set in. On some low-grade level of consciousness, that whole episode had bothered me, Cynthia and Knutson and Maggie Lane. An odd threesome any way you stacked it. Now it made a little more sense.

"Knutson her pimp?"

"Yeah. Her and some other hooker named Maggie . . . something. You had an F.I.R. on her somewhere in there—"

"Maggie Lane. And Knutson? I can't believe—where did you get this?"

"Posey, over in Vice. He's a friend of mine. He stopped by the house Saturday to watch the game, then come on down here to the lab when he found me gone. He'd read about the Kincade killing and he just passed it along in conversation. He said he'd been trying a long time to bust her and that girl Maggie, but they have a select clientele and a pretty good cut-out operation going, and he hasn't been able to touch them."

"No wonder Knutson was upset. He's out on parole." I moved out into the hallway.

"They tag him for pimping, he won't be out long." He stopped in the doorway and leaned against the jamb. "Where you gonna start?"

"With the family, I guess."

"I don't envy you," he said, shaking his head. "That's one hard luck family. One murder at a time's tough enough to take, but two . . ." He let it drift away.

I nodded. "See you later." I turned and walked down the corridor, a sudden sense of urgency gnawing at my vitals. Almost half a day gone and nothing accomplished except learning that Cynthia Kincade was a whore. But that had little significance other than social, and the knowledge did nothing at all to improve my frame of mind.

19

I lit a cigarette when I got to my truck, climbed in and drove across town toward Sunnyvale thinking about what Baskin had said about hard luck families.

I knew something about that. I had been a part of two families in my lifetime before Susie, both of which I had lost because of bad luck, or unkind fate, or whatever it is that pursues some people like a witch's curse.

My mother died first, at the beginning of my last year in high school, from an illness that came like a thief in the night, leaving my father and me alone and devastated. I learned to cope because I had to or die; my father turned to an old, tried-and-true friend, dove headfirst into the amber bottles he had been nursing on for years. And acre by acre, the land I grew up on began to slip away—poor management and more bad luck, a river of booze to curb his insatiable thirst—into the pockets of barroom cronies more cunning than he.

When he died, drunk and frozen in a Texas norther, I was the temporary guest of little brown men with inventive minds and treacherous hearts, Viet Cong guerrillas who lived in the ground like rodents, fought and died like religious zealots, and hated Americans with a hatred so intense it would have been fascinating if it hadn't been so frightening.

By the time I was rescued and the Red Cross caught up with me, my father was long dead and buried, and I could do little more than cry drunken tears over his grave and curse the hard luck.

When I was thirty-three my wife, Barbara, died almost as suddenly as my mother, only this time they knew enough to label it cancer. A year later, almost to the day, my son, Tommy, wasted his life against a concrete abutment, a stolen car and a lonely road, head buzzing with a load of amphetamines. Two companions died with him, the three bodies so intertwined within the car's interior they could never be sure who was driving.

It took nine months of my spare time to find the pusher, and when I finally took him in, they charged me with police brutality. For once they were right, and midway through the thirty-day suspension that followed, I gave my badge to Homer with explicit verbal instructions. He had never forgotten that moment, but he had forgiven me the way I knew he would. He was a great one for forgiving, just so long as you understood there was something to forgive.

Madge LeClair was short and plump and motherly, a round, troubled face not yet seized in the unforgiving grip of time. She had large eyes so brown they were almost black, and cracked, worn hands not usually found on a lady of means. She wore a no-nonsense nylon robe and matching pajamas, satin house shoes, and her hair, mousey brown streaked with gray, was pulled back and bound into a knot as large as my fist. Her neck was trenched with wrinkles, but her face was remarkably smooth and unblemished. I guessed that she had been small and round and dainty as a young girl, the kind of girl men want to cuddle and protect. She looked wasted by sorrow, dark circles under her eyes, ravaged hands clenched tightly in the hollow of her lap as if to hide them from disapproving eyes.

As Naomi Kincade had done, she sat on the edge of her seat, intently scanning my face as I told her who I was and what part I would have in the investigation of her daughter's murder. Unlike Naomi Kincade, she asked no questions.

"I don't know what I can tell you, Mr. Roman." She took a deep, sighing breath. "It was just a Sunday morning like any other Sunday. We had breakfast at the usual time. It was the staff's day off, so Julie and I prepared it, nothing elaborate, just bacon and eggs for Paul and I, and a poached egg for Mr. LeClair. Julie was feeling a little squeamish, so she had a piece of toast and some orange juice and later a small glass of milk."

"The chauffeur didn't eat with you?"

"No. He has his own small apartment above the garage. He usually prepares his own food. Sometimes he eats over here with the rest of the staff. We leave that up to him."

"I understand he's been with you a long time. How about the rest of the staff?"

"Yes, quite a long time. Juanita is the latest member of our little group and she's been here almost six years. Juanita is one of the maids."

"Any problems with the staff? Disputes over money, jealousy, dissatisfaction with their jobs?"

She shook her head firmly. "None. We keep a small, select staff. We treat them well, and they're intensely loyal to us."

"I understand, but things do happen from time to time. How about Mr. LeClair, he ever have any problems with the servants?"

She gave me a sharp look that confused me for a moment. "The staff. Absolutely not. Mr. LeClair, like most elderly people, was irascible at times, but never with the staff. He understood the necessity for kindliness when dealing with . . ." She hesitated for a second, as if searching for an impeccable word. "Employees." It was a good choice of words, but I wouldn't have been surprised if she had said menials.

"And Julie? No friction between her and any of the staff?"

Her face changed for the first time, lower lip quivering, eyebrows bunching, a spasm of pain crossing the plain plump face.

She shook her head silently, then after a few moments answered, her voice steady again.

"No, Julie got on very well with everyone. The staff adored her."

I found myself wanting to sigh. I pushed it down and took another tack. "Did Mr. LeClair have any enemies that you know about? An ex-business partner, perhaps, a disgruntled employee he may have had to let go? Someone who just flat didn't like him?"

"No, not that I'm aware of. I don't know anything at all about his business affairs, and I've only met a few of his friends. Since his wife died ten years ago, he has never entertained here at his home." She paused. "That's when we came to live here so that I . . . we could take care of him."

"And after your husband died you still stayed on to take care of him."

"Yes, of course. Mr. LeClair has always been a kind, generous man. He seemed as much a father to me as . . . as my own. I felt that I could do no less."

I nodded and studied her downcast face for a moment. The conversation was going nowhere, accomplishing nothing. I decided to introduce a new subject.

"Mrs. LeClair, are you familiar with the name Ralph Kincade?"

She pursed her lips thoughtfully, then slowly shook her head. "No. No, I don't believe I am."

"You haven't heard it recently? On the news, perhaps?"

She made a faint smile and shook her head again. "I rarely watch the news, Mr. Roman. It's too depressing. If it's not crime here at home, it's famine and terrorism in other lands. I prefer watching sitcoms. They may be inane and useless, but they usually have a happy ending."

Another blind canyon. That left only one unexplored trail.

"Did Mr. LeClair ever discuss his will with you, or possibly show it to you?"

She stiffened slowly, a stern look passing across her pale face. "No, of course not. I told you we never discussed his business."

"That's not exactly business," I said, but decided to let it pass. I felt the sense of urgency again, the need to move on. She had passed my internal polygraph test with flying colors, but it didn't matter much, since she had nothing new to tell me. "I'd like to talk to Paul now, Mrs. LeClair, if it's convenient."

She stood up immediately. "Yes, of course. I asked him to wait. He'll be in the music room, but I'll get him for you." She gave me a formal nod and turned away, then hesitated and turned back. "He's terribly upset over his sister, Mr. Roman. I hope you won't—" She broke off, chewing on her lower lip, the dark eyes pained.

"Won't what?"

"Won't . . . agitate him unnecessarily. He is—Paul is a very sensitive boy, and as you may know, a very gifted musician. People tend to spoil him, and sometimes he can be . . . well, temperamental."

I gave her my friendliest smile. "One summer in Wyoming I broke wild horses, Mrs. LeClair. Don't worry."

She looked confused, vacillating between reassurance and concern. "I see," she said, almost smiling. "I'll send him down to you."

After she left, I looked around the large, dimly lighted room. A study of some sort, a heavy masculine touch. Ornate, but not overly ostentatious, a clever mix of dark and light colors that soothed the eye and lulled the senses, the kind of room one could doze peacefully in, tranquilized by the monotonous chatter of TV. I suspected it might have been Timothy LeClair's favorite place before the advent of age and illness had forced retreat to his upstairs bedroom. His icons were here: a life-size portrait of Henry Ford, busts of Lincoln and Alexander the Great, the flags of Texas and America prominently displayed. A proud man without a doubt, one who understood the responsibilities of wealth, the power of a kind word, the impact of understated elegance that spoke of good breeding.

"We've already talked to you people once." The voice was round and firm, each syllable enunciated clearly, almost musical, spoiled only by a trace of petulance near the end.

I twisted in my soft leather chair and found myself looking at pure masculine beauty, fine features etched in bronze, a heavy mane of hair so black it looked blue, dark smoldering eyes. I understood immediately what Mrs. LeClair had meant about people spoiling him—people being defined as women.

"Humor me," I said, making no attempt to rise, waiting to see if he would shake hands.

He didn't. He moved away from the door and dropped to the arm of the facing couch, his tall gangling body detracting somewhat from the overall image of male perfection. He had narrow hands and long thin fingers, appendages no doubt suited to his alleged mastery of the piano. They drummed restlessly on his thighs, flitted to the narrow lapels of his blue blazer, fingered a fold of silk cloth gathered at his throat.

"I don't see the necessity for going over this again. It's—it's very disturbing. My mother and I don't understand why you're not out catching this . . . this animal who killed my sister instead of coming in here making a pest of yourself."

"I don't mean to be," I said. "A pest, I mean. And your grandfather was also killed, I believe."

"Yes, of course, my grandfather, too. It's just that my sister and I were very close. She was such a warm, caring person—"

"Your grandfather wasn't?"

He looked up, startled. "Wasn't what?"

"Warm and caring."

"Oh . . . yes, I suppose he was, in his way. But he was terribly old and not very friendly much of the time. Oh, I know he was ill and had a lot of pain and all that, but I think sometimes he used that as an excuse to be . . . to be mean."

"How old are you, Paul?"

"Nineteen. I'll be twenty in a few months."

"Going to college, I guess?"

He made a face. "Yes. Or at least I've been going to Texas A&M. I hate it. I was accepted at Juilliard in New York, but Gramps insisted I go to Dad's old school." He stopped, a sly look crossing the handsome face. "But now I'll be going to New York in January."

"That should be fun."

He frowned. "No, it won't be fun. They make you work all the time, but at least I'll be among people like myself, people in the arts, in music. All they care about at A&M is sex and football and playing soldier." His voice rang with a fine edge of contempt for the plebeian pleasures of the masses. He had a faraway look in his eyes, as if envisioning an existence of hard work, an absence of football and sex.

"Your sister was seventeen, I understand."

He came back with a lurch, a look of pain gathering in his face, the black eyes instantly moist. "Yes. My God, only seventeen! She had everything to look forward to."

"Did she have a boyfriend?"

"No, not really. She dated a few times after she passed sixteen, but she always seemed disappointed. She thought most boys acted silly on dates and were only interested in sex. I don't think she ever went out with the same one twice."

"Do you recall if she was wearing panty hose Sunday?"

His brow puckered, one thin finger prodding the corner of his mouth. "Yes. I'm certain of it. She always dressed well for church, nice shoes, not too high, and that would call for panty hose." His hands clasped tightly in front of his chest. "I understand why . . . why you ask. I saw . . . saw her . . . without—" He stopped and took a deep breath. "Yes, I'm certain of it," he repeated. He looked at his watch. "I'm really going to be late for my business management class—"

"Does it matter if you're going to Juilliard in January?"

He stared at me, then smiled for the first time, a winning smile, even white teeth that gleamed like newly minted coins. I knew women who would have died for that smile, others who would have fought to be near it. "Yes, of course, that's right, isn't it? I'm really flunking, anyway. I hate that kind of thing." He fingered his cravat again, looking pleased at this thought of newfound freedom.

"Then you won't mind a few more questions?"

One hand moved in an airy, graceful gesture. "Not at all. Although I don't know how much help I can be."

"Does the name Kincade mean anything to you? Ralph or David or Cynthia?"

His lips pursed, much as his mother's had done. "No, I don't think so. Why?"

"David is about your age, maybe a year younger. Ralph was in his late fifties."

His eyebrows arched. "Was?"

"You don't watch the news, either? Or read the papers?"

"No to both questions. When I'm not studying, I'm either going to or from class or sleeping." He smiled wryly. "Occasionally, I have a date. Who are the Kincades?"

"It's not important. What high school did you go to?" I recognized the futility of the question even as I asked it. Midway City had four high schools, one of which, Armbruster High, was located on the north side, the elite section of town. The chances that Paul LeClair and the Kincade kids had attended the same school were practically nil.

"Armbruster."

I nodded and made a mental note to check David Kincade's alma mater.

We talked for a while longer. I asked some of the questions I had asked his mother and received the same answers. Timothy LeClair had kept his business affairs away from his small family. Perhaps because they had evinced no interest, perhaps for his own reasons. Finally, I ran out of questions and gave up. Paul LeClair's knowledge of the murders seemed even more limited than my own.

At the end, he initiated a handshake, nodding cordially, muttering a halfhearted apology for having been boorish in the beginning. When I asked if I could speak to the chauffeur, he hastily agreed, bobbed his head again, and left with alacrity.

I looked around the room, wishing I had a cigarette, wishing I were outside in the beautiful day, wishing Homer had his damn case back and a million dollars, and I were home with Susie, and we'd all live happily ever after.

20

Peter Johnson was tall and spare. Steel-gray hair cropped close
to his skull. Small eyes the color of smoke. His face was long
and narrow, deeply eroded by gravity and time, a wide thin
mouth that seemed fixed in a rigor of cynicism and bitterness,
a face not meant for smiling. No wonder the LeClair kids had
been afraid of him.

He presented himself to me without a word, short-billed cap
in hand, lean body erect, the pale eyes calm and incurious, yet
somehow radiating defiance—and something else that might
or might not have been contempt.

"Peter Johnson? My name is Dan Roman—"

"Yes, I'm Mr. Peter Johnson." His voice was as harsh as his
countenance, his meaning clear: years of being called Peter had
taken their toll and he wasn't about to take any intimidating
shit from a lowly civil servant.

"Mr. Johnson," I said, acknowledging his rebuke with a small
smile. "I understand you've worked for the LeClairs for
twenty-five years or so, and—"

"No. I've worked for Mr. Timothy LeClair for twenty-five
years."

"I see. Well, the question is still the same. Having worked
for him all those years, it seems to me you're in a unique position. You must have known him pretty well, maybe even
picked up a bit of knowledge about his business affairs from
time to time, about his friends, his enemies, his social life over
the years, bits of gossip even, little tidbits concerning his . . .
shall we say, extracurricular activities, if any?"

His lips arched briefly, but they weren't making a smile. "No," he said flatly. "It was none of my business what Mr. LeClair did or didn't do. I was hired to drive his automobiles. That is what I did." There was no longer any doubt about the contempt; I began to understand what Homer had meant.

"Didn't you find that difficult?"

His eyes glimmered. A moment of silence, then, "I don't understand what you mean?"

"Being deaf, dumb, and blind. How did you manage all those years?"

The thin shoulders moved, an almost imperceptible shrug. "It isn't the staff's place to hear or see or tell. We perform our functions as discreetly as possible so as not to intrude into the daily life of the family. We are paid for our ability to function as unobtrusively as is humanly possible."

"Part of the furniture, huh? Come on, Mr. Johnson, that's bullshit and you know it. Aren't you interested in seeing your boss's murderer caught?"

He nodded quickly. "Very much." A flicker of something like pain crossed his face.

"Then talk to me, dammit! If people won't talk, we can't learn. If we don't learn, we don't catch. It's as simple as that."

The long arms spread in a helpless gesture. "I don't know anything. I—we were at church when it . . . it happened. How could I know anything? I didn't even see the . . . the bodies. Mrs. LeClair and the boy, they found them."

"I understand that. I'm talking about other things. Murders sometimes erupt out of small things: arguments, everyday friction, differences of opinion, jealousy, small things that can explode into violence in the heat of passion." I had injected passion into my own voice. I had seen a chink in his crusty facade with the glimmer of emotion in his failed face, and I went to a full court press. "Help us, Mr. Johnson. Cops are only human. We have no secret prescriptions for solving crimes, no special insight into other human beings. You know the LeClairs, probably better than they know themselves, certainly better than anyone else knows them. I'm not asking for family secrets. You be the judge, but tell me something." I finished quietly. Playing to his vanity might do the trick, but it might not, either. Then there was always the possibility that he knew nothing to tell.

He looked around the room, the wide mouth growing tighter, thinner; a conflict of emotions, or control reasserting itself? I couldn't tell which, and began to wonder if it mattered.

He spread his feet apart, both long-fingered hands now gripping the cap. He wet his lips and brought his smoky gaze back to me. "There is—" He stopped, started again. "There was friction between Mr. LeClair and . . . and the boy."

"Paul?"

He nodded stiffly. "Yes. Always was, from the time he was twelve or thirteen. Even before the boy's father died. Mr. Tim had very definite ideas about how to raise a boy, and Mr. Marvin always let him have his way. Mr. Tim was a hard man to defy." He stopped and appeared to sigh. "After Mr. Marvin died, Mr. Tim took over completely. He was bound and determined that Mr. Paul would be molded in his own image, would someday take over his business, build on his fortune. Mr. Paul had other ideas. He wanted to go to that school in New York, some music school. He wanted to be a piano player. He hated the thought of business." He stopped, a tight ironic smile briefly touching his lips. "He never had anything against spending the money that business made, though."

"They fight about it?"

He nodded, looking around again, still ill at ease in his role as betrayer of family secrets. "Sometimes. Mr. Tim always won. Mr. Paul was no match for him, but he still had to try sometimes. They fought about other things. Cars and girls. Companions. And what was expected of a LeClair, the need to excel at college, the need to be a leader in society—that kind of thing." He placed the cap on his head and checked the buttons on the dark blue worsted suit that had the look of expert tailoring. "I don't see how this will help you. Mr. Paul certainly didn't do it. He was right there at that organ in church all through the service." He shook his head and went on, as if talking to himself. "And even if he hadn't been, he'd never have harmed his sister. Mr. Paul never showed much affection for anyone, but he loved her, that was plain to see."

"I hear that she was a sweet, lovely girl."

The ironic smile touched his lips again. "Yes. Now that she had about grown up. Years ago she was a little holy terror. They both were." There was a softness in his harsh voice that had not been there before. For the first time I wondered about his family, if he had one other than the LeClairs.

"Kids," I said. "They're pretty much all alike."

He moved restlessly, shifting back to his at-attention stance. "Will that be all, Mr. Roman?"

I studied his face while I thought about it. There were other questions I could ask, but he had been more cooperative than I had expected, and maybe it would be wiser not to push my luck, come back to him at another time.

"For right now," I said, and pushed to my feet. I stuck out my hand and took a step forward.

He looked startled, but took my hand in his, pumped it once, and quickly released it. He seemed pleased, and for a moment I thought he might smile a real smile. But he only nodded and turned toward the door.

"One last question, Mr. Johnson. Does the name Ralph Kincade mean anything to you?"

He stopped, turned, and answered without hesitation. "Yes. I heard it at least a half-dozen times over the weekend. If you're talking about the Ralph Kincade who was shot last Friday night?"

"That's the one. Did you happen to know him?"

"No. I heard the name on the television newscasts. TNS ran it four or five times. I have a lot of free time. I watch a lot of television. Besides, I have a sister who lives in that part of town, just a couple of blocks from there. She called to tell me all about it. She met his wife a few years ago at a PTA meeting or something like that." He ended on a wry note, a bit of unexpected humor. "My sister's head of the neighborhood news network."

"On your way out," I said, "would you mind sending in the housekeeper—Mrs. Mullins, I believe?"

He turned at the door. "Mrs. Mullins didn't come in this morning. She called and said she had the flu."

"Okay, how about one of the maids?" I scratched through my memory, but couldn't come up with either name.

"Very well." He ducked his head and disappeared.

I used up another thirty minutes talking to the maids, Juanita Gomez and Hilda Lawrence. Both were married, both had been in church with their respective families at eleven o'clock on Sunday. They worked from nine until six, six days a week, and neither woman admitted knowledge of the LeClair family life beyond that acquired from an occasional meeting with family members throughout the day. They liked their jobs and their employers, felt they were well paid and well treated, and exhibited genuine surprise when asked about friction between Timothy and his grandson. They each expressed great sorrow over the loss of two beloved family members, and had no knowledge of anyone named Kincade.

My interrogation of the cook, a middle-aged woman named Matilda Kelly, proved even less fruitful, if possible, and took only ten minutes. She was hard of hearing and refused to wear a hearing aid because if God had wanted people to wear mechanical contraptions, he would have given us all one at birth. She lived in a small apartment adjacent to the kitchen, far removed from the family living quarters, and worked only those hours necessary to provide the family with good, solid food. Sunday was her one day off, and she invariably spent it with her son and his family in Dallas. She knew nothing about the comings and goings of the LeClair family and cared even less. She spent her time off reading the Bible and writing messages to God, which she left prominently displayed at the home of her son each Sunday. Besides being almost deaf, she had arthritis, a blister on her colon, varicose veins, and chronic sinus problems. There was nothing wrong with her mouth, however.

I watched her waddle out the door and decided I'd had enough of questions for a while. I desperately needed a cigarette, and my throat felt tight and dry as sawdust. I got up and followed the voluble little woman into the hallway, turned to my left, and let myself out.

The day was living up to its promise, a tad cooler than the day before, but still bright and warm for one of the last days of October. Wispy clouds drifted across the sky like strings of cotton candy, and orange and brown leaves wandered aimlessly downward from the LeClair's majestic oaks. Off to my right, a bulky man in a light-colored jumpsuit guided a riding mower in and out of the trees, an attached bag slowly filling with shredded leaves and yellow-green grass.

The gardener, I thought. Another interrogation. More questions with unlikely answers. But not for now. I needed sustenance for an empty stomach, balm for my scratchy throat.

I drove into downtown Midway City. I found a parking space within easy walking distance of Willy's Barbecue Joint, a fairly decent eating establishment catty-cornered from my bank. I also needed to cash a check. My unexpected reimbursement to Maggie Lane had left me short.

Since Willy's was on my side of the street, I ate first—a barbecue sandwich with cole slaw, an order of shoestring potatoes and a beer.

Feeling slightly better, I crossed to the bank, cashed a three-hundred-dollar check, discussed the beautiful weather with the teller, then strolled back outside and almost ran head-on into Maggie Lane.

21

"Danny! Hello." She was wearing jeans, black with white stitching, form-fitting and undoubtedly expensive. Flat-heeled black shoes, a long-sleeved green blouse, and a matching sweater vest completed her catchy ensemble, highlighting the green eyes and auburn hair, emphasizing the healthy glow of unblemished skin. She appeared flushed, almost breathless, eyes clear and sparkling with humor. It was a knack rather than a condition, a mechanism she could initiate at will to make you feel important, exciting, loved. I wasn't fooled, but I was stirred.

"Hi. I was just cashing a check," I said, wondering at my need to explain my presence on a downtown street in my own hometown.

"Well, imagine running into you like this. Twice in just a few days . . . and after all those years." She liked to stand close and look up into your face, lips parted in anticipation of the next wondrous thing you might say. I hadn't forgotten that about her, either, but I didn't move away. I dredged my mind for something wondrous to say, but my wits were scattered too widely.

"Karma, I suppose," I said, then followed with something even more inane. "I see you're not working this afternoon." I could have bitten off my tongue, but she only chuckled and took my arm.

"Yes, I'm not working. I was going to do some shopping, but I can do that any time. I think I could use a drink. Would you like a drink, Danny? My treat."

I looked at my watch and frowned, a token show of resistance that fooled her about as much as it fooled me. "Well, yeah, sure, I think I could use a drink."

"Good." She squeezed my arm and turned us in the other direction. "Is Charley's all right with you? Remember when we used to go there?"

"Charley's is fine," I said, trying to recall what it was I wanted to ask her.

"It's just down the street," she said unnecessarily, guiding me along the sidewalk, then suddenly changing arms, tripping around to the inside, gripping my arm again. She smiled up at me. "The lady always walks on the inside," she said. "You told me that. Nobody pays any attention anymore." Her feet tapped quickly, matching my longer stride.

"Maybe nobody ever did," I said. "It was just something my grandfather told me once." We passed a bakery, the pleasing smell of baking bread mixing with the aroma of her rose-scented perfume. That, at least, hadn't changed.

"Your grandfather was a smart man."

I looked down at her. "How do you know that?"

"You told me," she said, and shook my arm. "Don't you remember?"

"I guess he was. He told me a lot of things. Over the years, I've found out most of them were right. He knew a lot about people, and what he didn't know he guessed at." A quartet of teenagers parted to go around us. I caught their appreciative glances at Maggie, heard a low wolf whistle behind us. I glanced down at her; she was smiling. Our feet grated loudly on the gritty sidewalk; a stray current of wind sent her hair swirling forward across her face. I resisted an impulse to brush it back.

"Like what?" she asked after a small silence, and I was momentarily confused.

"Oh, you mean my grandfather? Well, it was elementary stuff. He believed there was good in the worst of us, evil in the best. He said that we could control our lives only up to a point, that fate had the last word, made the hard decisions, that nature had built within us all the mechanism for self-destruction in one way or another, that circumstances and luck were triggering devices that determined when and if we would destroy ourselves."

"I'll buy that," she said, almost murmuring. "I told you he was a smart man."

"Maybe not so smart. He had a bad heart and he died in the bed of a neighboring widow lady at age sixty-six. He oughta had better sense."

She stopped, threw back her head and laughed, clear, bell-like tones that rang along the thoroughfare. Heads lifted and faces smiled. Some free soul behind us laughed along. I held myself to a manly chuckle and pulled her the few remaining feet to Charley's door.

It was dark inside after the brilliant sunlight. I stopped just beyond the door, waiting for night vision, trying to ignore the fact that Maggie was still giggling, clinging to my arm.

Off to our right, the bar stretched endlessly into gloom, lighted only by beer signs and whiskey ads, dark shapes posted along its gleaming length like lonely sentinels on the road to perdition. To our left I could hear voices, the muted clink of glasses, an occasional laugh. Straight ahead, a slender form in a mini skirt and a V-necked, sleeveless blouse materialized out of nowhere, a welcoming smile on her face.

"Two of you." It was a statement more than a question, and when I nodded, she led us along the bar and through a wide arched doorway into an almost vacant room with booths along three walls. Two other couples occupied booths at opposite ends of the room; our hostess ushered us to one near the center of the third wall.

"More privacy in here," she said cryptically, taking a courtesy wipe at the table. "Would you like something to eat?"

I looked at Maggie. She shook her head. "Dewar's on the rocks and a vodka martini." I looked at Maggie again; she nodded and smiled. The waitress went away.

"It's been a long time," Maggie said. "The name's the same, but they've changed the decor, and I didn't see Charley behind the bar."

"You won't," I said. "He had a stroke. Last time I heard, he was in a nursing home somewhere, taking his food through a tube." I suddenly remembered what it was I wanted to ask her.

"Oh, that's a shame. He was a nice man."

"You know what they say, nice guys go out first."

"Or something like that," she said, and laughed, taking her arms off the table as the waitress arrived with our order.

I sipped my drink, watching the waitress move down the row of booths to the couple at the end.

I brought my gaze back to Maggie; she was watching me over

the rim of her glass, eyes squinted and twinkling, the way she had always looked just before she said something funny or outrageously personal.

I decided I didn't want to hear it, decided that I was enjoying myself far too much. She was a hooker and I was married to the woman I loved. That said it all. There was no room in my life for clandestine adventures, however appealing the thought might be. No need for it. My uneasy feeling crystallized into fear, fear of myself. I felt a sudden need to distance myself from temptation.

"Why didn't you tell me Cynthia Kincade was a hooker like you?"

Her face fell; the sparkle died in her eyes. She put the drink down without tasting it, her lips curving in an unhappy, lopsided smile. "I don't know, Danny. I didn't think it was important. Is it? Does it really matter?"

"And that Gregory Knutson was her pimp?"

Her face closed down, the green eyes darker, veiled. "Boyfriend, pimp; they're pretty much interchangeable words in my business, Danny."

"And yours, too?" I asked, my voice unaccountably thick. "Boyfriend or pimp, Maggie? What ever happened to independent Maggie Lane? Free spirit. Her own woman. Determined not to be beholden to any man. Pimps control whores, Maggie. Don't tell me I'm wrong. I used to be a cop, remember?"

She stared at me, eyes burning, mouth crimped into a cupid's bow of resentment. "Don't judge me, Danny. Independence is only a girlish dream. It may work sometimes in the straight world, but not in mine. There are too many parasites, too many freaks. No matter how careful we are, they slip through. Johns who take what we offer and walk out laughing, without paying. Johns who only want to hurt, to inflict pain. Men like Knutson are necessary evils. We have to have somebody."

"Everybody needs somebody," I said, unable to keep contempt out of my voice, a part of me watching, appalled, as I deliberately smashed what little was left of our feeling of camaraderie, the residual affection that time had not been able to erase. I understood that it was only my own insecurity at work, but she didn't know that, and she shoved abruptly to her feet, gathered her purse under one arm and stalked out, head high, flat-heeled shoes tapping a resolute rhythm on the wooden floor.

"You didn't touch your drink," I said, but, of course, she didn't hear me. I finished mine, lit a cigarette, and dropped a ten-dollar bill on the table. I got up and followed her trail outside, into sunny brightness that burned my eyes but did little for the cold empty place in my chest.

22

I found Ted Baskin and Homer Sellers holding a council of war in Homer's office. Mitsi was gone from her desk, on a coffee break or an errand for Homer. I went in without knocking, and Homer looked up with a scowl that quickly dissolved into a grin.

"Well, well, speak of the devil." He pushed back from the desk and ran both hands through mud-colored hair, doing little to correct its usual disarray. He was wearing his contacts, and his blue eyes were bleary and rimmed with red.

Baskin swiveled in his chair. "Hi, Dan. We were just wondering about you. How'd it go with the LeClairs?"

"Smooth as silk. Easy as picking out an Aggie by the piss stains on his sneakers."

"Hey, now," Homer protested halfheartedly, smothering a smile, slamming a hand on the desk.

Baskin laughed.

I pulled the other chair around beside Baskin and sat down. I grinned across the desk at Homer and took out my cigarettes. "Before you start getting hostile, Homer, you'd better remember I've still got a full day left, and since you're not paying me a damn dime, you'd better make up for it in nice."

"You're a real prince," Homer said, lacing his hands on the clutter on his desk. "What'd you do, zilch out with the Le-Clairs?"

"Pretty much," I admitted. "The LeClairs are out of it unless one of them hired a hit man, and the staff are all original stone monkeys: see no evil, hear no evil, speak—well, you know how it goes. The housekeeper, a Mrs. Mullins, and the gardener still need to be interrogated." I blew a ball of smoke at Homer. "The housekeeper is out with the flu, and I thought you might want to take her since you just got over it and are probably immune."

"Immune, my ass," Homer growled. "There's fifty different kinds of flu bugs."

"I found out about the will," Baskin put in. "Sharpe, Billings, Dockwell and Sharpe. They were surprisingly cooperative. At least Ronnie Sharpe was. He's the grandson of old man Askew Sharpe, and the newest member of the firm. No big surprises that I could see. The daughter-in-law, Mrs. LeClair, gets fifty thousand dollars a year and use of the family home for as long as she lives. All maintenance expenses paid, of course. The fifty thou is spending money, I guess. He left his oldest son, Robert, the grand sum of one million dollars and divided the rest of the estate equally between Julie and Paul."

"Which means Paul will get it all," Homer said sourly.

Baskin nodded. "There's a proviso to that effect. Surviving grandchild, and all that."

"Unless Robert suddenly appears and ties it all up in court," I said. "Any progress in locating him?"

Baskin shook his head. "Nothing in the computer chain. I've got a query in to the FBI and the IRS. But you know how them bastards are at the IRS."

"You don't pay well enough," I said. "Give me his full name and social security number and let me try my luck."

Homer glowered. "You mean you'd bribe a public official?"

"Quick as a wink, Homer. How do you think I find people in this great bastion of democracy of ours? A night letter to Ann

Landers? I don't have computer banks, or electronic surveillance equipment, or police departments I can query across this great nation. I've got a little money and a devious mind and a certain knowledge of human nature. Mostly, that's all it takes."

"It still ain't right," Homer grumbled. "Man's got a right to some privacy. That's privileged information."

I gave him a mocking grin. "Tell that to the next company that sends you an unsolicited credit card only because they already know how much money you make. Come on, buddy, grow up."

Baskin stirred uneasily and cleared his throat. "We got the makes. Everybody connected with the LeClairs. Not a clinker in the pile. The staff is clean, and so are the LeClairs themselves, except for Paul. He's in the computer, coded JRS. That's juvenile record, sealed. Have to get a court order to bust in."

"Maybe we oughta," Homer said thoughtfully, obviously unaware that our bickering had made Baskin uncomfortable. "I'll tend to that. I know a judge that'll sign most anything I give him if I take along a fifth of Black Label."

"You mean you'd bribe a public official? That just ain't right, Homer."

Baskin laughed, and Homer turned red.

"Ain't no bribe, boy. Me and this feller are friends. We're always exchanging little gifts like that."

"We've been friends a long time, Homer. I don't remember your bringing me a bottle of Black Label, or a bottle of Ripple, for that matter."

"Yeah, well, you can afford to buy your own." He dabbed at his leaking eyes with a ball of tissue, shuffled the papers on his desk. "Okay. So what have we got here? We've got two robberies that misfired, or do we have some crazy bastard running around shooting people for fun? What do you guys think?"

I looked at Ted Baskin; he looked at me. We both turned back to Homer.

"The way I see it," I said, "we don't have a shred of evidence either way. Taken separately, I'd say no robbery in the Kincade case, and maybe in the LeClair case. But I'd be guessing either way. Some junkies will hit an outdoor toilet looking for something to steal when they're hurting bad enough, so it's possible both of them started out as robberies. I just don't know, Homer." I looked at Baskin.

He nodded slowly, a distressed expression on his plain face. "I hate to say it, boss, but that's about the way I'd call it, too."

Homer snorted and ran a hand down across his face. "What you're saying is you really think they're random murders, that we might be playing host to one of them serial killers, somebody like that guy Lucas or his buddy Toole."

"Could be the homegrown variety," I said. "Everybody has to start somewhere."

"Some nut," Baskin said. "Somebody who just lately flipped out."

"He doesn't operate like a nut," Homer said. "Nuts make mistakes. Far as I can see, he ain't made a damn one."

"He made three," I said. "He killed three people."

Homer ignored me and turned to Baskin. "We need to check with Dallas and Fort Worth—hell, make that every city in the area. See if maybe he's been working anywhere else close by."

"Can do," Baskin said. He took a pad and pen out of his pocket and scribbled a note. "How about outlying cities, the big ones? Houston, Austin, like that?"

"Maybe later. Work the close ones first. We can go statewide later if we have to. Also, there's that computer information center, VI-Cap, at the FBI Academy at Quantico and the Justice Department computer bank in Dallas. Run it by both of them. If we have got a serial killer, chances are he's done it before somewhere."

"One thing that argues against a serial killer," I said. "Most of them are sexually motivated."

"Yeah, well, maybe he gets off pumping bullets into somebody's head." Homer dug around in his coat pocket and came up with a rumpled handkerchief. "Don't forget he took the panties off that LeClair girl."

"Panty hose, according to her brother."

"Same difference." He blew his nose lustily, took a deep breath and blew it again.

Baskin stood up. "I'll get moving on this. Any more suggestions?"

"Yeah," Homer said placidly. "Get a haircut."

Baskin laughed and went out with the quick, bouncy strut of a short man who has always wanted to be tall. He said something to Mitsi, and her raucous laughter invaded the room.

Homer winced. "Twenty years, and I'm still not used to that laugh."

I lit another cigarette and looked past his shoulder out the window. Gloomy and gray, the time between twilight and dark; the hour of the wolf was fast approaching. I felt a shiver in my stomach that had nothing to do with Tennessee superstition. I thought of Maggie Lane and understood the feeling: guilt. I had acted like a jackass at Charley's, and the reaction was locking in. I felt restive suddenly, filled with a flood of inexplicable emotions. I stood up.

Homer squinted up at me. "You running out on me, too?"

"Be getting dark soon. I want to get home before *they* start coming out."

He looked puzzled, frowning. "They who?"

I moved toward the door. "You know, vampires, werewolves, zombies—they're all out there, just waiting for darkness." I used my one and only imitation: Peter Lorre.

"Shit," he said, wagging his head, going back to his work.

Mitsi was gone again, and it was just as well. I was stoned on conversation, in no mood for more frivolous chitchat.

23

I sat across the street from Maggie Lane's duplex for twenty minutes, wondering if she was at home, and if she was, if she might be working. Yellow light beamed faintly through the living room windows, but what I could see of the rest of the house was dark. I had about decided to forget the whole thing when a light came on in a small window that could only be a bathroom. A few minutes later, it went out.

I waited another ten minutes, smoking, arguing with myself. A part of me—the same part that loved dogs, horses, and little old ladies—wanted me to apologize for my churlish conduct at Charley's. And that seemed logical, the gentlemanly thing to do.

But there was another part of me that sneered. A low, coarse part I had heard from before, an insinuating voice that said I was here for something other than forgiveness. And that, of course, was an egregious lie.

I snorted away doubt, climbed out of the Ramcharger, crossed the street, and walked up the driveway feeling noble and righteous, an honest man on his way to right a wrong.

I drew up at the now familiar door. I worked the knocker, then stepped back uneasily, not knowing what to expect. At worst, she would probably tell me to get lost, and even at best, I didn't expect to find love on her face, or loving on her mind.

I found nothing, got nothing. Not even a sound. I dropped the knocker again, waited while I counted to ten. She was in there. Bathroom lights didn't go on and off all by themselves.

I waited and listened. Still nothing. A car passed in the street. A dog barked somewhere down the line of elegant houses. Darkness gathered quietly.

I abandoned the clapper, rapped on the glossy wood that looked like steel. While I waited, I searched the door for a peephole.

Maybe she knew it was me; maybe my fractious behavior had wounded her more deeply than I had known; maybe she was sleeping—Christ—maybe she had a man in there after all.

I was turning away when I heard the snick of the lock. Another, and the door swung open a crack: two inches, no more. I stepped closer, peered in at one eye and a slice of cheek, the pink corner of a mouth that didn't appear to be smiling.

"Hi," I said. "It's me."

"Go away, Danny."

"Look, all I want—"

"Please, Danny, go away!" Her voice sounded strange, thick, slurred. Drunk? Half asleep?

"All right, but I just want—"

"I can't let you in!"

"I don't need to come in, Maggie. Dammit, I just wanted to tell you I'm sorry I acted the way I did at Charley's."

I saw a faint nod. "Okay, thank you."

"Right," I said crisply, and it would have ended there if the telephone hadn't rung.

She turned involuntarily to look, the door swung open another inch, and the light caught the hidden part of her face.

My stomach rolled, surged. I felt bile rush into my throat. I cursed and shoved the door open against her protesting weight, pressed steadily until I was inside the foyer, staring at her, at the discolored, misshapen part of her face she had tried her best not to let me see.

Her left eye was blackened, swollen almost shut, lacerations streaking down across the flawless cheek, lips broken at the corner, crusty with dried blood, a blue-black lump the size of a robin's egg nestled just below her hairline, another at the juncture of her jaw. Even her neck had not escaped; blue-green bruises marred its slender length, disappeared beneath the collar of the flimsy robe. I cursed again.

Her shoulders slumped; her face turned downward and away. The phone kept on ringing.

"Who did this to you?" I had to struggle to keep my voice below a shout.

She shook her head, one hand coming up to hide her shame. "It doesn't matter, Danny. Please go." It was a slurred whisper I had to strain to hear.

I took her shoulders in my hands, turned her to face me. "Who, Maggie? Who is he, goddammit!"

"I won't tell you!" She spoke thickly, through the right side of barely parted lips. "You may as well—please go."

I caught her chin gently, lifted her face. One eye watched me, shrinking, a smoky look I couldn't fathom, a punishing brightness that made me suddenly ashamed to be a man. I felt like cursing again, felt like crying; I wanted to tear something apart with my bare hands.

"It was Knutson," I said softly. "Nobody else would dare. He's too damn big; they'd be afraid of him." I watched the flicker in her good eye and knew.

She shook her head. "No! Danny—please, it doesn't matter. I'll be fine. I'll just need—" She stopped, the eye widening, fixed on my face.

And abruptly, I realized that I was smiling, my cheeks creaking from the strain, a dry, keening noise in my head that drowned out the pealing telephone. It was a sound I had heard only a few times before.

My head began a slow, steady pounding; I felt chilled all over.

"I'll be fine," she repeated, managing a wry tone despite the whisper. "I'm tough."

"I know you are." I touched the good side of her face and backed away toward the door. "I'll see you, Maggie."

She took a faltering step forward. "Danny. Don't interfere—please."

I started to smile again and found I couldn't. I nodded instead and backed out the door.

*　　*　　*

I gave him no warning, no chance to get set. He had four inches and fifty pounds on me, arms at least three inches longer. I couldn't hope to match him muscle for muscle, so it would have to be down and dirty from the very beginning, with surprise my only ally.

I hit the door with my shoulder the moment it began to open, hoping he would be looking around the edge the way he had before.

He was.

I heard the satisfying crack of wood on bone, felt the door hesitate momentarily before breaking away from my onslaught, slamming back against the wall. I caught it on the rebound, let it swing shut behind me.

Knutson tottered a few feet away, one hand clapped against his forehead, the other reaching for the back of a chair to steady his wobbly legs. He grunted with pain, or maybe anger, rivulets of blood dribbling from beneath his palm. He looked stunned, eyes out of focus, coordination momentarily out of sync. I figured we were about even.

I moved closer. "Maggie Lane. What you did to her wasn't nice, Gregory."

"That bitch," he mumbled, shaking his head to clear it.

"Yeah, that bitch." I snapped a left into his face, feeling his nose melt under my knuckles. I followed with a right, full into his twisting lips, into the cascade of blood spilling from his ruined nose.

His head snapped backward; he howled with pain.

I hit him high on the left cheekbone, another left, crossed with a right to his neck just below the hinge of his jaw, followed with a jab to his other cheek.

He staggered, but stayed on his feet. I began to worry. I was marking him, but I wasn't hurting him much.

He whirled drunkenly away from me and crashed into an end table beside the couch, lamp, ashtray, and an empty beer bottle spilling to the floor. His mouth was already puffing, nose skewed to one side, blood seeping from a cut on his cheekbone. He looked like a walking wreck, but he was backed against a wall, digging blood out of his eye sockets, shaking his head as if to clear it, mumbling curses.

His eyes blinked rapidly, focused on me, blinked again, and he came bellowing away from the wall, spitting blood, long arms outstretched, a crazed grin on his bloody, broken lips, blood-smeared teeth giving him a ghoulish look.

I watched him come and realized I had broken the most basic rule of hand-to-hand combat: I had given him time to recover, allowed him to take the offensive, and I had a sinking feeling that I was going to pay dearly for my lack of initiative.

I went to meet him. I had no choice. The room was too small, too crowded, the only space to maneuver the long, narrow area just inside the door, and his long arms more than covered that.

I couldn't go back, around, or over, so I took the only way open: I went under—crouching, diving, throwing myself beneath the massive arms, slamming a fist into his heart area as his momentum carried him past.

My own momentum carried me to my knees. I kept going, tucking my shoulder into the threadbare carpet and thrusting with my legs, coming to my feet in a slow-motion roll that seemed to take forever.

Too long.

I heard him grunting with effort behind me, felt his hands slip under my armpits and snake up behind my head in the opening moves of a full nelson. He was incredibly strong, even for a big man, forcing my arms upward, fingers digging into the back of my neck as his hands crawled toward each other and the lock that would leave me as helpless as a babe in arms. His breath jetted against my ear, harsh and ragged and filled with spittle.

I let my body go limp. He grunted with surprise, the sudden weight sliding his fingers farther apart.

I stomped on his right toe, bowed my neck, and jammed my arms downward with all my strength. His fingers slipped again, sliding down across the sides of my throat, giving up the hammerlock, settling for a bear hug.

It was only a small improvement. His arms tightened around my chest. I could feel my ribs creaking, folding, air rushing out of my lungs in a sour-tasting torrent.

I tried to break his hold, gripping the thick wrists and pulling, twisting, wrenching, but pain was sapping my strength, the loss of air bringing spots that danced before my eyes like black snowflakes, strings of bright lights exploding like holiday fireworks.

He grunted again and increased the pressure. I realized that I was slowly being crushed; I was starving for air, weakening.

I scratched the back of his hands, dug desperately for a handhold on something, anything, my sense of time and place receding, my mind flirting with oblivion.

So this was how it felt to die, I mused. Peace, contentment, drifting into darkness, into nothingness ... the thought brought a small burst of adrenaline.

Do something, goddammit! Even if it's wrong!

I stomped again, blindly, looking for his toes, finding nothing under my boot heel but solid flooring.

I heard him chuckle, a harsh, sobbing, triumphant sound against my ear.

I raked the back of his hands again—and found a thumb.

Protruding slightly from the rest of the pack, thick and hairy and slick with blood, it was something to attack, and I dug at it with both hands, scratching and clawing it away from his clenched fingers, filling my palm with its slippery length, jamming it backward with my last remaining strength, the dancing dots in my eyes congealing into a solid wall of darkness.

I felt it give and heard his pain-filled oath. I renewed my attack with both hands and experienced more than heard the crack as the thumb broke free of its mooring, moved easily backward to lie against his wrist, mushy and strange, rapidly filling with fluid.

For one blinding second I thought he might ignore it, against all known principles of animal pain, thought the crushing steel bands around my chest would go on and on—

His arms flew open.

He screamed.

I fell forward against the wall, sucking air, coughing and sucking air, hot dry air that seared like tiny fingers of flame. Light came back to my eyes, reason and caution to my brain. I whirled.

Knutson staggered, five feet away, bent double, cradling his left hand in his right, moaning, blood still oozing from his ruined nose, one eye already swollen shut, the broken lips small, red-crusted sausages.

I worked on my breathing, watching his big, hulking frame begin to shiver, listening with very little compassion to the threatening sounds coming from his throat.

Without warning, he dropped to his knees, his body racked by violent tremors, retching, gagging, finally spewing out a noxious mixture I didn't try to see.

"Take a deep breath," I advised.

I leaned back against the wall and closed my eyes, wishing for a cigarette. But I had left them in my jacket in the truck, along with anything else that might slow me down or provide a handhold for big Gregory Knutson.

I listened to his nauseating sounds and took inventory, mildly surprised that I had come out of it so well—bruised ribs and a few scratches on my neck, a knuckle or two that might be sore for a while.

Better than I deserved, I thought ruefully, for a stupid trick comparable to invading the den of a hibernating bear. Someday my runaway temper would get me into something I couldn't luck out of. And for what? The relationship between pimps and whores had existed since the dawn of time, since the first caveman offered his woman for a chunk of dinosaur meat. And there was damn little I could do to change it, even if I tried.

I pushed away from the wall and stripped the top sheet off the single bed in the corner. I tossed it at Knutson.

"Wipe your mouth; you're making me sick." I walked around behind him so I wouldn't have to see his ragged face or the mess he had made on the floor.

"You understand, asshole, what this was all about?"

He rocked, cradling his hand against his stomach, dabbing tenderly at his mouth with a corner of the sheet. His left hand was big and bulbous; he made no sound.

"Talk to me, pimp. Maggie Lane. She's off your roster, scarface. You ever go near her again, I'll come back here and hurt you." I realized how silly that sounded. "I mean, *really* hurt you. You understand me?"

His head moved minutely in what could have been a nod.

I kicked the sole of his shoe with my toe. "Talk, man. I want to hear you say it."

"Yes." His voice was hoarse and scratchy.

"Yes what?"

"Yes, I understand."

"The reason—the only reason I'm not having your ass pulled in for parole violation is the fact that Maggie would be dragged into it. She's got all she can handle right now. But that won't stop me, you son of a bitch, if you so much as speak to her on the street. You have any problem with that?"

"No . . . no problem. Why don't you just leave?" There was a thread of pleading in his voice, a note of humility I didn't believe for a moment.

I opened my mouth to say more, then closed it again. More threats would be fruitless. I had stated my case; he would either abide by my rules or he wouldn't. I had two options: I could wait and see, or I could do what I had promised, really hurt him, something that would keep him in traction for a while.

But I was tired and hungry and sore, and had no heart for more violence.

"Okay, you got it, Knutson. You lick your wounds and I'll go about my business. Just don't go making yourself my business again."

I got no answer, but I hadn't expected one. I crossed the few feet to the door and let myself out.

The night had turned chilly; I shivered all the way to my truck.

24

I drove home slowly, drained of emotion and most of my strength.

I threw a Hungry Man TV dinner into the oven and went into the bathroom to shower. The front of my shirt was streaked with blood, the collar dappled with spots and splotches where Knutson had huffed and puffed while he tried to put out my lights.

My neck burned, but the scratches were surprisingly light. Evidently Knutson kept his fingernails trimmed back or bitten down. Other than that, it was the same old tired face, and I marveled again that I had paid so little for such a foolish act.

I had no feeling of relief, no sense of a job well done. I had acted hastily and without plan, leaped willy-nilly into a game I had no business playing. In my monumental rage, I had acted out some long-smoldering adolescent fantasy, avenging the fair maiden, understanding even as I did so that it wouldn't matter one iota in the long-term cosmic balance of things.

"Someday," I told myself as I stepped into the hot, pelting water, "you're gonna let your temper overload your ass, and look out ass."

I came out of the shower humble and refreshed, but not repentant, went into the kitchen and ate hot beef and grainy mashed potatoes, a soggy pile of mushy green peas. Washed down with beer, it wasn't half bad.

I settled in the den with another beer, a cigarette, and a sigh. I flipped the channels to TNS and its continuing news programming, hoping I might catch a rerun of Susie's five-minute spot from the night before. Running nothing but news eighteen hours a day, TNS had to repeat a lot. I wondered how they'd manage when they went to twenty-four hours.

But it was a forlorn hope. I watched for an hour and saw nothing of Susie, only the usual potpourri of killings and assaults, robberies and rapes, and malfeasance in high places.

Sixteen people arrested in the second largest drug bust in Dallas. Mexican brown heroin, a rarity only a few years ago, was rapidly becoming the staple base for American heroin distributors. . . .

A clerk executed gangland style in a convenience store robbery that netted the grand sum of forty-seven dollars—Dallas police had no suspects. . . .

Another teenage girl raped on the north side of Midway City. Believed to be the work of a man dubbed the Creeper, so called because of his penchant for invading second-story apartments, his seeming ability to appear suddenly out of nowhere, leading one detective to remark that he must creep through the cracks in windows or under doors. . . .

Ex-State Senator Winston Pryor Bearcraft sentenced to seven years in the penitentiary following his conviction on charges of selling civil service jobs to women in exchange for sexual favors. . . .

Congress deadlocked on President Reagan's tax reform bill. . . .

Approximately two hundred and fifty soldiers killed in a chartered plane crash near Gander, Newfoundland. Ice buildup on wings suspected. . . .

It was enough, too much. I punched the remote control until I found a sitcom, something I could doze along with without taxing my brain, without the twinges of horror that came with news of death and devastation among my fellow *Homo sapiens.*

I was well into a laugh-track comedy about youth and its horrendous problems, about unrequited love and expanding libidos, when the trilling notes of "Moonglow" seeped through the raucous laughter, invaded my consciousness like the shriek of mating cats.

I thought about not answering it. Warm and cozy and half-asleep in my own home, I needed no intrusions, wanted no distractions from the innocuous nonsense that was lulling me into oblivion with the sweet seduction of a mother's soothing croon.

They came again, the same notes, but more insistent, more demanding. I cussed a little, stubbed out my latest cigarette, padded into the entry hall, and opened the door.

David Kincade stood there. Dressed much as he had been the time before: blond hair in meticulous disarray, framing the handsome, apologetic face.

"Sorry to bother you again, Mr. Roman, but I—"

"Come on in, David," I said, managing to keep the weariness out of my voice, the irritation out of my face. I turned and went back into the den, leaving him to close the door, to find his own damn way across the eight feet of barren terrazzo tile. I felt put-upon, childishly aggrieved. I wondered if he had come to tell me another damn lie.

"Sit down, David." I dropped into my seat and lit a cigarette, feeling a little embarrassed as good humor returned. "Something to drink? I've got some Cokes, orange juice—"

"No, thank you, sir." He stood watching the TV for a moment, then turned to me with a broad smile. "I like that one. They've really captured today's youth, the pressures we face, the temptations, drugs, sex, cars, fast living." He dropped to the edge of the couch.

"Yeah, well, we never had things like that back in my time." I turned off the sound.

He smiled and ducked his head. "That sounded a little nerdy. I guess every generation has the same problems."

"More or less. But one thing never changes. We all believe we're the first generation to discover sex and the true meaning of life."

He laughed. "I guess that's true."

We looked at the silent figures on the screen for a moment. I took a drag on my cigarette. He cleared his throat and coughed into his palm.

"I wanted—well, I thought I ought to come and tell you something, Mr. Roman. I've been worrying about it and—well, I told you something that wasn't quite true." He stopped and cleared his throat again.

"You mean about seeing your mother in the stands?"

He made a face, then gave me a lopsided grin. "Yes, that's it. I didn't really see my mother until the meet was over."

"I know that, David. I knew it at the time."

His blue eyes widened. "Why didn't you—?"

"Call you on it? Well, as it happens it didn't much matter, and I don't think a boy trying to help his mother is such a bad thing. I would have done the same thing, I think. I hope I would have, anyway."

David flashed his engaging grin. "Man, I've been worrying like crazy about that, and here you've known all along."

"You shouldn't lie, David. You're no good at it."

He slapped his knees and stood up. "I know it. Everybody tells me I'm like an instant replay. I make a bad call and an instant later my face makes a liar out of me." He laughed again and ran the zipper up on his jacket.

"Being a good liar takes a lot of practice. It's usually not worth the effort."

He nodded, his face abruptly serious. "I want you to know how much we all appreciate what you've done, helping to find Dad's . . . Dad's killer, and all."

I stubbed out my cigarette and stood up. "All I've done is prove who didn't do it. Maybe that will help, I don't know."

I followed him to the front door. He smiled and reached for the knob.

"I've been meaning to ask someone, but I keep forgetting. Where does your sister work?"

He swallowed before he answered, averting his face slightly, speaking with a deliberate casualness that told me he knew about her, if not all of it, enough to be ashamed. "Some little . . . company over in Dallas. I forget the name. They make parts for airplanes, I think." His face had turned faintly pink, the blue eyes veiled.

"There's a lot of those around," I said, and thumped him on the shoulder. "Thanks for coming by, David."

"You bet. Thank you, Mr. Roman, for not—well, you know." He stuck out his hand.

"Take care," I said and watched him cross the yard to his mother's old Buick parked at the curb. He had a jaunty stride, loose, yet controlled, the look of a determined young man on his way to something better than he had.

I wished him well.

Nostalgia and self-pity sometimes go hand in hand.

By the time I got back to my chair, thinking of David's shame for his sister had brought me full circle to my own eighteenth year—the year my mother died; the year my father finally became the drunkard he had spent most of his adult life trying not to be.

Once, near Christmas of that year, on a blowy and rancorous day, I came home to find him dead drunk for the very first time. Sprawled inelegantly along the length of the living room couch, wearing muddy boots and vomit-stained clothing, he breathed raggedly through his mouth, a whiskey flush staining his pallid skin like a fading tan.

I tried not to care, tried to laugh in the way we all sometimes laugh at careless drunks, tried not to despise him for what he had become. But at eighteen forgiveness does not come easy, and in the end, I turned around and walked away and left him there, sneering angrily at my tears, trying my best not to hate this one last person I had left on earth to love.

25

I was up and about early the next morning, eager to hasten the day. The night would bring Susie, and I found myself looking forward to it the way a glutton anticipates a gourmet meal.

I ate cornflakes with rare pleasure, vowing to lay in a decent store of victuals at the first opportunity. While I ate, I made a mental list of the supplies we would need for the cabin: bacon and eggs and the makings for pancakes, precooked ham, charcoal and lighter fluid and a slather of steaks for barbecuing, canned biscuits and Italian bread.

Roughing it in style: a fireplace for lollygagging in front of, tall timber, and a spring-fed brook just outside the cabin door. Farther down the hill, a three-acre, teardrop-shaped lake stocked with catfish and bream provided a fisherman's dream and offered all the delicious fillets we could hope to eat.

Five days alone with the woman I loved. It would be hard to take, I thought wryly, but with a little ingenuity, a little careful thought, I'd probably be able to manage very nicely.

As early as I was, Ted Baskin was in his office before me, hunkered over a stack of paperwork on his cluttered desk, humming tunelessly, whistling the high notes through his teeth, an irritating habit that had driven me wild when we partnered in a patrol car. He looked up and found me watching from the doorway and grinned guiltily.

"You still miss my music?"

"Like a wart on the end of my tongue." I went in and sat down, lit a cigarette. "You're in pretty early."

He nodded soberly, leaned back, and laced stubby fingers behind his head. "Made a pass through Communications on the way in. Believe it or not, we got an answer from Quantico on our four-point."

"Four-point?"

"Computer lingo they use. We break the M.O. down into facets of comparison called points."

"Anything?"

He made a wry face. "Nope. If our man's a serial nut, he must be just starting out. Either that or he's been doing it some other way." He rubbed a hand across his face and yawned. "Haven't heard from Dallas, though."

"That figures. They're too close by. Probably take three, four days."

"Not if I can help it. I'll be on their ass by noon if we haven't heard." He rose to his feet. "You want some coffee? This stuff we got here ain't worth a shit, but it's hot."

I shook my head and stood up. "You know, if we do have a serial killer here, our chances of catching him are somewhere between nonexistent and none."

He nodded glumly and sat down on a corner of the desk. "Yeah. Not till he makes a mistake of some kind, leaves some prints or other physical evidence. Something we can get our teeth into."

"You mean the next time?"

He sighed. "Yeah, I guess that's what I mean, all right."

"And if he doesn't make a mistake next time?"

His chin jutted, a hint of belligerence in his eyes. "Then we won't catch him the next time, either." He studied my face, his green eyes gleaming. "But, goddammit, Dan, we gotta try."

"Okay," I said, and smiled. "I just wanted to be sure we were on the same frequency here."

"Shit," he said. "I thought you were getting ready to dump it back in my lap."

I looked at my watch. "Not for another eight hours or so. In the meantime, I'll have to dig up something to do—"

"The Mullins woman," he said quickly, smiling faintly. "She went to work today. She goes in at six. I just talked to her at the LeClairs'. She said she'd be available all morning."

"Nice of her. What happened to Homer? He was supposed to take her."

"High-echelon meeting this morning. He don't know when he'll be able to get away. Then he's got to go see that judge friend of his on that juvenile record thing."

"After he stops by the liquor store," I said sourly.

Baskin chuckled. "You had him going a little on that bribery thing last night. Matter of fact, you guys had me going. I'd forgotten you were old friends. I never was around Homer much until the last few years, and then only on business. I'd always heard he's got a short fuse and a loud bang."

"Mostly he's fuse. He sizzles a lot but rarely goes off. We came from the same small country town and Homer never outgrew it. He tends to take people at face value, and there's no way you can convince him that a friend can look him in the eye and lie. He should never have been a cop. You can't always do the right thing and be a good cop. He'd make a good minister, not because he's particularly religious, but because he loves to preach." I turned in the doorway and looked at Baskin's smiling face. "As it happens, I'm his favorite congregation."

He laughed and picked up a letter opener lying on his desk, scraped at a rind of black beneath his thumbnail. "I'm sending Babbitt out to the Kincade funeral today. Thought we'd get some long shots of the mourners, particularly anyone who didn't look like they belonged, somebody hanging back, you know. I plan on doing the same thing with the LeClairs tomorrow, maybe do some comparing." He shrugged. "It's a long shot, but long shots have a way of paying off big sometimes."

"Good idea, Ted. It's been done before with some good results. Some killers like to see the results of their work. Keeps the thrill going, I guess."

He walked with me as far as the coffee machine. I declined his offer of coffee again and left him dropping coins into the slot, muttering imprecations at the squat, blinking machine.

Outside, the weather had shifted gears as it has been known to do in Texas: a low-hanging gray blanket of clouds and mist as fine as steam from a boiling pot. Wind-borne dead leaves scuttled along the gutter, and across the street in the little city park, two old men in colorful windbreakers talked animatedly, arms waving, arguing, no doubt, the abysmal state of world affairs.

I climbed into my truck and lit a cigarette and thought about the last three days and the impending trip with Susie to our cabin in South Texas. Anticipation of the latter did a lot to balance out the frustration of the former.

I had almost forgotten how tedious and unrewarding a murder investigation could be, the pressures of time, the inevitable feeling that each passing hour added to the probability that the killer would go unpunished. Statistics and time favored the perpetrator, while the detective's greatest allies were tips, perseverance, and a lot of luck.

But I was running out of time and so far there had been no tips. That left luck, something I had stopped counting on a long time ago. So, in all likelihood I would fail, I thought glumly, surprised at a sudden sharp pang of regret. I had started this unlikely investigation as a favor to Homer, as a way to get through a dull weekend. Expecting nothing, I had gained little, and somehow that made me feel guilty of some indefinable offense against the Kincades and the LeClairs. The feeling was unreasonable and I didn't like it. I owed them nothing beyond an honest effort and I had at least given them that.

But, sometimes, a defeatist attitude can prove to be a fatal handicap, and I drove across Midway City to the LeClair mansion with country music ringing in my ears, the gravelly, one-note voice of Johnny Cash driving all thoughts of my incipient failure right out of my head.

26

People were up and about at the LeClair home. A red Porsche 211 sat in the circular driveway, and as I negotiated the bumpy turn in from the street I could see two thin-butted figures with their upper torsos hidden under the upraised bonnet. A few yards closer and I recognized the lanky form of Peter Johnson, the black-haired graceful figure of Paul LeClair.

They stood watching while I coasted to a stop. I switched off the engine and lit a cigarette, remembering the smokeless environment inside the big house. I climbed out of the truck and lifted a hand in greeting.

"Good morning," Paul LeClair said pleasantly. He said something to Johnson and walked toward me, dusting off his hands. Johnson dropped the bonnet on the Porsche, checked to make sure it was latched, then turned and disappeared around a corner of the house.

"Good morning," I said, advancing to take the proffered hand. "Good-looking car."

He nodded indifferently, dropping my hand after one quick, hard pump. "Back again so soon?"

"Mrs. Mullins. I understand she came in this morning."

"Yes, she did. She's inside. Just ring the bell, she'll be the one who answers the door." He hesitated, a frown ditching the narrow forehead. "Any particular reason you have for talking to her?"

I shrugged. "No more than anyone else. Just routine, the same as yesterday."

He nodded. "I was hoping when I saw you . . . well, that you might have some news—something to tell us about the . . ." He let it trail away.

"No, nothing definite." It was my turn to hesitate. "I do have another question for you, since you're here handy. And I might tell you, you don't have to answer it if you don't want to."

The frown came back. "What? I don't understand. I told you everything I know about what happened."

"Not about that. Something that happened before you turned eighteen. Something that happened to you, or that you caused to happen. Do you understand what I mean?"

His face tightened, lips pulling down in a crippled grimace. The thin nostrils flared. "I thought that was over and forgotten. Christ, I was just a kid! They told me the records would be sealed when I became eighteen."

I chuckled easily. "Your lawyer told you that, huh?"

"Yes, goddammit!" The profanity seemed forced, as though alien to the well-shaped mouth. His face worked angrily. "I don't know what that has to do with anything. It was four years ago, for Pete's sake."

"Routine. We automatically run the records of anyone connected with a murder victim."

"I don't care. Those records were supposed to be sealed."

I shrugged again and fieldstripped the cigarette. "Civil servants. What can you do?"

"I didn't do it, anyhow. That little bitch was lying through her teeth. She was just afraid—" He broke off, choking on the words, the black eyes burning.

"Afraid of what?"

He sucked in a deep breath, his handsome face pale. "Getting pregnant. She was afraid she'd got pregnant, that's why. I didn't use anything and she wasn't on the pill and she was too damn dumb to know you don't get pregnant just like that the first time you do it." He stemmed the tumbling flow of words, fisted hands thumping each other in spasmodic twitches.

"So she yelled rape on you?"

"Yes," he said sullenly. "And it wasn't. We'd been to a school dance. Christ, she was all over me on the dance floor. Everybody noticed it. We parked on the way home and . . . and we did it and the next day she told her old man that I had forced her to. Crazy damn broad. Christ, she was a year ahead of me, a year older than me."

"How old were you?"

"Fifteen. I was a sophomore and she was a junior. We'd been dating for over two months and that was the only time I didn't stop when she said for me to. And that time she didn't want me to, either. I could tell. She kept saying stop and then kept coming on. Christ, I didn't know what to do, so . . . so I went ahead and did it." He gave me an earnest, imploring look. "You can understand that, can't you?"

"I'm not sure."

"Well, what did you do when a girl told you no, told you to stop after letting you do everything but?"

"I never had that problem a whole lot, but when I did, I stopped."

"Yes, but things were different back then, girls were different. Now, most girls don't want you to stop, and no doesn't mean no, not really."

"What was the disposition of your case?"

"They—" He stopped, staring at me, the narrow face hardening with suspicion. "I thought you'd seen the record. You said—"

"No," I said gently. "I didn't tell you I'd seen anything. I haven't, as a matter of fact. All I did was ask you what happened when you were a juvenile."

"You tricked me!"

"I'll have to admit that. But don't feel bad, I've tricked people a lot older than you." I gave him a friendly grin. "Would you like to tell me how it came out?"

He started a shrug, then turned it into a grimace. "Nothing. Not much, anyway. I had to go—" He stopped abruptly and gave me a hard-faced smile. "No, I don't think I will. I don't enjoy being tricked, being made a fool of. If you want to know, you can try to find out." His face was flushed. He seemed more annoyed that I had conned him than at what he had revealed.

"It's no big deal, Paul," I said. "Like you said, it was a long time—"

"Mr. LeClair," he said crisply, the thin smile back on his face.

I returned his smile. "How about Mr. Paul? That do all right?"

"As long as it's there," he said. "And while we're about it, the servants' entrance is around back."

I grinned full into the blaring black eyes. "Mr. Paul. Anybody ever tell you, you're an arrogant little prick? You have to study up for that, or did it just come natural?"

He pulled himself erect, gave me a withering look and turned on his heel, disdain in every inch of the tall graceful body.

Moments later he folded himself into the red Porsche, and the peaceful morning erupted into violent sound and movement. He peeled rubber all the way around the circle, the juddering rear end of the little car missing my truck by no more than four inches. He took the dip at the street far faster than was good for the car or for him, and screamed off down the curving street.

I looked at the ugly black marks on the driveway and shook my head. "Oh, oh, Mr. Paul, Mama ain't gonna like that."

But then it occurred to me that maybe he didn't give a damn what Mama liked or didn't like. With the old man dead, his sister dead, he was the big cheese around the LeClair mansion.

Of course, he didn't know that yet.

On the other hand, maybe he did.

Mrs. Cornelia Mullins was a tall spare woman. All angles and knobs. No makeup, and no frills on the severely cut gray dress that hung on her rawboned frame like a nightshirt. She had strong plain features, accentuated by steel-gray hair pulled back from her face and wound into a smooth, hard-looking knot behind her head.

I had seen a hundred just like her in the movies over the years, quiet, controlled and efficient, a woman you would not take lightly, would not joke with, or tease, or proposition.

She had a warm, liquid voice, a Southern voice that brought to mind green-capped mountains, dark hollows ridged with pine, slow-smoked hams and fried bread, black-eyed peas. I listened to her slow melody and didn't wonder when she told me that she had eleven children, had buried two husbands, and was working on her third. I didn't question that she came from Virginia, old genteel stock, that she had married beneath her all three times, that she had given her life to the care of her children and the family LeClair.

I listened with rapt attention while she chronologically listed the LeClairs, their family history, their good traits and their foibles, and I couldn't disagree when she told me that Mr. Paul was too prideful, way too far up on his high horse to ever do anything but fall.

And, finally, when I asked her if it wasn't against the staff code or something to talk about the family that way, she sniffed with disdain and said, "What family, Mr. Roman? That old man and that little girl was the LeClair family to me. Mr. Tim was like a father to me, and that little girl was as much as my own. I want that scoundrel caught, Mr. Roman. I want it in the worst way. I want to see them strap him down and put him to death, though Lord knows it'll take a dozen years for that."

"If ever," I said. "He could be a psychopath, Mrs. Mullins. We almost never kill crazy people."

"They ought to kill this one, if that's what he is."

"You were off on Sunday. In church with your family, I suppose."

"No," she said sharply. "I don't believe in it. That's the only thing me and Mr. Tim ever disagreed about all those years. I believe everybody's got to make his or her own peace with God. I don't have to go kneel in some big tabernacle to do that."

"That's true," I said. "What do you do on Sunday?"

"*Last* Sunday," she said, a meager smile flitting across her face, "we stayed home and watched the Dallas Cowboys whup up on the New York Giants. Me, my husband, and four of my married daughters along with their families. That's about eighteen people all told, Mr. Roman."

"That ought to do it," I said. "Have you ever heard of a family named Kincade?"

"There's some Kincades back in Virginia I went to school with when I was a child. Other than that, I don't believe I have."

"Do you know of any enemies Mr. LeClair had, someone in business possibly? A personal friend he might have had a falling out with?"

"No. I didn't know anything at all about Mr. Tim's business affairs, and most of his old friends have passed on, or are old and sick like he was."

"What was wrong with him exactly?"

"Rheumatoid arthritis mostly. He had some other problems with hardening arteries, diabetes, chronic bronchitis, but mainly arthritis."

"Did you ever hear Mr. Paul and Mr. Tim fighting?"

She nodded sagely, the slick cap of hair gleaming in the artificial light. "Oh, yes, they fought a lot. They were both hotheaded and stubborn, but Mr. Tim would win, of course."

"Why 'of course'?"

She smiled—a warm, wide smile that did wonders for her face, brought a twinkle to her eyes. "Mr. Tim had the money. That's why 'of course.' He'd just cut off Mr. Paul's spending money and that young man would come around right smartly. The man with the money, Mr. Roman, he's just always bound to win."

"Who gets the money now?" It had suddenly occurred to me that maybe everyone knew what I thought might be a secret.

"Lord, I don't know. He was a dear old man, but he kept his own counsel about money matters. My guess would be Robert; he's the only son left."

"He's also gone," I said. "A long time, from what I understand."

"Oh, he's gone, all right. Must be fourteen, fifteen years. But that don't mean that old man didn't love him. I can remember when he was the apple of Mr. Tim's eye."

"Do you know what happened?"

"That I do," she said stiffly, "but I don't reckon that's got anything to do with this."

"You never can tell."

But her mouth was crimped, a solid disapproving line across her worn face, and after a long ten-second silence I decided she had said all she was going to say. Her features were once again stern and austere, all the friendliness gone, her dark eyes remote, veiled.

I thanked her for her time, said good-bye, and left.

Despite the cold wind and seeping damp, the gardener was out on his mower, moving in and out of the mist-shrouded trees like some lonely wraith lost in the fog. He was the last one on my list, but he was a quarter of a mile away heading in the wrong direction, and I had no stomach for chasing ghosts.

Besides, I had whiled away a good part of the morning. Lunchtime was coming up and I needed something in my system other than cold milk and cereal. I needed a beer and some good solid food.

What I really needed, I thought morosely as I followed Paul LeClair's ugly black tracks out of the driveway, was to catch a killer.

27

His name was Malcolm Sledge. A short, blocky man in coveralls and a bulky, quilted windbreaker, thick-soled work shoes and white socks. He shut off the mower and peered at me out of small bright eyes almost hidden behind puffy lids and hedgerow brows. His face was round and fat, cheekbones stained permanently red by a network of broken veins. His lower lip protruded grotesquely on the right side, creating a lopsided effect that did little to enhance his overall attractiveness. He folded his hands on the steering wheel, leaned to one side and spat a globule of dark-colored spittle into the yellow-green grass. An unpleasant mix of insecticide, hot crankcase oil, and body odor wafted around him like protective armor.

"You'd be that detective feller, I reckon. Mr. Johnson told me all about you."

"Nothing derogatory, I hope."

The bright eyes scanned my face; I couldn't decide if they were gray or blue. But, whatever their color, they watched me with a cold, unwavering stare, as if I might be just another old stump that needed uprooting.

"I guess so," he said finally, leaning to spit again. "You'll be wanting to ask me a lot of questions, I reckon. Mr. Johnson told me not to fret about it."

"Only one or two, Mr. Sledge." I lit a cigarette and looked around, shaking my head. "I guess all this land keeps you pretty busy just cutting the grass and trimming the trees and such."

"Ain't doing this to cut the grass," he said, a faint note of scorn creeping into his voice. "I'm mostly whipping up the leaves. Grass don't grow no more this time of year." He looked away, his expression clearly adding, "Any fool would know that."

"By damn, that's right," I said. "Beats the hell out of raking, I'll bet."

He stiffened. "Ain't no call to talk dirty."

"You're right," I said. "Pardon me." I pinched out the cigarette and threw the butt into a nearby pile of leaves. He watched in disapproving silence.

"Mr. Sledge, they tell me you don't work on Sundays—"

"That's right," he said. "That's the Lord's day."

"Then I take it you were in church last Sunday?"

"Nope. I don't hold with that folderol. Money-grubbing preachers. I can read my own Bible my own self without some preacher yelling at me and asking for my money."

"You were home last Sunday then?" I edged around the front of the mower, trying to get upwind.

"Nope. Not all the whole day. That old lady of mine lost her car keys." He leaned out to spit, touched the corner of his mouth with a crooked thumb, settled back.

"And?"

"And what?"

"You said your wife lost her keys. What does that have to do with . . . anything?"

He gave me an annoyed look. "I had to make her some new ones, that's what."

"Okay," I said patiently. "You went out to buy your wife—"

"I didn't go out to buy her nothing. Them things cost about two dollars apiece." A sly expression crossed his face. "I can make 'em over here for nothing."

"Over here? You mean here, at the LeClair house?"

"Out in the garage. We got this dandy little key-making out-fit. Grinds 'em out in just a few seconds. Don't cost nothing hardly except the blanks and they're real cheap."

"You mean you came over here Sunday?" I felt a faint stirring in my stomach, a coolness behind my ears.

He was silent for a moment, the sharp eyes studying my face. He stirred uneasily on the metal seat. "Yeah, I did, but Mr. Tim don't care. It don't cost hardly nothing and he—"

"What time, Mr. Sledge? What time of day was it?"

"Well, I don't rightly—it was before noon, I know that. I wanted to watch the Cowboy game and—"

"How long before noon?"

He looked up at the overcast sky and traced the bulge in his lip with a stubby forefinger. "I reckon about an hour or so. The old lady was gonna fix us some dip and stuff and I had to stop by the store and get some mustard and chips—"

"Around eleven o'clock, would you say?"

"Somewhere around there. I know I got back home before noon. I had to make four keys, but that didn't take very long. I guess I was here thirty minutes, maybe."

"You didn't see anyone?"

"Nope. Nary a soul. They was all in church, I guess, except old Mr. Tim."

"Did you see a car? In the driveway or out on the street, maybe?"

"Nothing in the driveway, that's for sure." He stopped and squinted his eyes in an elaborate impression of a man thinking hard. "I did see a car—out on the street, down a ways. One of them big old gas guzzlers, as I recollect."

"Do you remember the make, the year, type?"

"It was a sedan, I think. Big, but that ain't unusual around here. These rich folks gotta have their big cars to go along with these big, fine houses."

"You don't remember the make?"

"I'd say offhand General Motors. I don't know which one. They been making them all look alike for ten years."

"Old or new?"

"Not new, I don't think. Tell you the truth, I didn't pay much attention. Just another car. Anyhow, I was in a hurry."

"Color? Do you recall the color?"

He scratched his jutting jaw. "Light-colored, I reckon. Yeah, I'm purty sure of that. Light-colored."

"Did you hear anything? Loud noises, five or six loud noises?"

The sly look came back to his face. "You mean like gunshots? Naw, I didn't hear nothing—" He broke off, looking faintly alarmed. "You mean that's when it happened?"

"You didn't know?"

He shook his head, the small eyes widening. "No, I sure didn't. They didn't say on the TV."

"You haven't talked to any of the other staff?"

"No, sir. Mr. Johnson is the only one I talk to when he tells me what to do. He didn't say nothing about the killings, and I sure wasn't gonna bring it up. He can be real mean when he gets riled up."

"Are you sure you didn't hear a car drive up, or a door slam while you were in the garage?"

"No sir, I didn't. That little machine makes a lot of noise and the garage is a right smart way from the house, anyhow. I didn't hear nothing."

I sighed, feeling deflated, the small spurt of adrenaline fading. A false alarm. If he was right about the time, then he must have been inside the garage during the murders, or at least during the murder of the girl. I wondered if the killer had seen him arrive and depart, wondered how close this smelly little man had come to being a victim himself.

"Where was your car while you were in the garage?"

"Around in back. I parked it near the door of the little workshop we got back there." He looked a little pale, nervous for the first time, the artificial flush on his cheekbones giving him an almost healthy glow. He wet his lips. "Good Lord, you don't think he was . . . doing it to them while I . . ." He let it fade away, the dark little eyes flickering, clearly seized with intimations of mortality. "Good Lord!"

I had to smile a little. He was obviously shaken to the core, his expression frozen between self-realization and morbid fascination. He stared at the house as if he had never seen it before.

"It's okay," I said. "The killer's long gone." I reached out and touched his plump shoulder.

He jumped and turned to glare at me. He snorted something unintelligible, twisted the key switch on the mower, then wheeled it in a tight little semicircle, heading back the way he had come.

He drove erratically, with none of his former precision, staring over his shoulder at the gleaming white mansion as if he had just discovered that hordes of wyverns and goblins resided there, and might come tumbling out at any given moment.

| *28* |

I stopped by Homer's office when I got back to police headquarters. Mitsi was eating a late lunch at her desk. Homer was
gone. I chatted with Mitsi a few moments, then went in to
Homer's desk to make out my last reports on the LeClair murders.

I filed out F.I.R.s on Mrs. Mullins and Malcolm Sledge, made
out another detailing the gist of my conversation with Paul
LeClair. Dribbles and dabs of new information, none of them
particularly significant that I could see. Sledge had been there
during the murders, that much was obvious, but since he saw
nothing, heard nothing, it mattered little. The business about
seeing the car wasn't new, the girl who had driven Julie home,
Carol L. Gibbons, had said much the same thing. Again, without a clearer description, it wouldn't help a hell of a lot.

Paul LeClair's revelation was new, even mildly interesting,
but I could see no connection between it and his grandfather's
and sister's murders four years later. Besides, Paul LeClair had
a perfect alibi.

A perfect alibi. I rared back in Homer's chair, lit a cigarette,
and thought about that for a moment.

As far as I could see, the only similarity in the two murder
cases was the fact that all of the survivors had impeccable alibis. Unusual, but not unknown. Everyone had to be somewhere at any given moment in time. It all came down to being
able to prove it.

Cynthia Kincade stood to gain from her father's death, and
while her alibi wasn't perfect, it was provable.

Paul LeClair stood to gain the most, and his alibi was beyond
reproach with a hundred, maybe two hundred, good solid

churchgoing citizens ready to step forward and swear to his and his mother's presence in church at the fateful moment. Alibis didn't come much better than that.

David Kincade's alibi was perfect. His mother's was not, but again, it was provable. And, think as I might, I could find no motive for either of them to kill Ralph Kincade.

So?

I crashed forward in Homer's chair. So nothing. So back to a random murderer again, some slimy little creep with a Saturday night special, one of the growing breed of losers who roamed at will, controlled only by the dictates of a diseased mind, a stalking predator, his natural prey fellow human beings.

I stacked the reports on Homer's desk and surrendered to overwhelming feelings of defeat, futility.

I had given it my best shot, but what I had wasn't nearly good enough. I had solved nothing, proved nothing. We knew precious little more than we had known the morning Homer rousted me out of bed. Bits of information, unrelated facts; flotsam along a barren shore, the fallout of murders that had no rhyme or reason.

But even as I admitted failure, steeped myself in self-pity, deep down at the core of my awareness I sensed that we were wrong, that we were taking the easy road that had been traveled by many others before us. Henry Lee Lucas, serial killer buffoon. Six hundred murders had been laid at his door, hundreds of cases closed on his unsupported word, later to be reopened when he gleefully recanted, denouncing his captors as naive incompetents. A lot of law enforcement faces had been stained a permanent red by that one.

Would the Kincade/LeClair murders end up in a pending file, waiting for more depredations against the citizens of Midway City or some other place? It seemed likely, even probable. And there was damn little I could do about it. I had given my time and effort to the chase and the quarry had eluded me with ease. It was hard to accept, but there it was.

A rough booming voice sounded out in the corridor, and I heard Mitsi laugh. A moment later Homer loomed in the doorway, hair spilling across his broad forehead like strands of dried Johnson grass. He looked tired, red-rimmed eyes peering from dark burrows, thick shoulders rounded from some intolerable weight.

"Well, there you are. I was thinking about going by your house, see if maybe you'd snuck home for your afternoon nap."

I got up and went around the desk, plopped down in his visitor's chair. "I may as well for all the good I'm doing."

He stood behind his desk looking down at me, big hands going through the pockets of his coat. "You look as bad as I feel, little buddy. You letting the pressure get to you?" He tugged a folded sheet of paper from an inside coat pocket, then did a free-fall into his swivel chair. "Christ, I'm tired."

"Bad meeting?"

He shook his head and sighed, a heavy wheezing sound. "You wouldn't believe the simpleminded assholes we've got running this town. Time was, they'd pretty much leave you alone, let you do your job. No more. They've got computers; they've got statistics, numbers for everything. Little smiling jerk-offs in blue blazers with stacks of printouts, just waiting to spout numbers at you." He slapped the sheet of paper on his desk and gave me a weary smile.

"Life is hard, Homer. When you came into this world, red-faced and naked and squalling, nobody told you it was gonna be easy."

He grunted and took a cigar out of his inside coat pocket. "Uh-huh. Well, I take it you've been working? See that Mullins woman?"

"And the gardener. The reports are there on your desk."

"Tell me, will you? I'm tired of reading reports." He held a kitchen match to the cigar, huffing blue-white smoke across the desk, the pungent cloud stinging my eyes, opening my sinuses.

"Not much from the housekeeper. She corroborated the fact

that Paul and old Timothy battled a lot. Said Timothy always won because he had the money. She has a lot of respect for money."

"Don't we all."

"I don't know. It's not the most important thing in life."

"That's because you got some," he growled. "Go on."

"She gave me a pretty good rundown on the LeClairs, but none of it helps that I can see." I paused and waited until he looked up at me. "The gardener was a slightly different story. He was there when the murders took place."

Homer's eyebrows shot upward. "There? At the house?"

"Not at the house. In the garage workshop making some keys for his wife. But don't get all hot and sticky. He didn't see anything, hear anything. He came and left, and if he was right about the time, the killer was probably there all the time. The girl must have come home while he was in the garage. She went in, got herself killed, and old Malcolm didn't see or hear a damn thing."

"You believe him?"

I nodded. "I think so. Those little key-making machines make noise, and anyhow, that little gun wouldn't have made all that much racket. He did remember seeing a car, a big car, he said, not new, and maybe made by General Motors. It was parked out on the street, down a ways from the driveway."

He nodded slowly. "The part about the car matches pretty well what Carol Gibbons told us." He stirred restlessly. "Think we ought to bring him in, squeeze him a little more?"

I shrugged. "You can, but I don't think it'll amount to anything. His story was believable and he volunteered it. He's not a lovable character, but I don't think he was lying."

"Shit!" Homer said. "A witness on the scene and he turns out to be another damn stone monkey."

"It's a bummer, Homer."

He glowered at me. "You're taking it pretty damn well."

I shrugged again. "I've accepted defeat. Once you do that, nothing touches you."

He snorted and picked up the sheet of paper, unfolded it.

"Uh-huh. Well let's see if this touches you. We broke in Paul LeClair's juvenile record and he was—"

"Rape," I said nonchalantly.

His head snapped up. "How in hell did you know that?"

I grinned. "Good detective work, Homer. A good detective never—"

"Yeah, I know. Well, it was a rape, but it was what they call a date rape. The girl called a halt, but Paulie baby was way beyond that stage and he went right on. He evidently roughed her up some, blacked an eye, squeezed her throat a little. Anyhow, he got a year in juvenile detention, probated on condition that he attend a teenage counseling session once a week for the same period at a place called the Juvenile Rehabilitation Center. Looks like he did, and that was the end of it."

"Not much for rape and assault."

He sighed. "Guess they figured there were mitigating factors. He'd been dating her a month or so, and anyhow, they don't seem to consider a date rape in the same class as a stranger rape. The girl admitted they'd been doing some heavy petting—making out, she called it." He gave me a cynical smile. "The fact that Paul's granddaddy was richer'n the Bass boys probably didn't have anything to do with it."

"Of course not."

He dabbed at the paper with a long index finger. "Interesting, but I don't see that it helps us none."

"I agree," I said, and pushed to my feet.

"Where're you going?"

"Home."

He leaned back in his chair. "You really are giving up?"

I glanced at my watch. "I can give you a couple of more hours if you can think of anything I can start and finish in that length of time."

He shook his head. "Naw, go on, take off. I won't bitch at you. I don't want to seem ungrateful."

"Sorry I couldn't do you more good, but I guess I've lost the touch."

"Cut out the shit," he said mildly, making an airy, expansive gesture. "Man can only do so much in a given amount of time. You promised me four days and you've given it to me. What more can I ask?"

I looked at him closely. "You sure you're feeling okay?"

He laughed and heaved to his feet. "Go on, get out of here. I got work to do. Where're you and Susie going, anyhow?" He took off his coat and hung it on a rack in the corner.

"Just down to the cabin," I said, regretting it immediately. "Or," I added hastily, "we may fly to Acapulco."

He laughed again. "Don't worry, I'm not going to bother you two lovebirds. Looks like the weather's turning on us, though. You might have to spend all your time indoors."

"That would be a shame." I wandered to the door. "See you in a week or so, Homer."

He sat back down. "Yeah. Take it easy. Give my love to Susie."

"You got it," I said, but he was already bowed over his desk, papers in hand, a frown on his broad forehead, and I wasn't sure if he heard me.

29

I was dozing in front of the TV when Susie came home, cold hands and a flushed laughing face as she threw herself over the arm of the chair and into my lap, eyes flashing, happiness radiating like heat from a burning building.

We nuzzled for a while, murmuring small inanities, arguing over who missed who the most. She won, of course, smothering my arguments with warm kisses and overwhelming enthusiasm. Not willing to be outdone, I did some smothering of my own, and with no less enthusiasm.

After a while she broke away, went into the kitchen and fixed a cup of coffee for herself, uncapped a bottle of beer for me. I lit a fire in the fireplace. Fetchingly disheveled, she sat down in the other recliner and told me about her trip.

I listened with grave attention, chuckling at appropriate places, clucking at others, watching the firelight dancing on her lovely face and marveling at my change of luck.

She talked with vigor and animation, graceful gestures, but our eyes kept meeting, breaking apart only to come back again, lingering, and it wasn't long before we arose without a word and walked down the hallway arm in arm to the bedroom.

I had already showered and shaved, anointed my body with a manly aroma, so that time, I had to wait for her.

We arrived at the cabin a few minutes before eleven o'clock, later than I had planned, but not bad considering the early morning traffic, the skittering horde of nine-to-fivers who blocked our passage out of Fort Worth, their pallid city faces cast in permanent molds of frustration and unseemly anger.

The weather didn't help: glowering skies, low and convoluted, promising rain, giving nothing but a fine, annoying mist that necessitated an occasional flip of windshield wipers. Gusty winds buffeted the truck, bringing commingled aromas of wet mesquite, sagebrush and cedar, an occasional whiff of burning diesel oil from passing eighteen-wheelers.

Undaunted by the elements, rosy-cheeked and effervescent, Susie helped me unload the Ramcharger and stored the supplies while I went around checking things, turning on the electricity, the water, the bottled gas. Roughing it in style. All the comforts of home and then some.

A satellite dish, almost hidden behind a screen of young oak saplings, gaped toward the southern sky, a recent addition I had let myself be talked into by Homer and the rest of our deer hunting buddies who saw nothing incongruous in watching an X-rated movie from Sweden in a cozy log cabin out in the middle of nowhere.

True, we were only twelve miles from the Interstate, but thanks to the giant earth-raping machines, all of the ranches and farms on my side of the highway had been eliminated, and my nearest neighbors were fifteen miles away in my hometown of Butler Wells.

My four hundred acres had not escaped, three hundred and ninety acres smashed flat and gutted for the soft black gold that was to be our answer to OPEC: lignite coal. I had been as greedy as all the rest of them, closing my eyes to the desecration of the land, holding out my hand for the money.

But the ten acres of timber on the hill, the cabin, and the small teardrop-shaped lake had been another matter. My father and I had worked too hard and too long to build the cabin, and it was all I had left of him. I had bowed my neck and taken a stand, and they had finally capitulated, declaring in their reports that the hill was nothing but solid rock, anyway, and not worthy of their time. Actually, it was sandy soil with a clay base, a modicum of rocks along the ravine that housed the lake. But they needed to save face and I needed the small victory for my soul, and so the bargain was struck in a spirit of equanimity.

The coal money brought me a small measure of wealth and, what was more important, a large measure of freedom in choosing the type of cases I wanted to work.

And slowly but surely the timber was coming back. Five years after excavation there were towering willows bordering the creek, pines and hardwoods head-high along the lower slopes, mesquite and elm spreading across the creek bottom. There were small patches here and there that would probably never grow anything again, nature's rebuke for the carelessness of man.

"What do you want for lunch?" Susie spoke from the rear of the front room, a long narrow space that served as kitchen and dinette, sectioned off from the rest of the room by a console TV and a low, crowded bookcase. "How about ham sandwiches, chips, and a Coke?"

"How about ham sandwiches, chips and a beer? Coke's not good for my macho image."

"Beer's not good for your mucho belly," she said and giggled.

"You trying to tell me something? Like maybe I'm getting too much muscle around my middle?"

"No, sire," she said, aghast, striking a wide-eyed pose of maidenly innocence. "Thou art a perfect speciman of a man."

"Maybe I'll have tea," I said thoughtfully, and listened to her bubbling laughter.

We ate lunch in front of the fire, pausing occasionally to watch some particularly awesome bit of mayhem on the TV news: body bags and grim faces, ogling crowds and bloodstains on the sidewalk. I turned it off when the soap operas came on; entirely too much sex and violence for my taste.

We talked for a while. Susie told me about the rest of her latest adventure, the frightening rush of swirling muddy water along the reaches of the Rio Grande, the agony of people watching their life's accumulations slowly disappearing before their eyes. I watched the play of emotions on her face as she relived the nightmare, soft and compassionate one moment, then flushed and tight and filled with pride as she described someone's heroic action in the midst of peril; I could almost feel the swelling of her heart. Mine did a little swelling of its own.

Near midafternoon we bundled up and walked the hundred yards down the hill to the lake. Bright and sparkling despite the overcast day, it yielded no fish to our rods and lines and, after an hour of frozen fingers and runny noses, we galloped back up the hill to sweet warmth and rum toddies, to cuddling before the dancing fire, and inevitably, to the nearest of the single beds in the other room.

Not long before dark, I braved the elements again to scorch a couple of steaks. Susie built salads, microwaved two potatoes, and baked biscuits in our little gas oven.

I could hear her singing contentedly in the cozy warmth while I ducked swirling smoke and fought the biting wind, my nose running again, eyes tearing, a raw spot spreading in my throat. A woman's lot is hard, I thought, and wondered if she'd care to change places.

Drifting on the wind came the moldy perfume of dying vegetation, the whispering rattle of dried sycamore leaves, the sough and creak of towering hardwoods, the pungent tang of pine needles. Sights and odors and sounds, earthy and restorative, a panacea for my country-bred soul. I watched the darkening woods close in and despite the angry weather felt rich and warm with discovery and contentment.

An armadillo wandered by, oblivious to everything around him, nose in the leaves and wilted grass, rooting in likely places. He crossed my path no more than a quick step away, then scampered like a charging rhino when I stamped my foot. Upwind, three ghostly forms materialized out of the gathering darkness, stood watching me from the edge of safety, a dense thicket of shinnery that may well have been their bedding ground for the night: two does and a fawn, all ears and knobby legs, graceful bodies tensed for flight, white-tipped tails flagging.

Beside me, Susie tapped on the window and made cooing sounds, watching the deer with delighted eyes. I smiled and nodded and looked back at the shinnery thicket. The deer were gone, as quickly and as quietly as they had come, and I wondered again how I had ever had the heart to kill one of those delightful creatures.

We ate with much gusto, cleaning the steak bones and scraping the potato skins, wiping out the salad down to the last crouton. We left two small, lonely-looking biscuits, a spoonful of peas, and a handful of no-sex-tonight green onions when I saw that Susie wasn't having any. She picked them up with a cryptic little smile, wrapped them in aluminum foil and stowed them in the fridge.

"You didn't eat your onions," she said innocently, wiping the table in front of me.

"Huh-uh," I said, grabbing her around the waist. "Maybe tomorrow." I pulled her into my lap, burrowed through the mane of black hair and nibbled on the lobe of an ear. "They make my breath too exotic. You might get ideas."

She squirmed sideways, caught my neck in an elbow lock.

"I've *got* ideas. I just wanted to see if you had them. It's a sure sign when you don't eat your onions."

"You know me too well. That's a bad omen. There's no mystery anymore."

She leaned back to look at my face. "That's not true at all. I tell you every little thing that happens to me and you hardly tell me anything. You're as inscrutable as a rock. For instance, I don't even know the name of your first girlfriend."

"I never had a first one," I said. "I lived a lonely, chaste life."

"Come on, now. I told you all about my early years—"

I laughed. "You're *in* your early years."

"I mean high school and college."

"Okay, let's see. I think her name was Matilda. They called her Matilda the Hun. She had hair on her lip and on her chest—"

"All right," she said, and made a mock motion to rise. "If you can't be serious for one—"

"Okay, her name was Melissa. We dated during our sophomore year."

"Was she pretty?"

"Not as pretty as you."

"Was she—all right, I'm not going to ask questions and get silly answers. You just tell me about her."

"She was pretty, Susie. At least I thought she was. She was nice and . . . and sexy, I guess. We went together for that one school year, and the next year she dropped me cold and began going with my best friend. End of story."

"Were you sad? Or mad?"

"More sad than mad, I suppose. Losing a girlfriend is one thing, but I didn't want to lose my buddy."

She tightened her hold on my neck, stabbed me in the belly with a stiffened finger, then laughed. "Well, I guess I know what to expect when you get tired of me."

I squeezed her until she grunted. "You're different. You're my woman. You're my wife."

"Uh-huh," she said, but I could tell she was pleased. "How many other girlfriends have you had?"

"Not many. I wasn't always this good-looking."

"Don't give me that. I see women looking at you."

"Yeah. They'll watch an old dog scratching, too, but that don't mean they want his fleas."

She tried not to laugh, but it came bubbling forth. She yanked my head against her breasts. "Danny! I'm trying to have a serious conversation—"

The phone rang.

I grinned into her flushed face. "Saved by the bell."

She grimaced and released my neck. "You don't have to answer it."

"I've got this compulsion," I said. "If I don't answer it, I won't sleep a wink all night."

"You might not, anyway," she murmured as I deposited her on the couch.

I laughed and yanked up the receiver on the third ring.

30

"Danny!" It sounded so much like Susie I was momentarily confused, half turning to look before realization came smoking in. Maggie Lane.

"Yes. Hello," I said, my voice more formal than I intended.

"Danny, I'm sorry to bother you like this, but after what happened I don't think I have any choice but to tell you the truth."

"What happened? And what truth?"

"You know what happened. Cynthia called me this morning and read me the riot act because of what you did to Knutson. You know better than I do what you did."

"That's true."

"Whatever you did he deserved it . . . and more. I made a terrible mistake with him, and with Cynthia, too. I thought we were friends, but after what she said—" She broke off, breathing deeply, the sound competing with the white noise on the long-distance line.

"What was that?" I looked at Susie. She quickly looked away, staring fixedly at one of the darkened windows.

"I'm sorry, Danny. I'm sorry I lied to you."

"About what, Maggie?"

"About the trip. The trip to Galveston. I—I was right here . . . working all the time."

I felt something turn over in my chest, a numbing sensation in my solar plexus. "How about Cynthia and Knutson? Do you know if they went?"

"No, I don't. I don't think they did. Why else would they want me to lie for them?"

"Why did you do it?"

"I—Cyn asked me to. And Knutson, he—I'm sorry, but I was afraid of him."

"Did she give a reason?"

"Yes. She said she was afraid that her mother and brother would find out about her being a . . . well, a hooker, if the police started digging too deep. She said if I told you she was with me in Galveston that you would . . . believe me."

"Why would she think that?"

"I don't know," she answered quickly; too quickly, I thought.

"That doesn't make sense, Maggie. You'll have to do better than that."

Another silence, a deep, shuddering breath. "All right. I told her once about you and me . . . about us. Just a girl-to-girl talk one night not long ago. When her mother hired you to go to California, she asked me if you were the same one and I told her you were. So she knew . . . not all of it, but enough, I guess. After you talked to her, she told Knutson and they called me. She asked me first, and I said no, and then Knutson came on the phone. . . ." Her voice faded, returned, muted, fragile. "I'm sorry, but he frightens me."

"Not too much or he wouldn't be your pimp."

"He's not, not really. He's Cynthia's pimp. I let her talk me into using him to take care of my problem johns, to screen new johns. He gets twenty percent for that, just to meet the first-time johns and let them see him, how big he is, so they would know they would have to . . . so they wouldn't try anything funny. That's all he did, but he wasn't satisfied with that. He wanted to bring in new business—"

"I get the idea."

"Does it really matter, Danny? I'm sure Cyn wouldn't do anything to hurt her daddy. She was always talking about him. I think she loved him very much."

"Then why are you telling me this?"

"I—I'm not sure. I guess because I'm mad . . . and I hate that I lied to you. I never did that before."

"I never thought so at the time."

"I never did. I don't have much pride left, but I've never been a liar."

"Why did Knutson beat you?"

She made a soft sound that could have been a sigh. "Someone, probably someone in Charley's, saw us together and called him. He goes there a lot. He thought I was lying when I said that it was just a friendly little drink. He thought I was telling you the truth about Galveston. He kept staring at me in that scary way he has when I kept telling him I hadn't said a word about that to you. I told him to leave and that just made him madder. Once he hit me, he—he couldn't seem to stop. I think he liked it, Danny."

"Don't let him in. If he shows up, call the police."

Her laugh was sharp and brittle. "Sure, I'll call the police."

"Do it, dammit. He's on parole. He won't risk going back to prison if he knows you mean it." I hesitated. "Or you can call me."

"All right," she said, but she didn't sound convinced. "I'll let you go now. I just wanted to set things straight. I'm sorry."

She broke the connection. I listened to the empty line sizzle for a moment, then cradled the receiver. Susie was leafing through a magazine, her face composed and unreadable, one foot swinging with a metronomic cadence from the fulcrum of her crossed legs. A sure sign of agitation.

I sighed, got up and went to the refrigerator. I uncapped two bottles of beer, went back into the living room area and held one out to her. She made no move to accept it. I set it on the table at the end of the couch and dropped into a heavy leather chair that Homer had provided for his own comfort on our sporadic visits to the cabin.

I lit a cigarette and sampled the beer. She finished the magazine and reached for another.

"That was a woman on the phone," I said. "A woman named Maggie Lane. She's a hooker. She's involved peripherally in the Kincade murder case. Once, a long time ago, she was involved in my life. I'm willing to tell you about it if you want to listen."

She tossed the magazine back on the coffee table and smiled crookedly. "I thought you'd never ask."

"You asked me about old girlfriends a while ago, well, Maggie Lane and I were friends, more than friends, for almost a year. For a lot of reasons I won't go into it didn't work out—"

"You can go into them," she said sweetly. "I watched soap operas for years."

"It's not important. What is important is how she came back into my life, why she just called me long-distance on the phone—"

"Is it important? You didn't sound very excited . . . except that one time there when you were cursing."

"Do you want me to tell you about it, or not?"

She nodded firmly. "Yes, I do. But let's not start with the premise that I've been sitting here burning with jealousy just because you received a telephone call from a woman. That seems to be what you are thinking."

I stared at her, a little nonplussed; that was *exactly* what I had been thinking. I felt an involuntary smile breaking across my face. "I guess I was, at that."

She smiled, a genuine smile that lit up her face. "I'm jealous as hell of you, Danny. But I'm not jealous of old girlfriends.

They had their chance and they struck out. I didn't. Now, do you want to tell me about it?"

"I do," I said.

And I did. Beginning with the delivery of Ralph Kincade to his door. Everything that had happened during the four days since his murder. A lot of talking. It took another beer and a half-dozen cigarettes, one pause for a trip to the bathroom. She listened well, dark eyes intent, her gaze rarely leaving my face as I talked, speaking only to ask an infrequent question for clarification of a point.

My sorry little tale touched her emotions, faithfully mirrored on her mobile face: horror and compassion, a fleeting bit of humor now and then, fearful joy when I told her about my battle with Gregory Knutson, and sadness when I described what he had done to Maggie Lane.

When I finished, I got up and went into the kitchen area again. I opened another beer, lit another cigarette, came back and told her what I had been dreading most.

"I have to go back to Midway City," I said.

She nodded without comment, her expression noncommittal.

"I don't know if Cynthia is capable of killing her father, but Knutson is. It's my fault they're not under suspicion, not being checked out. I accepted Maggie Lane's word and I shouldn't have."

She nodded again, not pointing out that all I had to do was pick up the phone and call Homer.

"I need to do this myself, Susie. It may not amount to any-thing, but it was my mistake."

"All right," she said, and stood up. "I'll start packing."

"You don't have to go. I can come back probably by tomor-row evening."

She gave me an enigmatic little smile and shook her head. "I'll pack."

31

Both cars were in the driveway: Cynthia Kincade's red Toyota and the tan family Buick. Light still glowed faintly around the living room draperies although dawn had come and gone a half hour before. I stretched the kinks out of my driving muscles as I crossed the dew-shrouded lawn to the front door.

We had left the cabin before five o'clock, drove the ninety-five odd miles to Fort Worth and slipped through the waking city a good fifteen minutes before the early morning traffic madness. Susie slept most of the way, or pretended to, rousing fully only when we reached our house. She had slipped out of the truck with a quick kiss, a terse "Be careful," and I had waited until her slender figure disappeared through the door. I knew she was unhappy, and I was sorry about that, but as far as I could see, there was nothing else I could do.

Cynthia Kincade answered my knock, hair still up in curlers, almost-pretty face bereft of makeup, hands clutching the edges of a frayed nylon robe. If she was making a lot of money as a high-priced call girl, she didn't appear to be spending it on clothing.

"What do you want?" she asked coldly, her face squeezed into a tight, forbidding frown, the blue eyes bright and hard.

"I think you know."

"I don't want—" She broke off, wincing, as a cheery voice came from behind her.

"Who is it, dear?" Naomi Kincade appeared in the background, a white cloth coat across her arm, her left hand grasping a purse. "Oh, Mr. Roman. I thought you were my ride to work."

Before I could answer, a car turned into the driveway behind me, a horn tooted lightly. "I believe your ride is here," I said.

"Oh, dear. I'm sorry, Mr. Roman. I must go to work today. I haven't been since—and we're in the middle of an inventory and I'm the only one who knows—could you come back another time?" She looked haggard despite a heavy coating of makeup.

"It's quite all right," I said. "Actually, I wanted to talk to your daughter." I looked at the stone-faced young woman beside her. "If I may."

Cynthia Kincade's face tightened again, but when she turned to her mother, she was smiling amiably. "Of course." She took her mother's coat and helped her into it, kissed her on the cheek. "See you later, Mom."

Naomi Kincade hesitated, then kissed her daughter's cheek in return, gave me an apologetic smile, and hurried down the steps to the waiting car.

"What do you want?" Cynthia hissed again, leaning a shoulder against the doorjamb as if to deny me entrance.

"The truth," I said. "That'll do for openers."

"That bitch called you! Surely you don't believe her. She—"

"If you're talking about Maggie Lane, that was my problem from the beginning. I did believe her. I believe her now. I think it's time for a little truth from you, Ms. Kincade."

"I never lied to you," she said sullenly. "I was with Gregory Knutson."

"That's true, you didn't. You left that up to your pimp."

She straightened, her face blanching. "I—she . . . she told you that I was . . . that I—" She broke off, the words clogging her throat.

"No, she didn't. It came from a vice detective with the Midway City police. Did you think it was a secret? You're lucky you haven't been busted. All Maggie Lane told me at first was that the three of you went to Galveston to meet a friend of Knutson's. I knew she was a prostitute, and I suppose it says something about my powers of deduction that I didn't tumble to the fact that you were one also."

She stared up at me, the blue eyes moist with tears, the slender fingers of one hand cupped at her lips. She blinked rapidly; one solitary tear drifted down along her nose and into the corner of her mouth. She shivered, clutching the edges of the robe together at her throat. If she was acting, it was a damn good job, I thought.

"It would be warmer inside," I said.

She nodded woodenly and stepped back. I followed, closing the door, letting her lead me toward the fireplace where we had stood before, the focal point of the drab room. A small fire crackled cozily, giving off the sweet smell of burning oak.

She stopped at one end of the mantel. I walked around the overstuffed chair and staked my claim to the other end. I lit a cigarette and offered her one. She declined with a shake of her head.

"Where's David? Is he still in bed?"

"No, he . . . he had to go in to work at six o'clock."

"Pretty early. Where does he work?" Small talk. Giving her time to pull herself together, time to understand that her moment of truth had arrived.

"Armbruster Supermarket. They let him fit his hours into his class schedule. They're open all night, so . . ." She let it trail away, as if suddenly realizing the unimportance of my question. She looked at me. "I didn't lie to you, Mr. Roman. Not exactly. I was with Greg all night last Friday night, but . . ." She faded again.

"But what?"

She took a deep breath. "But from six o'clock to eight o'clock I was with another . . . man."

"A john?"

She nodded, facing me squarely. "A trick," she said dispassionately.

"Where?"

"In—in Greg's apartment."

"Where was Greg?"

She shrugged slender shoulders. "Out. He left before the man came—a few minutes before."

"Did he tell you where he went?"

"No. Charley's, I suppose, or some other bar. He had been drinking. I could smell it."

"Who was the man?"

She turned to the fire. "I don't know. Greg called him Mac. I suppose Greg knew his last name. I didn't ask him."

I flipped the cigarette butt into the flames. "I hope he does," I said. "I also hope he can prove where he was during those two hours."

Her head came up, eyes widening. "What do you mean?"

I sighed. "You're not naive, Cynthia. We're right back where we were Saturday. You can't prove where you were at the time of your father's death, and now there's another worm in the apple: Gregory Knutson."

"My God, you can't . . . you can't believe I had anything to do—" She choked again, whether from anger or pain, I couldn't tell.

"I wouldn't have believed you were a whore, either," I said harshly, "the day I met you. You didn't look like one or talk like one, but maybe that says more about my idea of a whore than it does about you. You don't look like a killer, either, but how can I trust my judgment having been so wrong about you before?"

She shook her head, both hands trembling, gripping the robe above her breasts. "How can I make you believe—?"

"You can't," I said roughly, taking a step toward her. "Not until you start telling me the goddamned truth!"

She stared at me mutely, lips trembling, real tears starting in her eyes. I glared down at her—the prince of bullies, the brow-beating cop personified—but now was the time if there was going to be one. She was disoriented and cowed, all her attention focused on me, her stricken face reflecting a kind of terrified fascination as I moved another half step forward.

"Another goddamned thing," I snarled, attacking from another direction unforeseen until that very moment. "You and David both told me you hadn't been in contact with your father. Why did you lie?"

It was a random shot in the dark, bursting out of my subconscious of its own volition. But even as I spoke the words something clicked in my memory, and I realized that she had indeed revealed contact with her father, directly or indirectly. Obliquely to be sure, the surprise she had expressed at Kincade's California job, giving as a reason his fear of heights. I hadn't told her the job was in high-rise construction, but she had known. How else but from her father? Good deductive reasoning, albeit a little late.

And now, watching her face crumple, disappear into cupped hands, I felt a visceral tug of dismay, a feeling of inadequacy. I should have caught it at the time, not six days and two murders later.

I found an unused handkerchief in my rear pocket and pressed it into her hands. She stood slumped against the wall by the fireplace, making liquid, sniffing sounds.

"When was it?" I asked, more or less gently. "Late Thursday afternoon?" It was another swing in the dark, but not quite so wild. I had left Kincade in his apartment packing while I went to exchange the little Datsun rental car for something more suitable for a fifteen-hundred-mile trek across country. He had been alone for more than two hours.

After a moment of hiccuping and blowing her nose into my handkerchief, she nodded, her face downcast. "Yes."

"Why didn't you tell me?"

"David—David said we shouldn't. After that other detective talked to him, he . . . he said they acted like they thought we . . . we might have had something to do with Dad's death, and that we'd better wait and see. . . ." She blew her nose again.

"Which one of you talked to him?"

"Both of us." She walked around and sat down in the overstuffed chair. I crossed in front of her to the couch. "When he called I was here alone. We talked for a few minutes about . . . well, just about what had been going on, what everyone had been doing, like that. He told me about his job, how much trouble he had because of the heights, but that he had pretty well overcome it. He—he said he was coming home and then . . ." She stopped and took a deep breath, looked at me for the first time in minutes. "And then he started crying. I guess he was drinking, or had been, anyway. He told me he was sorry he had been so hard on me, that—that I was still his beauti- ful . . . beautiful little girl, and . . . and . . ." She shook her head, tears again brightening the blue eyes. "I guess I started crying, too. He kept saying he was sorry, so sorry, and that he'd make it up to me, that he had been wrong about me . . . and about David, too." She poked at her nose with the balled-up handkerchief and shook her head.

"I don't know what he meant about David. He always treated him like a . . . well, it doesn't matter." She thumbed the edges of her eyes, rubbed them gently. "David came home about then and I gave him the phone and I went into my room and . . . cried."

"Did he tell you about the insurance policy?"

She nodded without looking up. "Yes, he said he had one. That if anything should happen to him on his way home, an accident or something, that I'd . . . that I'd get twenty-five thousand—" She stopped, slowly raised her head, a look of in- credulity dawning on her face. "My God, that's what this is all about, isn't it? That's what you came here to find out. You think I killed my father for the money!"

I gave her a bleak smile. "It had occurred to me. You, or someone close to you." I paused, let a couple of long seconds tick by. "Don't put your faith in Knutson, Cynthia. He'll dump you like a bag of trash when it suits him. Talk to me."

But her face had closed down again, as stiff and hard as a plaster cast, eyes motionless, staring into the distance.

Minutes later, I tried again, but she sat like a graven image, giving no indication that she heard.

Finally, I gave up and left, leaving her to whatever it was she saw behind those unblinking blue eyes.

I had most of what I came for, more than I had a right to expect, a possible motive for the murder of Ralph Kincade. Mo- tive and, unless she could prove differently, opportunity. I should be elated, I kept telling myself, as I pulled into the downtown Midway City traffic.

But I wasn't.

If Cynthia had killed her father, either with or without Gregory Knutson, then who had killed the LeClairs? And why? There was still the undeniable evidence of the gun, the similarity of M.O.s to contend with. The modus operandi could be simple coincidence. It was possible. But the gun was a stumbling block I couldn't jump over or go around. Ballistics was a science; unlike people, it didn't lie.

I drove straight to Knutson's apartment. The old Mercury was gone, the blinds drawn in his front windows. I knocked anyway, once, twice, three times, then kicked the door and headed back to my truck.

Jud Harmon was waiting at the corner of his apartment, teeth gleaming in the early morning sunshine.

"Went to work this morning. First time this week. Musta had a wreck or something. Looked all banged up, like."

"How do you know he was going to work?"

"Had on the coveralls he wears to work, that's how. Had him a sandwich bag when he come out of his place. Reckon that's his lunch. He looked mad as hell, the way he always looks when he goes to work."

"What time was that?"

"Twenty minutes ago. He goes to work at seven."

I thanked him and climbed into my truck, continued on east toward city hall. One more stop to bring Homer up to date, then I was going home, pick up my unhappy wife, and head south to try again. I had some making up to do and, anyhow, it was Homer's problem now.

32

Mitsi's alcove was empty, Selectric neatly covered, desk clean, her small computer terminal dark and silent.

Homer was in his office, leaning back in his chair, one hand holding an open file folder propped on his stomach. He looked up as I came in, looked back at the file, then did an exaggerated double take. He had gone back to bifocals and reflected light turned the thick glass into opaque discs.

"Hey, little buddy! I thought you and Susie was living the good life down in South Texas."

"Was, is right." I plopped down in his visitor's chair and took out my cigarettes. "We got weathered out."

He gave me a disbelieving look. "You kidding? We got a beautiful day shaping up out there."

"Think back to yesterday, Homer, and the day before." I lit a cigarette, blew smoke across the desk at him. "But that's not really why I'm here."

"Never thought it was. You couldn't just drop it, huh?" He smiled crookedly, blue eyes distorted behind the bifocals.

"That's not it at all. I got a call from Maggie Lane last night."

"Maggie Lane. That's the pross." His voice was flat, the broad face suddenly expressionless, and I knew that somewhere along the line he had made the connection between Maggie Lane the hooker and the Maggie Lane I used to know.

"Right. The hooker who corroborated Cynthia Kincade's story about being in Galveston Friday night."

"So?"

"So, she said she lied. She was home . . . working. She has no idea where Cynthia and Knutson were."

He came forward in the chair, his face still unreadable. "That takes us back some, I guess." He stood up and went to a water cooler in the corner. He fished a pill out of his vest pocket and washed it down with a small cup of water. He came back and sat down. "I read your report on her, Dan," he said quietly. "And . . ." He let it fade away.

"And you wondered why I took the word of a hooker?"

He shrugged, looking uncomfortable, not something he did often. "I figured you had your reasons. That was when I remembered the Maggie Lane from the Zero Club."

"The same. I shouldn't have accepted her word as gospel, but I did, and I'm sorry for it."

He shook his head. "My blame as much as yours. I read the reports. I could have questioned it. But I didn't, and the reason I didn't is because you're good with people. You were never wrong much in the old days. I didn't figure that's changed."

"I was wrong about Maggie. People change and I didn't take that into account. As it turns out, Gregory Knutson was her pimp, at least a pimp of sorts. Cynthia was her friend and she was afraid of Knutson and I guess the combination was enough." I stubbed out the cigarette in his big metal ashtray. "There's more to it," I added, and told him about the beating Knutson had given Maggie, about our fracas in Knutson's apartment, Cynthia's telephone call to Maggie, about what I had just learned from Cynthia Kincade.

"You dumbass," he snorted. "Who the hell you think you are, Sir Galahad or something? Fighting over a hooker—"

"She wasn't always a hooker, Homer."

"—and with a guy who could break you in half without half trying."

"He tried his best."

"Dammit, you spook me sometimes, Dan, the fool things you do. You oughta—"

"I oughta killed the son of a bitch."

He grinned. "Yeah, that, too." He slammed a platter-sized hand on the desk top. "Well, by God, better late than never.

Tell you what I'm gonna do, I'm gonna get on the horn here and have little Missy Kincade picked up, her and that rooster-brained pimp of hers—"

"On what charge? Lying? Or fornicating without a license?"

He gave me a startled look. "Hell, no, by God, suspicion of murder."

"I don't know about that. What does that do to our theory of a random killer wandering around the countryside? Two days ago that was the only possible answer as I remember."

"One damn thing at a time, boy. Hell, maybe Knutson killed them all. Maybe he killed Kincade so his girlfriend would inherit the twenty-five thou and then decided he needed some quick cash in the meantime and went in on Tim LeClair."

"Good clean line of thought, but I don't see a lot of evidence backing it up."

"They lied to you, didn't they?"

"If that was a crime, half the people in this town would be in jail."

"Well, what're you getting at? What would you do?"

"Put a man on them. On each of them. Knutson's at work. I just left Cynthia in a kind of funk. I think she'll be there for a while, and it's doubtful if she can get in touch with Knutson at work by phone."

"This ain't Dallas. I ain't got that kind of manpower. Hell, I doubt—"

"It won't be for long. If Knutson is guilty, he'll run the minute Cynthia gets to him. Maybe they both will. If they do, then pick them up."

He stared at me thoughtfully, then let a sly grin crease his face. "Hey, how about you—?"

"Sorry, Homer." I stood up. "I came back today to do what I should have done five days ago. I have a very unhappy wife at home with three more days of vacation. I'm going to spend them making her happy if it gives me lockjaw."

He smiled faintly, reaching for the phone.

I lit another cigarette and listened to him rattle off instructions to Baskin. When it seemed he was about to run down, I eased toward the door, lifting an unseen hand in farewell, getting the hell out of there before he got off the phone and talked me into staying.

"I don't think so, Danny," Susie said coolly, tossing her head to clear a straying clump of hair from her face. "There's too much to do. I have two weeks' wash, and this house hasn't been cleaned in . . . I don't know how long." She reached into the clothes hamper again, came out with a shirt and a frilly silk blouse. She tossed them into separate piles. She was wearing a fuzzy red sweater and black jeans, both new, not her usual attire for working around the house.

I dropped the lid on the commode and sat down, lit a cigarette. "You remember the pact we made right after our first fight? If one of us started acting childish, the other one would—"

"Childish? Is cleaning house and washing clothes childish? They sound like very mature activities to me."

"The activity doesn't matter; it's the mood. Okay, you're pissed off at me, and maybe you have a right to be, but you're punishing yourself as well—"

"Punish?" She gave me an incredulous little laugh. "I can find much better ways of punishing you other than washing your dirty clothes and cleaning your dirty house."

"*My* dirty clothes? *My* dirty house? You live here, too, you know." I almost added "occasionally," but bit it off in time. "And I see quite a few blouses, panties, and slacks in that pile, not to mention them little doohickeys you use to hold up your boobs."

"What?" She straightened and tugged on the red sweater, turning to look in the wall mirror behind the sink. "I don't need anything to hold up—"

"Yeah, you do," I said, and came up behind her with a rush, slipping my hands under her arms, cupping her breasts, burrowing through the mass of hair to nibble on her neck.

She squirmed around to face me, locking her hands behind

my head. "No, you don't, buddy. You think sex is the answer to everything."

"Maybe not, but it can stop a silly argument dead in its tracks."

She sighed. "I don't want to argue, or fight, either. But we do have all of this work to do, and since we're here . . ." She left it hanging, eyebrows raised, a small lopsided smile making it clear what my next words should be.

"Okay. We'll both pitch in. We should be done in plenty of time to drive to the cabin before dark. The weather's turned around, and maybe we'll be able to spend the next two days doing what we wanted to do in the first place."

"Taking walks, fishing, and hunting pecans." She gave me a hug, a passionate kiss.

"No, clearing out the brush around the cabin."

We were finished by twelve o'clock. Clothes washed, dried and folded, the house vacuumed and dusted, kitchen floor mopped. Not exactly spring cleaning, but everything was in its place, spotless and shining, as neat and orderly as the habit of a nun.

Susie made ham and lettuce sandwiches for lunch, a glass of milk for her, a beer for me, a side dish of deep-fried onion rings. She was talkative again, good humor completely restored, eyes sparking with their usual effervescent fire.

I was biting into my second sandwich when the phone rang.

I chewed, swallowed. We looked at each other while it rang a second time.

"Don't answer it," I said. "You're not supposed to be in town and I don't want to talk to anyone."

It rang again; Susie squirmed in her chair. "Danny, it might be—"

It rang again. Before I could stop her, she scrambled to her feet and yanked the receiver off the hook.

"Hello." She glanced at me and made an apologetic grimace.

"Oh, hello, Uncle Homer, how're you doing?" She wriggled her eyebrows and smiled, listened again, laughed. "Oh, you're just saying that because it's true." She laughed, listened, then made another face in my direction. "Uh-huh, he's sitting right here at the table . . . no, not at all, Uncle Homer, nice talking to you . . . I will, you do the same. Good-bye."

She came around the table, the phone cord pulling tight. "Uncle Homer wants to talk to you." She gave me a sheepish smile, her eyes avoiding mine.

"No kidding?"

Still looking at her, I spoke into the receiver. "Too bad, Homer, I've already left."

"Sorry to bother you again, Dan," he said, his voice ponderous and deep, and I felt a faint stirring of unease; he was using his calamity voice, impersonal and portentous, a tone I had heard only a few times before.

"What is it?"

"David Kincade," he said. "He's dead." He paused for a moment, then when I didn't reply, went on. "Shot. Just like the others. Two in the chest, one in the head."

"Dammit!" I said, something sliding in my chest, a tight-fisted hand squeezing my insides. "Dammit, Homer, what's going on?"

"I dunno, son. I wish I did. It's all crazy as hell."

I breathed deeply for a moment, feeling Susie's eyes on my face, unable to think coherently, trying to absorb this latest example of man's inherent absurdity. Finally, I blurted, "Where? When?"

"Right at ten o'clock, we think. Here at his house." He hesitated. "We found one of the slugs. It's a twenty-five caliber. Can't tell for sure, of course, but it looks like it might be the same gun. Baskin's on the way to the lab right now. We'll know in a little while."

"Cynthia," I said slowly, "where was she?"

"At that Cresson Sheet Metal place where Knutson works. I put Chester on her right after we talked this morning. She left about nine-thirty, drove out to Cresson's and met Knutson on his ten o'clock smoke break. They walked out to her car and talked for about ten minutes. He went back to work and she went home. She's the one found her brother. She called the police and when the patrol car got there, Chester went in with them."

"David was supposed to be working."

"He was. He got off at nine o'clock and rode home with one of his co-workers. He got home just as the girl was leaving. They talked for a minute out on the driveway. The girl drove off and David went inside. Chester followed her."

The line hummed emptily while I watched my Cynthia/ Knutson theory disintegrate and blow away. If the gun proved to be the same one used in the other murders, then they were in the clear. Unless, of course, they had brought a third person into the act. But that made no sense at all. There would be no monetary gain from David's death, and it could only result in a more extensive investigation by the police, a second and closer look at everyone concerned. That would be the last thing Cynthia and Knutson would want if, in fact, they had killed Ralph Kincade and the LeClairs. No. The answer lay elsewhere. And elsewhere was starting all over again.

"Dan?" Homer's voice cut into my dismal thoughts.

"You know what this means, Homer?"

"All I know is the girl and Knutson didn't do this one. If they didn't do this one, then I reckon they didn't do the others, either."

"It also blows your serial killer theory right out of the saddle."

"*My* theory? If I know anything about it, you and Ted Baskin both were—"

"Okay, our theory. I never heard of a serial killer circling back after almost a week and killing another member of the same family."

"Don't mean it couldn't happen," he rumbled, then harshly cleared his throat. "I might be inclined to argue with you about that if it wasn't for—hold on a minute." I could faintly hear him talking to someone nearby, a nasal voice responding. Chester?

I lit a cigarette and looked at Susie. She was staring out the bay window, arms stretched on the table before her, hands clasped, a bemused expression on her face, a cynical lift to the edges of her mouth.

"Hold on, sugar, this won't take much longer."

She cut her eyes at me, let the tilt to her lips grow into a cynical smile. "Uh-huh," she said, and went back to looking out the window.

Homer came back on. "Dan? There's some funny things about this one I think you ought to see. Don't make any sense to me. Think you could take a quick run over—"

"Dammit, Homer, we're getting ready to go back to the cabin. What kind of things?"

"Evidential things. I can't go blabbing them over the phone. No telling who might be listening."

"That's a crock, Homer. This isn't a party line—"

"It is over here. Ain't you been hearing them clicks? We've got an audience, buddy."

"I can't," I said, realizing there was no conviction in my voice, seeing Susie in my peripheral vision, standing up, coming around the table, taking the phone out of my hand.

"Uncle Homer? He'll be there in a few minutes." She hung up the receiver, bent down and brushed her lips across my cheek.

"Go," she said, and swept out of the room before I could get a look at her face.

34

They had removed the body, for which I was duly thankful, but the yellow chalked outline on the garish rug was still a grisly reminder, enough to send a chill across the back of my neck, a tightening in my throat.

Homer was there, and Ted Baskin was back from the lab. Chester and two patrolmen were out talking to the neighbors, and two of Baskin's tech squad were wrapping up their operation, preparing to leave.

The small logs in the fireplace had burned through in the middle and collapsed into the ashes, sending up an occasional tendril of smoke, a snapping spark, quickly extinguished; the smell of wood smoke still saturated the air.

We stood over the chalked outline, almost unrecognizable as a human form except for one outflung arm and the roundness of the head. It lay eighteen inches or so to the left of the over-stuffed chair I had used on my visits, next to an unpainted magazine rack that looked exactly like one I had made in a high school woodworking class. An open magazine lay near the tip of the outflung arm. I bent down to get a closer look.

"That's the cable TV log," Homer said. "That's one of the things I was talking about. Looks to me like he was maybe trying to tell us something, but if he was, we sure as hell ain't getting the message. Go ahead, pick it up. It's been photographed and dusted, and anyhow, we think he crawled over here and got it out of the rack after the killer left."

"Why?"

"You can't see it too clearly with all the wild colors in this rug, but look over there by the TV. There's a big spot of blood. That's where he was shot. That's where I found the bullet in the rug. It was from the shot in the head. It hit at a bad angle, followed the skull around under the skin and came out near his right temple. By the way, it was from the same gun as the others." Baskin looked at Homer, then back at me, his freckled face grim. "Perfect match, no mistake."

I nodded, following with my eyes the irregular smears of blood that went from the plate-sized spot in front of the TV toward the chair. A slightly larger smear, as if he might have stopped, then the trail veered off to the left, led directly to the chalked outline beside the magazine rack. I began to understand what Homer had meant.

"His first thought was probably the phone in the kitchen," I said. "But it was too far and maybe he realized he wouldn't be able to pull himself up to reach it. So he changed direction."

"That's what I mean," Homer growled. "He went for the rack, the TV log. He took it out of the rack—"

"How do you know that? Maybe it was already on the floor."

Homer shook his shaggy head impatiently. "No. The sister said it was in the rack. They always kept it there. Anyhow, she remembers putting it in there when she straightened up the room this morning, not long before she left to go see her boyfriend out at Cresson's."

"Maybe David watched TV after he got home," I suggested, a halfhearted attempt at devil's advocacy.

"It wasn't on when the girl found him," Homer said, raking a heavy hand across his face, a gesture of frustration. I was covering much the same ground he had already been over and he was impatient to get to the meat of the subject. "For the sake of argument, let's just say the damn thing was in the rack. Okay? He crawled over here deliberately, took it out of the rack, and turned it back to last Saturday—"

"Last Saturday?" I felt a tiny rill of something that could have been excitement—either that or a bubble of gas from the onion rings. I bent down and picked up the magazine. Homer was right. It had been opened to the previous Saturday, the pages clumsily folded back, heavily smeared with blood. The Saturday page was relatively clean, one thumbprint near the edge, a two-inch streak of blood across the middle of the page. Neat and precise compared to the other stains, it was a half inch wide and drawn across the seven o'clock listings for Saturday night.

I looked up. Homer and Baskin were watching me expectantly. "Was one of his hands, probably his left, smeared with blood?"

They nodded in unison. "His right hand was lying on top of the TV log," Homer said. "Looks like he dipped his forefinger in blood to make that mark. I think it was deliberate." He looked at Baskin. "Ted here thinks it might've been an accident."

Baskin shrugged. "Ain't no way of telling for sure."

Homer stirred restlessly. "Let's assume he did it on purpose. Whatta you think, Dan?"

I looked down at the magazine. Seven o'clock was movie time on the local cable franchise. Four movies were listed in tiny boldface print, within the smear of blood from David Kincade's finger. I read them aloud: *"Johnny Dangerously, The Karate Kid, Strangers on a Train, The Spirit of St. Louis."*

"Two new ones and two old ones," Baskin said. "I don't remember seeing the old ones, and the new ones don't tell me a damn thing." He cut his eyes sidewise at Homer.

"I've seen *Spirit of St. Louis,*" Homer said. "Jimmy Stewart playing Charles Lindbergh flying the Atlantic." He looked at me. "How about you? They tell you anything?"

"I remember *Spirit of St. Louis,*" I said. "And I saw the last half of *Strangers on a Train* the other night—"

"Stranger," Baskin said, his speckled face lighting up. "Maybe he was trying to tell us the killer was a stranger."

"Hey," Homer said. "That could be it, by God."

"It's possible," I said slowly. "He and I were talking about stranger murders the other night." I went on to tell them about David's two visits to my house, the gist of our conversations.

"Trying to protect his mama," Homer said. "I can't fault him too much for that."

"What a damned waste," Baskin said. He was standing in

front of the mantel, one of David's trophies in his hands, staring up at the family portrait. "He was a good kid. My boy, Rick, said everybody liked him, even the girls he went through like a dose of salts."

Homer grunted. "What the hell does that mean?"

Baskin carefully placed the trophy on the mantel. "It means he played the field. His senior class at Trinity Valley High had about two hundred girls. Rick said he seemed to be trying to work his way through all of them." He turned away from the mantel, smiling bleakly. "That's probably an exaggeration, of course, but Rick says David was with a different girl just about every time he saw him around. But I guess that's not too hard to figure. He was a handsome kid, a lot of charm, a terrific athlete—" He broke off and looked up at the portrait again. "Looks like the only thing he didn't have was a stable family life; his father a runaway, his sister a hooker."

"Cut it out," Homer said mildly, "before you get us all to crying. Tell Dan about the stuff you found." He looked at me. "This is the rest of what I meant about strange things."

Baskin shrugged. "I don't know. I've had time to think about it a little more, and I believe all those things are just mementos from some of David's conquests."

"Bullshit, Ted! Why would he hide them like he did? And what about the mask?"

Baskin shrugged again. "To keep his mother from seeing them, I suppose. After all, they aren't the kind of things a boy could keep in his bureau drawer."

"You guys mind telling me what the hell you're talking about?"

"Women's drawers," Homer growled. "And bracelets and rings and gold chains, even a couple of bras. He had them hid in a metal box under the floor of his closet, down in the entrance hole to the crawl space under the house."

"It was his hiding place," Baskin said. "He had some pornography down there, too."

"That don't mean anything," Homer said. "Every kid his age has a little porno lying around. How about the mask?" His eyes gleamed as he and Baskin exchanged glances. I had a sudden feeling that I was a spectator to some unfathomable private contest.

Baskin tugged the lobe of his left ear. "That's a little harder to figure. It's a good-quality mask, like you might get if you rented a Batman costume for a party or—"

"Batman?" Something stirred in my mind, surfaced, and sank without a ripple.

"Yeah, kinda like Batman. It's hard to tell. It's a cowl, sort of, with little ears. Covers the head down to the shoulders in back and just above the mouth in front. It has eyeholes, of course, and looks like it'd leave the mouth and jaws visible. Could be a kid's Halloween mask, but it'd be pretty expensive for that."

"Batman," Homer said, baring his teeth at me in a wolfish grin. "That mean anything to you, Dan?"

I stared at him, the blip of thought returning, skittering away, but this time not quickly enough. "Yeah, there's a man, a rapist they call Batman—"

"Exactly," Homer said. He glanced at Baskin, then back at me. "You knew him better than we did. You think David was capable of something like that? We talked about this some before you got here. Ted here don't think so, what with all David's amorous conquests at school. I say that wouldn't make a damn bit of difference if he liked to rape. The one thing don't have anything to do with the other. Rape is an assault, an act of rage, aggression; the sex is only a means to that end." He looked at me and brought back the smile. "I read a book about it once. What do you think?"

I shrugged and took out my cigarettes, vaguely annoyed. "I'd say there's no point in arguing about it. It should be easy enough to prove or disprove. Somewhere in your organization there must be a list of items taken by the rapist, if, in fact, he did take things. A simple comparison should do it. If that fails, there are plenty of pictures around here of David. I'd think some of the victims would remember a physique like his."

"Gee whiz," Homer said, the grin widening. "Why didn't I think of that?"

"Posey's on his way over to the lab," Baskin said, his face carefully neutral. "As it happens, there is a list of things taken by the Batman rapist. We'll know pretty quick if it matches what we got." He frowned. "Seems to me, though, that the description I heard made the Batman taller and thinner . . . and dark-haired."

I lit a cigarette and crossed to the door.

"Where you going?" Homer asked, his voice querulous, edged with belligerence, his normal reaction when a situation wasn't developing the way he wanted it to.

"Home," I said succinctly. "Where I belong. You got me over here under false pretenses, Homer. You don't need me on this. You put on that dumb act of yours, and all the time you were already doing what had to be done."

"I thought you might know what he was trying to tell us," he said, his tone aggrieved, the blue eyes gleaming, distorted behind the bifocals.

"Maybe you did, but that's not the real reason you got me over here. You thought I'd get hooked back into this mess of yours, mainly because you knew I liked this kid David. It's not going to work, buddy. I've got problems of my own, not the least of which is making it up to Susie for dragging her off the only vacation she's had in a year. I don't know any more than you do if David was trying to tell us something. He was dying, maybe out of his head with pain and delirium. He might not have known what the hell he was doing. At any rate, it's no longer my problem."

I opened the door and went out, crossed the porch and walked down the driveway. I flipped the cigarette butt in a vicious arc toward the street, torn by doubt and a smattering of self-disgust. My reaction to Homer's small subterfuge had been disproportionate to the crime. He was floundering and desperately trying to catch a killer. He knew the percentages of unsolved murders better than most, and I knew that deep down inside the knowledge that the killer might well get away with it would be gnawing at his guts.

35

Susie was gone when I got home. The house was empty but not silent: she had left the radio in the kitchen playing, wailing country music that did nothing to stem my rising sense of dread as I plucked the note from under the bilious green frog:

Danny:

Janey Petroski called, and since it is 2:30 and we obviously aren't going to make it to the cabin today, I've accepted her invitation to go shopping. We may have a bite to eat and go to a movie later on. Don't worry if I'm late.

Susan

Despite the crisp coolness of the note, I read it with a feeling of relief. At least she would be home later, hopefully in a better frame of mind. We still had two days, maybe three, since it would be unconscionable of Sy Deacon to demand that she return to work on Sunday. After all, Sunday was the proverbial day of rest, news or no news.

I opened a bottle of Miller and found a seat at the kitchen table. I lit a cigarette and opened the drapes, feeling relaxed and at ease for the first time that day, forcing all thoughts of human folly to the back of my mind, searching the foliage of the oak trees for signs of my resident squirrels, looking for the peace of mind that watching them always brought.

They were there, three of them as usual, going about their preparations for winter with a singlemindedness of purpose that I found fascinating, scouring the lawn for fallen acorns, a few nuts from my solitary pecan, zipping up and down the tree trunks with a deftness, grace, and precision equaled by no other living creature.

One of them had no tail: a natural bobtail, or, more likely, the victim of a marauding old buck raiding the nests, eliminating future competition by biting off the tiny baby nuts, in this case taking off too much, or grabbing the wrong thing. At any rate, bobtail had come out of the nest that way, a tiny hopping figure that I had at first mistaken for a baby rabbit.

Despite expert opinions to the contrary, the absence of the bushy appendage seemed to present no problem. He was at least as fast as his nest mates, skimming through the trees right along with the best of them, soaring from limb to limb with no apparent difficulty. Maybe he just tried harder.

I was down to the dregs of my beer, lighting my second cigarette, when the phone rang.

I thought about not answering it, leaving it for the machine to pick up on the fourth ring. But a moment later I decided it might be Susie having second thoughts about dinner and the movie, feeling guilty over her curt message, worrying about me being out there in a world of murderers.

"Hello."

"Dan. This is Ted. Hey, man, I just wanted to make sure that you aren't sore at me over—you know it was all Homer's idea, don't you?"

"Yeah, Ted, I know. Actually, I'm not mad at Homer, either."

"Well, you looked pretty well pissed off when you left, and old Homer stomped out of here looking like he just stepped in something smelly." He tried a halfhearted chuckle.

"He'll get over it."

"Yeah, well, okay." He paused. I could hear a deep intake of breath. "By the way, I just got a call from Babbitt—he's that chunky guy who works in my lab—and he said that metal box of David Kincade's, the one with the mask and things in it— well, it had been wiped clean. Not a fingerprint on it. Don't that seem funny to you?"

"Odd," I said.

"Yeah, odd. And he said he found some hairs inside the

mask, four or five hairs caught in the seams. The thing is, they're dark hairs, black hairs, not blond like the Kincade boy's. They're from a young male Caucasian, all right, but I don't see how they could be David's."

"That's even odder," I said, suddenly overwhelmingly weary of it all, determined not to let myself get sucked back into it, not even to the extent of fruitless speculation. "Ted—"

"One more thing," he said, breaking in hastily. "Posey's list checked out with the stuff in the box . . . but he said no way could David Kincade be his Batman rapist. He said his man was taller, thinner, and they've already confirmed that he has dark hair. They've also got a blood type of A negative, and according to the autopsy report, David's blood type is O positive. What do you think of that?"

"Odd," I said, and left it at that, let the silence grow.

He laughed. "Okay, I get the message. I just thought you might find it interesting, is all, considering all the work you've done on the case—"

"Thanks, Ted. I appreciate your thoughtfulness, okay? And tell Homer, who is probably standing right there beside you, that I said no sale." I hung up right in the middle of his braying laugh.

I opened another beer, sat back down at the table, and looked for my furry little friends. They were there, still doing their thing, but it wasn't the same. Somehow the spell had been broken, the magic gone; they were just three squirrels doing what squirrels do in the fall.

Besides, something had been added. Another ingredient, another dimension. Dark and silent and brooding, images of Ralph and David Kincade haunted the edges of my mind, as unobtrusive as distant clouds, as insistently nagging as ancestral fear.

Who had killed them, and why?

Who had killed Timothy and Julie LeClair, and why?

Was there a connection beyond the instrument of death?

Those basic questions remained intact, as far from resolution as ever. David's death had done nothing to clear away the murky shroud that cloaked all four deaths, dense and impenetrable.

Or had it? Had David, in fact, been trying to tell us something with his bloody finger mark on the TV log? If so, who had the message been meant for? Me? Or had the mark resulted from the spasmodic twitch of a dying hand? And, if not, what in hell could his message have been? I had seen all of the movies at one time or other. *Johnny Dangerously*, a so-called comic spoof of the gangster era, *The Karate Kid*, an innocuous tale about a ninety-pound weakling fighting back. Nothing there that meant anything to me, nothing that could correlate with the murder of an eighteen-year-old boy.

The Spirit of St. Louis I remembered only parts of—Lindbergh flying the Atlantic. Nobody murdered, a happy ending.

Strangers on a Train. Another old one. A murder mystery from what little I had seen of the last half, between dozing off and trips to the refrigerator and the bathroom, and interruptions by David—

I straightened slowly.

An interruption by David. He had come to the door at about the same time the movie began. I had missed the first part because of his visit—he had even commented on it, apologized for causing me to miss it, added that it was a good movie, a good plot, good acting.

Was it possible he had remembered that when he was dying? That he was telling me—what? What, goddammit? Could Baskin be right? Was *stranger* the key word, the message he was trying to convey, that he was being murdered by a stranger?

I pondered that for a moment, then slowly shook my head. Too tenuous, too much. The long crawl to the magazine rack must have been unbelievably painful, a monumental task for a dying boy, too much effort without a definite purpose. What?

On the other hand, if he knew the name of his killer, why hadn't he simply written it in blood? There had been plenty of blood, and he had obviously lived several minutes after the killer left.

The answer to that came blowing in on the tailwind of the

question: the long-napped, wine-and-black carpet would have resisted any attempts at legible writing, as would the soft, nubby, rust-colored covering of the couch. The face of the TV would have been the only logical place to leave a message, but it had probably been behind him, out of sight, out of mind, and anyway, it was probable that his first thought had been the telephone, a cry for help.

So, it was conceivable he had started for the telephone, decided he wasn't going to last long enough to make it, veered left to the magazine rack instead as an alternate plan took shape in his mind. It must have required a tremendous concentration of his waning strength, I thought, but wasn't that what it meant to be a great athlete, the ability to focus your powers, to draw on inner reserves you didn't know you had?

My head was whirling. Pure speculation. Conjecture. And I hadn't the faintest notion if any of it was valid. For days I had thought of little else and it had all come down to zilch.

I got up and paced the length of the kitchen, came back to my seat and plopped down, staring out into the slowly gathering twilight.

Maybe not. Maybe I knew more than I thought.

I got up again, slipped the phone receiver off the wall and sat back down. I dialed Ted Baskin's office number.

"Baskin."

"Ted. This is just a suggestion, mind you, and you don't have to bother calling me back, but you may want to check the juvenile record on David Kincade. Mitsi told me there was one. Okay? And you may want to check—maybe with the cable TV company—and see what the movie *Strangers on a Train* is all about. I know it was a murder story of some sort, but I didn't see enough to make any sense of it. Who knows? Maybe one of the character's names will tell you something. David saw it and liked it. He told me as much. We talked about it a bit. I don't know, these are just wild swings in the dark and probably won't amount to a fart in the wind."

He chuckled. "No wilder than what Homer's doing. Him and Chester just left here for the LeClair place. There was a pair of panty hose in David's box, and Homer's going to see if the boy or the mother can identify it as the girl Julie's. Man, all them panty hoses look exactly alike to me."

"Yeah, I guess, except for color."

"Thanks, Dan. Couple of good ideas there. I'll let you know—"

"No need for that." But there was no conviction in my voice and he just laughed and broke the connection.

36

Hard on the heels of sunset, darkness came swiftly, shrouding the trees in my yard with spectral solemnity, driving my furry friends into their leafy homes high in the upper foliage with flipping tails and chattering voices.

I turned off the radio and the sudden silence reverberated inside my head, echoing throughout the quiet house like muted thunder over distant hills. I felt isolated, suspended in time, the glow from my cigarette the only light in the universe, the thudding of my heart the only sound.

I felt strangely sad, inordinately guilty, a not uncommon reaction of mine to failure, and once again I wondered if maybe I shouldn't have chosen a saner occupation, one that had nothing to do with people—a desert prospector, a mountaintop ascetic contemplating the folly of man.

"Maybe in my next life," I said, speaking aloud just to shatter the silence, going into the den and flipping on the TV for the same reason.

I kicked off my boots and waited patiently for the six o'clock news, dreading it at the same time. There would be pictures once again of the Kincade house on Murray Street, pictures of David Kincade, a thirty-second accounting of the accomplishments of his young life, a requiem without regret delivered in curt, impersonal tones, the media doing its thing with sophistication and verve, fulfilling the people's right to know.

It came ten minutes and two commercials into the broadcast, no better or worse than I had expected, pictures of David's smiling face in a graduation cap and gown, his splendid body suspended between two iron rings, caught in graceful flight at the apogee of his parallel bar dismount. I closed my eyes and drank half my new beer.

The anchorwoman was crisply detailing the skimpy details of his demise when the doorbell began its melodic chiming.

I padded to the door in my sock feet.

Probably one of my neighbors wanting to borrow a cup of sugar, I thought, or maybe the paper boy collecting, some damned salesman ignoring the NO SOLICITORS sign, or some beautiful female admirer unable to stay away any longer. . . .

But I was wrong. Paul LeClair stood there, handsome as always, his smile ingratiating, his tall slender body impeccably adorned in a powder-blue suit that had never seen a price tag or a clothing store rack.

While I watched, the smile spread into an apologetic grimace, the dark eyes limpid and shining, as innocent as a puppy who has just pissed on your best pair of Justin boots.

"Mr. Roman, I, uh, I just wanted to come by and apologize for . . . well, I acted like a . . . a—"

"Arrogant prick," I said.

The winning smile flashed again. "Yes, that says it nicely. I'm very sorry and . . . and I wonder if I might speak to you for a moment?"

"Sure. Come on in. I'll even let you use the front entrance."

He tried out a halfhearted laugh as he went by me. "I deserve that, I suppose. I got a little carried away the other day. I'd like for you to forget it, if you would."

"Sure," I said, closing the door, waving him into the den. "It's all forgotten. Find yourself a seat, Mr. LeClair."

He turned in the middle of the floor. "Please, that isn't necessary. My name is Paul. Everybody calls me Paul."

"Except the hired help," I almost said, but stopped it in time. "Okay, Paul, you can call me Mr. Roman."

He laughed, a genuine laugh that lit up his handsome face in an extraordinary way and made me wonder what my reaction to him would be if I had happened to be a woman.

"Just kidding," I said. "Call me Dan."

He sat down on the couch, on the edge in much the same way that David Kincade had done. "I called the police department trying to get your phone number and they referred me to Captain Sellers' office. The lady there wouldn't give it to me, or your address, but she did tell me that you were in the phone book and that you were actually a private investigator." He hesitated, an uncertain look crossing his face. "Is that true?"

"It is."

"I see." He scooted back on the couch and crossed his long legs. "If that's the case, then I'd like to hire you."

"To do what?"

"To work for me."

"I understand that part. What I don't understand is what you want me to do."

"I want you to find my Uncle Robert."

I stared at him, a little off balance. "Your Uncle Robert?" I echoed. "The one who's been gone for fifteen years?"

"Yes."

"Why?"

"Several reasons. Primarily because I know nothing about running my grandfather's business and I need someone I can trust to take charge."

"He ran away from the business once, what makes you think he'd want to have anything to do with it now?"

"Things have changed. My grandfather's dead. Uncle Robert would have a free hand. Then, of course, there's the matter of his inheritance. He'll have to be located in any event. Grandfather left him a substantial sum."

"Fifteen years. It may be too long. Different name, a different life. He could be dead, could be a wino, could be in jail or in another country."

He nodded patiently. "Nevertheless, I'd like to try. You do find missing people, don't you?"

I studied his quiet, passive face. "Sometimes," I said, wondering if he could be as naive as he seemed.

"I'll give you five thousand dollars." He slid forward to the edge of the couch again, delved into his inside coat pocket, and came out with a small slip of paper. "I've already made out the check." He rose and quickly crossed the distance between us, laid the piece of paper on the arm of my chair. "That's just to go to work for me. I'll give you another five thousand when you find him." He went on quickly. "There's no big hurry. You can continue working with the police on my sister's murder, but perhaps you could go ahead part-time on my uncle's case. I'd expect you to keep me up-to-date on both cases, of course." He paused, his eyes bright.

"In other words, you want me to be a spy in the enemy camp." I tried to remember the last time someone had tried to bribe me.

"They are not the enemy camp." His lips had a petulant twist. "You're making more of this than there is. I—my family has a right to know what's going on and the police won't tell us anything."

"Maybe there's nothing to tell."

He nodded vigorously. "That's the kind of thing I want to know."

"I've never been a spy," I said, scratching my head. "It sounds risky. Not to mention illegal."

"That's why I'm paying you so much." He stopped and wet his lips.

I poked at the check with a cautious finger. "That's a lot of money, all right, but—" I broke off; the phone was ringing.

"Excuse me," I said courteously. With that much money on the table, the least I could do was be polite until I sent his ass packing. I went into the kitchen and snapped up the receiver.

"Dan? I know you said I didn't have to call you back but . . . well, anyway, since the Kincade boy is dead, I had no problem getting into his file. Seems he was involved in a near-rape back when he was fourteen, about four years ago."

"What does that mean, near-rape?"

"Well, it seems he and his girlfriend were nude-wrestling on the couch at her house one night, and the girl's old man came home and caught them. The girl saw him first and started yelling rape. That was David's story, anyway. I guess the judge must have believed him, at least partially, 'cause he gave him a probated sentence on condition he go to the Juvenile Rehabilitation Center for counseling. I think they considered it an attempted rape more than anything else. The girl's old man was a city councilman. Hadn't been for that it probably wouldn't have amounted to anything."

"I see. I take it this counseling is done by doctors. Does it give the name of David's?" A gossamer thread of thought wafted by, as fragile as an old spiderweb, as delicate as a baby's sigh.

"Yeah. Doctor named Alvin Buglemann. He's a volunteer. The center is staffed by volunteers although they hold the sessions on city property." He stopped and cleared his throat. I heard the rasp of his breath. "One more thing. That movie *Strangers on a Train*? I went over and talked to Fred Schinndarten in R and I. You remember him? An old movie buff. He remembered it right off, gave me a thumbnail synopsis . . . if you want to hear it."

"Sure, go ahead." I fished out a cigarette and lit it, then craned my neck to look at Paul in the den. He was watching the TV, sitting on the edge of the couch again, coat unbuttoned, long arms dangling between his knees, his right hand cupped loosely in his left. He looked at me; I made a vague gesture of apology and held up one finger. He nodded, his eyes in shadow, head tilted as if listening to the silent voices on the TV screen, or Ted's voice coming over the line.

"It's been a long time since Fred saw it, and he couldn't remember any of the characters' names, but it was about two men who meet on a train, strike up a conversation, booze it up a little. Well, to make it short, they end up finding out that each one of them has someone—a wife, a father—he would like to get rid of—he don't remember both reasons, but one of them had to do with an inheritance. So, anyway, they make this pact, see? They decide they'll trade murders—"

Trade murders.

"—timing it just right so each one will be able to set up a perfect alibi while the murder is taking place at his house—"

Perfect alibi.

"—and that way they won't be suspected. One of them is rich, and he promises the poor guy a lot of money when he gets his inheritance—"

Rich man, poor man.

"—well, it goes on like that and one of them does a murder, but, of course, something happens to screw it all up for them and justice prevails in the end." He ended with a hollow little laugh. "Things sure work out great in the movies, don't they?"

"How does it go? Life imitates art?" I could hear my voice but it seemed far away, disconnected from reality, flowing like warm honey and filled with an infinite languor. I looked at my hand gripping the phone. The hair seemed to be standing straight up above my knuckles, the palm sweaty against the smooth hard plastic. I looked at Paul LeClair. He was staring straight into the fireplace, as still as stone.

Ted made the laughing sound again, more uncertain than humorous.

"Well, I won't keep you—hey, Dan, are you okay?"

"I have to go now," I said. I hung up the receiver and took a deep breath. The air was heavy, a sickly sweet taste on the back of my tongue.

I got up and went back into the den. My beer was lukewarm, but I drank some just the same. It was flat, brackish, little better than the taste already in my mouth.

"You like beer, Paul?"

"Not much. Thanks, anyway."

"I wasn't going to offer you one," I said, grinning at him. "I just wondered if you drank it. Speaking of wondering, I'm still wondering about the disposition of your rape case."

He shrugged, smiled easily. "Nothing, really. I had to go to some stupid group counseling sessions for a while—"

"At the Juvenile Rehab Center," I said.

He blinked slowly, a mocking glint coming into his eyes. "Yes, that's right. So you did see my records, after all."

"Just a good guess. Doctor's name was Buglemann, I'll wager."

"Yes, it was. He handles all the so-called rape offenders."

"It's funny," I said.

His eyebrows shot upward, propelled by indignation. "I don't see anything funny about it."

"It's funny that you didn't meet David Kincade. He also attended Dr. Buglemann's group counseling sessions at about the same time you were going. Isn't that funny?"

Paul's smooth forehead wrinkled, brows bunching above dark, intense eyes. "I've been thinking about that—about knowing someone named Kincade. There was a boy named David there. We didn't know anyone else's last name, you know. A short boy, very muscular, blond."

"I see," I said, and finally I did see—clearly, painfully, the idea flowering hotly in my mind, bringing a warm, queasy slide to my midsection.

It wasn't a blinding revelation with crashing cymbals and French horns, but, rather, a dark gruesome tapestry unfolding, synaptic switches clicking soundlessly in my brain, pieces tumbling into place with the crisp precision of a domino-fall: *perfect alibis, connections, arrogant impatient youth, murder by proxy.*

I thought fleetingly of the .38 Smith & Wesson Airweight hanging in the entryway closet. But only fleetingly. He wasn't armed. The faultless lines of the tailored suit would have revealed the bulge of a gun at once. Observation told me that; deductive reasoning told me he had come not to kill, but to buy, to dazzle me with brilliant subterfuge, to blind me with his greenbacks.

"Why did David want you to kill his father?" I asked, dashing past the point of no return with reckless abandon, one tiny ripple of doubt fluttering in my stomach, dissolving in the silent wind of budding knowledge.

37

Maybe he had steeled himself for the moment if it ever came, practiced what he would do, how he would react, what he would say. But I doubted it. I had a feeling I was watching total control, the kind of control I had always wanted and never quite attained, the kind of control an executioner would need to flip a lever or push a needle into a vein.

Nothing happened. He brought forth a sheepish smile. He shrugged and dipped his head like a small boy with dirt on his best Sunday suit, his skin slowly darkening, a subtle transformation taking place in his face. The sheepish smile slipped away, eyes brightening, suddenly predatory. His left hand twitched in a gesture of careless acquiescence.

He also made a gesture with his dangling right hand and revealed a gun. A small gun, to be sure, an automatic with gleaming pearl handles, a .22 or, after I thought about it for a second, more likely a .25.

He let it slip from his palm to his fingers, pointed it at me. So much for observation and deductive reasoning, I thought, and something constricted in my chest.

He nodded as if he had read my mind. "This is it. It's the only gun we had. It used to be my grandfather's. He carried it on business trips. I think that's ironic, don't you?"

"More sad than ironic," I said. "Answer my question, please. Why did David want his father killed?"

"Since you asked so nicely." His features changed form, became sardonic. "David's father was going to put David in prison. To protect David from himself, to protect society from David. David's father was a loser, Mr. Roman. He called from California and told David he was coming home, that leaving had been wrong, that he and David would have to stand up to what David had done, go to the authorities—" He broke off and made a liquid hawking sound of disgust. "He was a stupid, stupid man. They would have thrown David in prison for fifty years."

"That's a long time," I said. "What did he do?"

"David called me. He was in a panic. We met on Thursday night and talked it over. We decided there was only one way out. We made another trade. His father for my grandfather."

"That sounds fair. What do you mean, 'another trade'?"

His face tightened. "Everybody dies, Mr. Roman. My grandfather had lived long past his time. He was making life unendurable for all of us. He had no right to do that. Mr. Kincade was going to ruin the lives of three people. He had become a zealot, a fanatic—"

"I don't believe it. I spent two days and a night with Ralph Kincade. He drank like a fish, swore like a stevedore, and tried his damnedest to fornicate with a waitress—"

"Not a religious zealot, Mr. Roman, although he might have ended up that way eventually. I didn't know the man, but I did know David. Mr. Kincade ran away because he couldn't face what David was doing, couldn't face what his daughter had become. He was essentially a weak man, a sick man in his own way. And David was smart enough to know there's nothing more destructive than a weak man who suddenly believes he has grown strong."

"What do you mean, 'what David was doing'?"

"I think you know by now that David was a rapist." He smiled thinly and let the hand with the gun settle to his knee.

"You mean the Batman," I said, treating him to my own meager smile. "That was a mistake, Paul. You can't pin that on David. They have a description of the Batman: a tall thin young man with black hair. They have some hair from his head. They have a blood type, A negative. Who do we know who fits that description?"

His face paled, but the expression didn't change. He shrugged narrow shoulders. "Everyone is entitled to one mistake. We'll let that be mine. But that doesn't alter the fact that David was still a rapist. He worked my end of town, and I worked his. I visited his ex-girlfriends, and he visited mine. We made selections for each other, aided each other by making diagrams of each girl's house, making impressions of their house keys wherever possible. In most cases it was ridiculously easy to do. They are a lot like sheep. You tell them they're pretty and you love them and they'll trust you with their life. In the end they think only of themselves, their vanity, their needs. We only punished the ones who deserved it, Mr. Roman. It began with the two lying bitches who got us into trouble. I punished his and he punished mine. It—well, it sort of grew out of that."

"Punished, huh? And you and David were jury, judge and executioner all rolled into two."

His upper lip curled a tiny bit; he flipped his shoulder again—his way of giving the world the finger, his metaphor for life. "That's it exactly. They were tramps, all of the ones we visited. There were no virgins among them." He hesitated, wet his lips, then formed an almost shy expression. "Why don't you ask me why I had David kill my grandfather, Mr. Roman?"

"Okay, why did you have David kill your grandfather? As if I didn't know."

"It wasn't for the money, if that's what you mean. He was stifling me, forcing me to stay here and study accounting when my only interest in life is music."

"And raping teenage girls."

His head bobbed angrily. "No, no! You are deliberately—you are far from stupid, Mr. Roman. I'm sure you can see what my grandfather and Ralph Kincade were doing to us. David was good; he had a real shot at the Olympics, but he could never have made it sacking groceries in his free time. He needed time to practice his routines, improve on them. I was going to help him with money, free up his time, get him the best coach available." He stopped and wet his lips, breathing deeply. "I, too, am good at what I do, but I need the best teachers to be the best. That means New York—"

"Then why lie about the money? You need money to live in New York, lots of money. Especially to live in the style you're accustomed to."

He shrugged. "Money is easy to come by."

"Bullshit. From what I heard your grandfather had a habit of cutting off your cash flow when you got a little too frisky."

He didn't answer, his features forbiddingly still, sullen. He made an angry, petulant gesture. "He was a mean-spirited, tightfisted old man. Ever since I can remember. He drove my father to his death with his harping and nagging, watching every business move he made, complaining all the time. I've hated him for as long as I can remember. Even as a small boy I hoped he would die." His words were harsh and venomous, wrung from some deep well of hate I couldn't imagine. He lapsed into silence, face composed again, eyes trained on me, cold and glittering. "It was time for him to die."

I felt a sliding thrill of fear. I made myself smile, hoping it looked more natural than it felt.

"Young, handsome, talented. Both of you. I'm sure there were a lot of girls interested in you—I know there were in David's case. Why rape? And don't give me any of that punish bullshit. You're not the avenging angel type."

"If you don't know," he said seriously, "I'm not sure I can explain it. You're right, there were a lot of girls and they were easy. Perhaps too easy, too available, no contest." He stopped and wet his lips again, eyelids lowered across the bright eyes. "Easy. Yes. And yet each of them had their silly little games, their ego rituals, their own particular mating dance. It grows tiresome after a while, empty, meaningless. You want to crash through all that to the sex—that's what it's all about, after all. But you can't do that. If you do, you end up in juvenile court or something worse. I found that out, as you know." He barked a short, humorless laugh and sucked in his breath. "It's the

challenge . . . the power rush. They can't tell you to stop or to
. . . or when to do it, or for how long, or what to do. They have
to do what you want them to do and . . . and they're eager to
do it because they're at your mercy and they know it and
they're scared . . . God, are they scared! You can smell—"

"I think I've got it," I said, interrupting the flow of words that
had reached the point of babbling, his eyes too shiny, his voice
too high, power-tripping right there in front of me. "You mean
it was all some kind of goddamned game?"

He shot me a challenging look. "A game? Yes, a game with
the highest stakes there are. Risking money is one thing, risking your freedom . . . that's something else entirely. It takes
guts and nerves of steel."

"And someone else's pain."

We looked at each other in silence. He was breathing hard,
through his mouth. He swallowed. "David felt the same way,"
he said, as if to share the load, to spread the evil and somehow
make it better. "He was the one they called the Creeper."

"Why did you kill David?"

A shadow crossed his face, a ripple of pain or a spasm of
hatred. It wasn't clear enough to determine which.

"He killed my sister. Even though he knew I loved her. He
lost control and killed her like a stray dog in his garden. I admired David for his control; usually it was even better than
mine. That's one of the things that brought us together, made
us friends. We knew the same truths, loved the same music,
admired the same people and, for the most part, had the same
dream. We differed in one essential way: I have conquered fear,
he hadn't. He went there to kill my grandfather. And he did,
just as planned. Then my sister came home. He was at Grandfather's safe, taking the money—as planned. She came into the
room, saw Grandfather lying on the desk and screamed. Then
she turned and ran." He paused, staring at the figures scrambling across the silent TV screen. "Maybe if she hadn't run . . .
David chased her, caught her at the top of the stairs. By then
he had lost all control. He let fear rule him. He said no, but I
think he meant to restore control by raping her. Being in

charge, that was always the important thing to David. She broke free and ran down the steps. He caught her again near the bottom, shot her twice with my grandfather's gun. Then, filled with rage, at her, at himself, he shot her again in the head. He couldn't tell me why he took the panty hose." He stopped the monotonous, almost breathless recital, sucking a deep breath of air, coughing. "I had to kill him. Julie was the only person I've ever loved in my whole life!"

"A crying shame," I said, and idly picked up the check. Fine-grained and creamy smooth, it felt more like cloth than paper. "How did Ralph find out about David?"

"David didn't know for sure what made his dad suspicious. He followed David one night to a girl's home. David had a key I made for him. He went in and raped the girl, came out with his ski mask still on his head. His father was waiting for him."

"Why didn't he turn David in right then? Why wait almost a year?"

"I don't know. David didn't know, either, except he said his dad looked like he went into shock. He left for California two days later. David was sure his dad had also found out about Cynthia by then."

"David knew about Cynthia?" I folded the check in half, folded it again.

He nodded, glancing down at his watch, then looking back at my fingers folding the check a fourth and fifth time. It was down to a small square no larger than a postage stamp, no thicker than a nickel.

"What are you doing?" There was more curiosity than alarm in his voice.

I cocked my head and gave him a silly grin. "I'm hungry," I said, and shoved the check into my mouth with two fingers, tongued it into the space between my lower molars and my cheek. I watched him spring to his feet and rush toward me and made gulping sounds, gagging motions, finally lifting my chin and swallowing noisily, visibly. I shook my head and made a hawking sound. "Shit, that scratched!"

"Goddammit!" he said, backing away from me, the expletive

once again sounding forced and unnatural coming from his lips. "Why did you do that?"

"Preventative medicine," I said. "That check is made of fine stock. Should take two, three days to disintegrate in my tummy. Plenty of time for the boys down in the autopsy room to find it if I should turn up among the nonliving. Might be a tad embarrassing for you. Hard to explain."

I grinned at him, mainly to flesh out my cheeks, to keep him from noticing the bulge in my left one.

He looked back at me, his face cold, speculative. "It will be messy, but I can find it."

I felt a shudder start in my stomach, crawl upward to lodge in my throat. Our gazes locked. Behind him, on the TV, cars chased each other down a city street. I could see them clearly in my peripheral vision, almost hear the scream of tires, the rush of wind. . . .

"It won't work, Paul. I was only one of a team. They know all about it, about you. They know everything I know . . . more."

"No." He fashioned a one-sided smile. "You figured it out after I came into this room tonight. Something you heard during that phone conversation a while ago. You worked it out for yourself, by yourself. I sat here and listened to you talk on the phone and watched it happen. Besides, I was with Captain Sellers a short time ago, and he suspects nothing. I'm very perceptive, Mr. Roman, or hadn't you noticed." He shrugged, the smile almost kindly. "Besides, what do I have to lose? They can only hang me one time."

"By the balls, I hope," I said, and laughed shakily, a hollow little sound. I fumbled for my cigarettes on the stand beside the chair, right next to the remote control. I shook one loose and felt around for the lighter, flicking a glance at the TV.

"I'm sorry," he said, "but you'll not have time for that cigarette. I'll need time to find the check, and I'm due at a recital in a very few minutes."

The speeding cars were out of the city now, careening along a narrow highway atop a series of jagged cliffs. The one in front began to fade on a curve, striking loose gravel, spinning out of control. . . .

I puffed on the cigarette, smiling up at him foolishly, a free-wheeling spurt of adrenaline singing in my veins. I ducked my head and stole another glance.

The lead car was juddering at the edge of the cliff, breaking free, sailing majestically for one fleeting second, then plunging downward like a failed missile. The camera panned back for a long shot as the rocks rushed upward to capture the doomed vehicle.

Paul made a clucking, impatient sound and raised the gun.

I dropped the cigarette into the ashtray, let my hand fall to the table, covering the remote control. I bared my teeth at him and punched the volume button, held it down.

One split second of eerie silence before the car impacted the rocks, and then the explosion rocked the room. Fire mushroomed on the screen.

Paul whirled.

I hurled the beer bottle.

He caught himself halfway around, began his turn back to me.

Too late.

The bottle was already there, catching him higher than I had planned, glancing off the ridge of his high aristocratic brow.

He staggered, knees buckling, but he didn't go down. The hand with the gun wavered, steadied, started its deadly swing again.

I came out of the chair, full-bore and bellowing, more a sound of fear than it was fearsome, pistoning legs and outstretched arms—one hundred and ninety pounds of scared detective trying hard not to be killed.

I caught him at an awkward angle, charged to my right, smashing our entwined bodies into the brick wall surrounding the fireplace. I felt the gun between us and prayed he was too addled to pull the trigger.

His head slammed the solid oak mantel; mine rammed into the brick wall, head-on, hard enough to bring sparkling stars and multicolored lights, yet not so hard that it prevented me from having one millisecond of thought before the darkness came: I had lost the fight, lost the game, lost my life. . . .

But, of course, it didn't work out that way. He was still in dreamland when I awoke, my head throbbing like a snare drum, little splashes of colored light skittering across my eyeballs when I turned my head too quickly. The check was no longer in my cheek; I wondered if I had swallowed the damn thing after all.

Other than that I was in fine fettle, a lot better than Paulie baby. He had a red, angry knot the size of a plum high on his forehead, a trickle of blood angling across one smooth cheek.

I stretched him out on the carpet, checked his pulse, then cuffed his hands behind his back and went in and made a call to Homer Sellers. I told him to get his big ass over to my place, hung up when he started asking damnfool cop questions.

I replaced the beer and sat down in my rocker; I lit a cigarette and looked at the slim figure on my rug, surprised at how empty I felt, how little feeling there was inside.

Relief . . . and something I couldn't pin down.

It wasn't until I heard a car door slam out in the driveway that I knew what was causing the stillness in my mind, the empty gnawing in my guts.

A need to understand.

Something beyond Paul LeClair's simplistic explanation of why he and David had raped, taken by force that which had been freely offered, and then went on to kill with casual disdain the very humans who had given them life.

Futile speculation.

They had been gifted young men with a better-than-average shot at life, but obviously that hadn't been enough, so maybe it was simple self-indulgence, low impulse control, outlaw genes. Born into a generation that had been encouraged to think only of itself, concepts like self-control and discipline had little meaning.

But, I thought, listening to Homer's heavy footsteps on the

pebbled walk out front, maybe there was nothing more to understand. Their roads had forked the way roads do for all of us at some point or other. They had picked their way carefully, deliberately, with malice aforethought, as they say, and no amount of specious reasoning could alter that fact.

They had chosen to do evil because to them doing evil was fun, exciting, their game of choice without consideration for their opponents.

So now Paul LeClair belonged to Homer, to the ponderous machinery of the law, to lawyers, cops, prosecutors, and judges, and inevitably to the shrinks. They would pick at his psyche like turkey buzzards on a fresh highway kill, declare him insane for the defense, label him depraved for the prosecution, reject out of hand the notion that there are some people who are born without morals, without conscience, people who are inherently evil and have no wish to change, who see life as a grand parade of hapless victims to feed their need for self-gratification, people who worship strange gods whose call is dearer to them than anything else in life.

38

"My God, you could have been killed!" Susie's eyes were wide and dark, her lovely features puckered in a taut mask of anxiety, hands plucking at me in a frenzy of concern, the trembling curve of her lips arcing straight to my heart.

"Not a chance," I said, surrendering to her tenderly probing fingers as she cautiously examined the lump on my head. "It's times like these when the old breeding comes through, when the tough get going—" I broke off and kissed the end of her nose. "When a cornered rat fights back."

"And it would have been all my fault," she wailed, hugging

my sore ribs so hard it brought back memories of Knutson's tender mercies. "If I hadn't acted like a spoiled brat and run off with Janey shopping we would have been gone to the cabin."

"Is that why you went? Doggone, I thought you were mad at me."

"Oh," she said, and hauled my head down and kissed me, then whispered against my lips, her breath warm and strangely exotic. "Will you forgive me?"

She kissed me again before I could answer, a long warm kiss, chock full of things that words can't adequately describe: invitation, demand, promises. . . .

What the hell, I can be as gracious as the next guy. I forgave her on the spot.